"PUT DOWN THE REMOTE AND PICK UP *REALITY BOY*— IT'S A **SHOWSTOPPER**."

—THE HORN BOOK

ı▮ı

PRAISE FOR *REALITY BOY*

A *New York Times* Editors' Choice
An Amazon Best Book of the Month
A 2013 *Publishers Weekly* Best YA Book
A 2013 *School Library Journal* Best Book
A 2013 *Kirkus Reviews* Best YA Book
A 2013 *VOYA* Perfect Ten Book
A 2013 Association of Booksellers for Children Best Book
A 2014 YALSA Best Fiction for Young Adults Book
A 2014 YALSA Quick Picks for Reluctant Readers Book
A Winter 2013–2014 Top Ten Kids' Indie Next List Pick
A 2014 Texas TAYSHAS Reading List Top Ten Book

"**A.S. King is one of the best Y.A. writers** working today.
She captures the disorientation of adolescence brilliantly."
—JOHN GREEN, *The New York Times Book Review*

★ "**Heart-pounding and heartbreaking**…a compulsively
readable portrait of two imperfect teens learning to trust each other
and themselves." —*Kirkus Reviews*, starred review

★ "A nuanced portrayal…This is **a story about healing**."
—*Publishers Weekly*, starred review

★ "King's trademarks—attuned first-person narrative, convincing
dialogue, realistic language, and fitting quirkiness—connect
effectively in this **disturbing, yet hopeful** novel."
—*SLJ*, starred review

★ "King's writing is tighter, more focused, and **better than ever**.... [An] intense and **incredibly fresh** plot."
—*VOYA*, starred review

★ "King offers a compelling look at possible long-term effects of reality shows.... **Thought-provoking and ultimately optimistic**." —*Library Media Connection*, starred review

"The hallmarks of [King's] strong work are there: magical realism, heightened emotion, and the steady, torturous, beautiful transition into self-assured inner peace. Like Gerald, it's **wonderfully broken**."
—*Booklist*

"[A] **smart and sympathetic** story about breaking free from the world's expectations." —*The Bulletin*

"**Timely, incisive, compassionate. A.S. King is always on the cutting edge of YA.** All her novels are must-reads."
—MATTHEW QUICK, *New York Times* bestselling author of *The Silver Linings Playbook* and *Forgive Me, Leonard Peacock*

"**A.S. King is one of the most powerful, resounding voices** in contemporary young adult literature. *Reality Boy* is **fearless and brilliant**, a seething pressure cooker of a masterpiece that will make you angry [and] heartbroken, and will lift you up and make you feel real." —ANDREW SMITH, author of *Winger* and *The Marbury Lens*

"**A.S. King at her best, and maybe then some.** If you don't fall in love with *the Crapper*, you shouldn't be allowed to read. This book is **tough and funny and smart** as hell. It was a total pleasure to read." —CHRIS CRUTCHER, author of *Period 8* and *Whale Talk*

"**A.S. King's best work to date.** Gobbled up for the sake of entertainment and spit out by the world, Gerald is the kind of character you keep pulling for long after the story is finished. **Touching and teeth-clenchingly emotional**, this story is an important reminder that behind every reality show...may be a totally different reality." —JENNIFER BROWN, author of *Hate List* and *Thousand Words*

"**A powerhouse of insight and empathy** toward the people who cruise the fringes of acceptable behavior. A.S. King takes all kinds of risks and every single one pays off. **Highly recommended**." —JONATHAN MABERRY, *New York Times* bestselling author of *Rot & Ruin* and *Fire & Ash*

"King never fails to surprise.... **We all know at least one teen who needs a book like this**; I didn't know I needed it until I turned the last page." —DODIE OWENS, editor, *SLJTeen*

"[King's] ability to show all sides of the story, while never detracting from the main characters and their intense frustration with the adults and circumstances of their lives, is **a marvel**. *Reality Boy* **showcases King's talent**.... It's also about first love, celebrity, therapy, and finding your own narrative despite the story your family—and sometimes the world—tells about you." —JENN NORTHINGTON, *Shelf Awareness*

"I'm not sure if there is a subject that A.S. King cannot handle with perfect dexterity. She wins your trust by creating characters that are real and then paves the story's way with glass shards, heartbreak, and ultimately, gold. *Reality Boy* is a **fascinating emotional dissection of life** under the watchful eye of the American public and the subsequent fallout for one angry young man." —JANE KNIGHT, *Shelf Awareness*

"In *Reality Boy*, Gerald finds his voice, fights the power, meets a girl, and makes some changes. A.S. King is consistently badass and **unflinching** in her approach to tough issues, and this [book] is no exception." —BookRiot.com

REA

LITY
BOY

A NOVEL BY
A.S. KING

(L)(B)
LITTLE, BROWN AND COMPANY
NEW YORK ◆ BOSTON

Copyright © 2013 by A.S. King
Author Interview copyright © 2014 by A.S. King
Discussion Guide copyright © 2014 by Little, Brown and Company
Excerpt from *Glory O'Brien's History of the Future* copyright © 2014 by A.S. King

Little, Brown and Company

Hachette Book Group
237 Park Avenue, New York, NY 10017
Visit our website at lb-teens.com

Little, Brown and Company is a division of Hachette Book Group, Inc.
The Little, Brown name and logo are trademarks of Hachette Book Group, Inc.

The publisher is not responsible for websites (or their content) that are not owned by the publisher.

First Paperback Edition: September 2014
First published in hardcover in October 2013 by Little, Brown and Company

Library of Congress Cataloging-in-Publication Data

King, A. S. (Amy Sarig), 1970–
Reality Boy / A.S. King. — First edition.
pages cm
Summary: "An emotionally damaged seventeen-year-old boy in Pennsylvania who was once an infamous reality television show star meets a girl from another dysfunctional family, and she helps him out of his angry shell" — Provided by publisher.
ISBN 978-0-316-22270-9 (hc) — ISBN 978-0-316-22271-6 (pb)
[1. Family problems—Fiction. 2. Emotional problems—Fiction. 3. Self-actualization (Psychology)—Fiction. 4. Dating (Social customs)—Fiction. 5. Fame—Fiction. 6. Reality television programs—Fiction.] I. Title.
PZ7.K5693Re 2013   [Fic]—dc23   2012048432

10 9 8 7 6 5 4 3 2 1

RRD-C

Printed in the United States of America

FOR TOPHER

Everybody's so full of shit.

PART ONE

I AM
REALITY BOY

I'M THE KID you saw on TV.

Remember the little freak who took a crap on his parents' oak-stained kitchen table when they confiscated his Game Boy? Remember how the camera cleverly hid his most private parts with the glittery fake daisy and sunflower centerpiece?

That was me. Gerald. Youngest of three. Only boy. Out of control.

One time, I did it in the dressing room at the mall. Sears, I think. My mom was trying to get me to try on some pants and she got the wrong size.

"Now you stay right there," she said. "I'll be back with the right size."

And to protest having to wait, or having to try on pants, or having to have a mother like her, I dropped one right there between the wicker chair and the stool where Mom's purse was.

And no. It wasn't excusable. I wasn't a baby. I wasn't even a toddler. I was five. I was sending a message.

You all watched and gasped and put your hands over your eyes as three different cameramen caught three different angles of me squeezing one out on the living room coffee table, next to the cranberry-scented holiday candle ensemble. Two guys held boom mikes. They tried to keep straight faces, but they couldn't. One of them said, "Push it out, kid!" He just couldn't help himself. I was so entertaining.

Right?

Wasn't I?

Gerald the spoiled little brat. Gerald the kid who threw violent tantrums that left holes in the drywall and who screamed so loud it made the neighbors call the police. Gerald the messed-up little freak who needed Network Nanny's wagging finger and three steps to success.

Now I'm a junior in high school. And every kid in my class has seen forty different angles of me crapping in various places when I was little. They call me the Crapper. When I complained to the adults in my life back in middle school, they said, "Fame has its downside."

Fame? I was *five*.

At five years old, did I have the capacity to write the producers a letter begging Network Nanny to come and help me stop punching the walls of my parents' swanky McMansion? No. I did not have that capacity. I did not write that letter. I did not want her to come.

But she came anyway.

So I got madder.

1

IT'S WWE NIGHT. That's World Wrestling Entertainment, or *Smackdown Live!* for any of you non-redneck-y people who've never watched the spectacle of heavyweight wrestling before. I've always hated it, but it brings in good money at the PEC Center.

The PEC Center is the Penn Entertainment and Convention Center. That's where I work.

I'm that apathetic kid in the greasy shirt at the concession stand who asks you if you want salsa, cheese, chili, or jalapeños with your nachos. I'm the kid who refills the ice because none of the other lazy cashiers will do it. I'm the kid who has to say *Sorry. We're all out of pretzels.*

I hear parents complain about how much everything costs. I hear them say *You shouldn't be eating that fattening stuff* right before they order their kid some chicken fingers and fries. I hear them wince when their kid orders a large sugary Pepsi in a WWE commemorative cup to wash it down. At WWE, it's the fried stuff, cups with wrestlers on them, or beer.

I'm technically not allowed to work this stand until I turn eighteen and take a class on how to serve alcohol responsibly. There's a test and everything—and a little certificate to put in your wallet. I'm almost seventeen now, and Beth, my manager, lets me work here because she likes me and we made a deal. I card people. I check for signs of intoxication—loud talking, lower inhibitions, glassy eyes, slurred speech; then, if everything checks out okay, I call Beth over so she can tap them the beers. Unless it's superbusy. Then she tells me to tap them myself.

"Hey, Crapper!" someone yells from the back of the line. "I'll give you twenty bucks to squeeze one out for the crowd!"

It's Nichols. He only comes to this stand because he knows I can get him beer. He comes with Todd Kemp, who doesn't say much and seems embarrassed to be around Nichols most of the time because Nichols is such a dick.

I wait on the three families in front of Nichols and Todd, and when they get here, they barely whisper what they want and Todd hands over ten bucks. Two Molsons. While I'm covertly tapping the beer, Nichols is saying all sorts of nervous, babbly stuff, and I do what my anger management coach taught me to do. I hear nothing. I breathe and count to ten. I concentrate on the sound of the WWE crowd cheering on whatever big phony is in the ring. I concentrate on the foam at the top of the cup. I concentrate on how I'm supposed to love myself now. *Only you can allow yourself to be angry.*

But no matter how much anger management coaching I've had, I know that if I had a gun, I'd shoot Nichols in the back as he walks away with his beer. I know that's murder and I know what that means. It means I'd go to jail. And the older I get, the more I think maybe I belong in jail. There are plenty of angry guys like me in jail. It's, like, anger central. If we put together all the jails in this country and made a state out of them, we could call that state Furious.

We could give it a postal abbreviation like other states have. FS. I think the zip code would be 00000.

I wipe down the counter while there's a short break in the hungry, thirsty WWE crowd. I restack the cup lids. I count how many hot dogs are left in my hot drawer. I report to Beth that I am completely out of pretzels.

When I get up from counting hot dogs in the next drawer over, I see her walking through the crowd. Tasha. My oldest sister. She's with her boyfriend, Danny, who is about two staircases more than a step down from us. We live in a gated community of minimansions. Danny lives in a rented community of 1970s single-wide trailers. They don't even have paved roads. I'm not exaggerating. The place is like the hillbilly ghetto.

Not like I care. Tasha is an asshole and I hate her. I hope he knocks her up and she marries him and they have a hundred little WWE-loving pale redneck babies. I wouldn't shoot her, though. I enjoy watching her fail too much. Watching Mom swallow her Tasha-dropped-out-of-college-and-is-dating-a-Neanderthal soup every day is probably the best thing I have going for me.

It's probably the only thing keeping me out of jail.

2

I LIVE ABOUT ten miles away from the PEC Center, in a town called Blue Marsh, which is not blue, not a marsh, and not a real town. It's just a bunch of developments linked together with shopping malls.

I get home at ten and the house is dark. Mom is already sleeping because she gets up so early to power walk and invent exciting new breakfast smoothies. Dad is probably still out with his real estate friends smoking cigars and drinking whatever equity-rich assholes drink, talking about this economy and how much it sucks to be them.

As I near the kitchen hallway, I hear the familiar sound of Tasha getting nailed by Danny the hillbilly.

If I brought a girl home and did that to her that loud, my parents would kick me out. But if Tasha does it? We all have to pretend that it's not actually happening. One time she was whinnying away down in the basement with Danny while Mom, Lisi, and I ate dinner. This was last year when Lisi still lived at home. Mom talked nonstop to block it out, as if the three of us would magically unhear what was going on. *And did you see that Boscov's is having a white sale this weekend? We could use new sheets and towels and I think I'll go over on Saturday morning because the selection is always better early in the day and I really would love some that are blue to match the upstairs bathroom and last time I ended up with those red sheets and as much as I like them, they still seem too rough and they usually have nice flannel this time of year and I think it's important to have flannel sheets in winter, you know? Blah blah blah blah blah.*

I got about seven mouthfuls into a nice plate of roast beef and mashed potatoes and I finally couldn't take it anymore. I went to the basement door, opened it, and screamed, "If you don't stop planking my sister while I eat dinner, I'm going to come down there and kick your ass. Have some fucking respect!" and I slammed the door.

My mother stopped talking about towels and sheets and gave me that look she'd been giving everyone for as long as I could remember. It said *Tasha can't help it.* It said *We just can't control what Tasha does.*

Or, in Lisi's words, "Tasha is out of control and for some reason our mother is totally fine with it. Don't know why, don't care, either. I'm getting as far from here as I can the minute I can."

And she did. Lisi went all the way to Glasgow, Scotland, where she's studying literature, psychology, and environmental science all at the same time while balancing a waitressing job and her years-long pot habit. She hasn't called since she left. Not even once. She e-mailed Mom to let us know she got there okay, but she never calls. It's been three months.

Anyway, Mom should have named Tasha "Trigger." Not just because of the horse sounds she makes when she's getting planked by the redneck, either.

She is my number one trigger.

That's the term the anger management coach uses to describe why I get angry. It's the self-controlled, acceptable word we use for *shit that pisses me off.* That's called a trigger. I have spent the last four years identifying mine. And it's Tasha.

At least on that night—the time we had the roast beef and Lisi was still home—Tasha and Danny shut up. Which was good, because I was completely serious. As I ate, I had my eye on the fireplace set in the living room, and I was wondering what kind of damage the iron fire poker could do to a human head. I pictured an exploding watermelon.

My anger coach would say *Stay in the present, Gerald.* But it's hard when nothing ever changes. For sixteen years, eleven months, and two weeks, I've been drowning.

■ ■ ■ ■ ■

Dad arrives home. He'll hear it, too, the minute he gets out of the car.

Basement sounds—especially Tasha's whinnying—go to the garage first.

Giddyup.

I hear his dress shoes *tip-tap* on the cement floor and the door open...and he finds me standing in the dark like some freak. He gasps.

"Jesus, Ger!" he says. "Way to give your old man a stroke."

I walk over to the living room doorway and switch on the main hall light. "Sorry. I just got in, too. Got distracted by the, uh—you know. Noise."

He sighs.

"I wish she'd move out again," I say.

"She doesn't have anywhere to live."

"So? Maybe she'll learn how to get a job and not sponge off you guys if you kick her ass out." I don't know why I'm doing this. It's just raising my blood pressure. "She's twenty-one."

"You know how your mother is," he says. *You know how your mother is.* This has been his party line since Lisi moved out.

We move into the living room, where it's quieter. He mixes himself a drink and asks me if I want one. I usually say no. But tonight I say yes.

"I could use it. Busy night."

"Hockey game?"

"Wrestling. Those people never stop eating," I say.

"Heh," he says.

"Is Lisi coming home for Christmas?" I ask. He shakes his head, so I add, "There's no chance she'll come back with Tasha in the house."

He hands me a White Russian and flops himself on the couch. He's still in the suit he wore to work this morning. It's Saturday, and he worked at least twelve hours before he went out with his real estate group. He takes a sip from his drink.

"Those two never got along," he says. Which is bullshit. Tasha never got along. With anyone. And it's partially his fault, so he has these excuses. *You know how your mother is. Those two never got along.*

"Thinking about what you want for your birthday?" he asks.

"Not really." This isn't a lie. I haven't been thinking about my birthday at all, even though it's just over two weeks from now.

"I guess you have some time," he says.

"Yeah."

We look at each other for a moment, and he manages a little smile. "So what are your plans after next year? You gonna leave me here like Lisi did?"

I say, "My options are limited."

He nods.

"There's always jail." I let a few seconds pass before I say, "But I think Roger has reasoned all of that out of me." Roger is my anger management coach.

At first he looks shocked, and then he laughs. "Phew. I thought you were serious there for a sec."

"About that? Who'd want to go to jail?"

Right then, Danny the hillbilly opens the basement door and tiptoes into the dark kitchen and grabs a bag of tortilla chips from the cupboard. He goes to the fridge and grabs the whole carton of iced tea. Dad and I notice that he is completely naked only when the light from the fridge shines on his pecker.

"Maybe next time you steal from me, you could put on some clothes, son," Dad says.

Danny runs back down the steps like a rat.

That's what we have. We have rats in our basement. Sponger rats who steal our food and don't offer us shit for it.

I'm still thinking about my last rhetorical question to Dad. *Who'd want to go to jail?* I thought about going nuts once and hitting the mental institution. We have one of those here, only a few miles down the road, too. But Roger said mental institutions aren't really the way they used to be. No more playing basketball with the Chief like in *One Flew Over the Cuckoo's Nest.*

"So where to, then, Ger?" Dad asks, swirling his drink with his index finger.

I don't know what to say. I don't want to do anything, really. I just want a chance to start over and have a real life. One that wasn't fucked up from the beginning and broadcast on international TV like a freak show.

3

EPISODE 1, SCENE 1, TAKE 3

YES, EPISODE ONE. As in, they did more than one show of the Crapper. I was such a big hit with all those troubled parents around the country, so they wanted more chances to watch poor little Gerald squat and deposit turds in the most peculiar places.

I could almost hear the relieved parents of normal tantrum-throwing children saying *At least our kid doesn't crap on the dining room table!*

So true. So true.

What they didn't know was this: I didn't become the Crapper until those cameras were mounted on our walls. Until the strangers with the microphones did sound tests to make sure they could pick up every little thing that was going on. Until I became entertainment. Before then, I was just a frustrated, confused kid who could get violent—mostly toward drywall . . . and Tasha.

If I was to give a postal abbreviation to my house while I was growing up, it would be UF. I was furious, yes. Livid. Enraged. Incensed. But only because everything was Unfair. Postal abbreviation UF. Zip code: ?????. (The zip code for UF probably changes every five seconds, so there's no point trying to give it one.)

I can't remember a time when I didn't want to punch everything around me, out of confused, unacknowledged frustration. I never punched Lisi or my parents. But then, Lisi and my parents never begged me to punch them. Walls did. Furniture did. Doors did. Tasha did.

From the moment I saw Network Nanny, I didn't really believe she was a nanny. She didn't look like a nanny or act like a nanny. She had starlet hair—something you'd see at a red-carpet movie premiere. She was skinny. Bony, even. She dressed up, as if she was attending a wedding. She didn't smile or possess any warmth. As if she was . . . acting.

They'd sent us a fake nanny.

I didn't know this for sure until I was older, but it was true. Nanny was really Lainie Church, who was really Elizabeth Harriet Smallpiece from a small town in the south of England, who'd wanted to make it in Hollywood since she was five. Her first acting jobs were in commercials, and then she got a stint for a while in Iowa as one of those fake meteorologists who don't know anything about weather but act like they do. She had a very convincing Iowan accent, too. But Network Nanny was her breakthrough role.

Alongside our fake nanny was a less camera-ready *real* nanny. She wasn't allowed to interact with us, but she winked at me sometimes. She told Fake Nanny what to do to play a good nanny. This arrangement made me mad. I remember sitting there watching them set up and wondering what I could do to really show the world how wrong things were in my life.

After meeting with her makeup artist for a half hour, Fake Nanny got into costume and character and came into the living room, where my family sat waiting. She clapped her hands and looked at the three kids. I was five, Lisi was seven, and Tasha was nearly eleven.

Then she looked exclusively at me while she talked. "Your parents have called me in because your family needs my help." She stopped and checked her reflection in the TV screen. "Your mother says you fight all the time and that's not acceptable behavior."

To imagine Nanny properly, you have to give her an English accent. She dropped her r's. *Behavior* was *behay-vyah*.

"Sounds to me like you need the three steps to success in this house. And we'll start with some old-fashioned discipline. Gerald, do you know what that means?"

The director told me to shake my head no, so I did. I tried not to look into the cameras, which was why it took three takes to film scene one. How can a five-year-old not look into a camera that's right in front of his face?

"It means we're about to start a whole new life," she said. "And this will be a whole new family, easy as one, two, three."

⁝ ▮ ⁝

Nanny only came around for a day and then she left her crew of cameras and cameramen there to film us being violent little bitches to one another. Then, two weeks later, she came back and decided, based on that footage, who was right, who was wrong, who needed *prop-ah punishment*, and who needed to learn more about *responsibility*. She taught Mom and Dad about the naughty chair and how to take away screen time. They made homemade charts with rows, columns, and stickers. (The girls got cat stickers. I got dog stickers.)

Nanny didn't actually help make the charts, because her fingernails were too delicate and chart-making wasn't in her contract. "Anyway, it's not my job to parent these children," she said to Mom and Dad. "It's yours."

What the cameras didn't see was: Everything that made us violent little bitches happened behind closed doors or just under the radar of those microphones. And so Nanny (well, really, the *nannies*) only saw part of the picture. Which was usually me or Lisi running after Tasha, trying to hurt her.

Or me squatting on the kitchen table that day—the most-watched YouTube clip from our time on the show—after Nanny took my Game Boy away for throwing a tantrum. That was my first crap—first of many. After I spent the rest of the day in my room, she asked, "You know pooping anywhere but the toilet is dirty, don't you?"

I nodded, but the word *dirty* just kept echoing in my head. It was what Mom had said to me when I accidentally pooped in the bathtub when I was three. "Why did you do this?" Mom asked. "Why would you be so dirty?" I was so little I didn't remember much else, but I remembered that five minutes before, Tasha had told me she was going to help me wash my hair. Which is not what she did.

Nanny said, "Every time you poop and it's not in the toilet, you clean it up yourself and then you go to your room for the whole day. Does that sound fair?"

I shrugged.

She repeated, "Does that sound fair?"

I ask you: Imagine any five-year-old who's surrounded by cameras. Imagine he lives in the postal area UF. Consider that he has so little giveashit that he has started crapping on the kitchen table in front of video cameras. Then ask him this question. He will not know how to answer.

So I freaked out.

I screamed so long and loud, I thought my throat was bleeding when I was done. Then Nanny came over to me and sat down and ruffled my hair. It was the nanniest I'd ever seen her act in the two weeks I'd known her. She asked me why I was so upset, but she laughed when I told her.

"Your *sist-ah* isn't trying to kill you, Gerald. Don't exaggerate."

4

ONE OF THE first things they told me at anger management class was that I should get regular exercise. I thought about training on the equipment Dad had in the basement and then you-know-who dropped out of loser college for the first time and moved home, so we packed up the treadmill, the weight machine, and the Ping-Pong table and moved them to the corner of the garage.

When I explained that my home weight room now housed my number one trigger, my anger coach suggested that maybe I go to a real gym. At first, my parents would drop me at the gym a few times a week. But then I saw a different gym inside the real gym—a boxing gym. I decided then that I should go there, because, you know, I liked to punch shit. When I told my coach that I'd joined a boxing gym, he sighed but eventually agreed—with one rule. No actual boxing. As in, no hitting other people. I was thirteen and a half and I'd already hit enough people, so I was fine with that.

The guys who train at the gym are nice, I guess, but there's this one new guy. He's got issues. Postal code FS all the way. He looks at me sometimes and smiles that provoking smile. I know what it means because I used to use it.

His name is Jacko. I have no idea what his real name is. He's Jamaican, but not really, because his accent is fake. His parents moved to Blue Marsh when he was three and he's a middle-class kid now—dreaming he could be as poor as his parents were so he could be as interesting as they are, telling stories about their fishing village and living in a shack with a tin roof or something. That's why he fights, I bet. Because being middle-class is boring as hell.

Anyway, I don't know why everyone is okay with me being in a boxing gym. The whole idea is pretty ironic. I mean, if I couldn't kick your ass before, I sure as hell can kick your ass now. And that's what I think about every single minute I'm in the gym. Kicking ass.

K-I-C-K-I-N-G A-S-S.

There is part of me that wants to kick that Jacko kid's ass so bad, I wouldn't mind going away for it. In jail I would be able to kick more ass and more ass until someone bigger than me killed me. And it's all anyone expects of me at this point, right? Jail or death, I guess. Jail or death.

I pound the punching bag. I pound it until I can't feel my fingers. Sometimes they swell for days. This sunny Sunday morning, they crack and pop, and I think about how badly damaged they'll be when I'm old and how I'll have to get cortisone shots like my great-uncle John, and I don't care. I jump rope for about fifteen minutes and then I hit the speed bag— my favorite because it has rhythm and it puts me in some sort of trance.

I like the trance. It unwraps me. For fifteen minutes I am unbound from the layer of plastic wrap I've been wrapped in my whole life. I can see better, smell better, hear better. I can *feel*. Sometimes the speed bag makes me want to cry, it's so good. I don't cry, though. I just lose the rhythm and wrap myself up again—head to toe.

Before I walk to the parking lot, I go into the room next door—an abandoned warehouse room that used to have a mail-order business in it. When I started coming here, the company was still operating. Now all that's left is the shelving units and the little cubicles from the offices.

It's dark.

I walk in fast toward one of the cubicle walls. It's the only drywall in the whole redbrick place. Then I slam my fist through it, but that isn't enough, so I pound another hole, too, lower down because I'm starting to run out of space.

My hand stings and my knuckle is bleeding, but it feels good. When I stand back, I count the holes. Forty-two.

I I ▮ I I

By the time I get home from boxing-not-boxing, Dad is long gone to his Sunday open houses and Mom is showered after her usual two-hour Sunday-morning walk and is in the kitchen, doing kitchen-y things. She loves doing kitchen-y things. If my mom had her way, she would live in the kitchen and everything would be happy. And if it wasn't happy, she'd whip up a batch of something and then it *would* be happy. Or she'd just walk more. You pick.

After I take a shower, I sit down and she puts a plate of breakfast in front of me. Scrambled eggs, turkey bacon, and a glass of water. Mom has a new centerpiece and it reminds me of Nanny. I must have crapped on this table ten times, easy. Maybe more.

"Did you have a good workout?" Mom asks.

"Yeah. I'm getting really fast on the speed bag. I love that thing."

"Good for you," she says. In a good way.

"Yeah."

"I'm glad you found that gym," she adds. "I never knew it was there."

Mom puts her fork on the edge of her plate and downs a handful of some weird pills—supplements and vitamins and whatever chronic power walkers eat to make them not disappear into thin air. I'd say at five foot two, she's now easily under a hundred pounds.

"I'm heading out to do some early Christmas shopping today," she says. "Dad will be back around four. Any chance we'll see you for dinner?"

Right when I'm about to answer, the rhythmic sound starts in the basement. *Ba-bang-ba-boom-ba-bang-ba-boom.* Mom automatically gets up, runs the water in the sink full blast, loads the dishwasher, and then starts it, although it isn't even half-full.

"Nah. Double shift today. Won't be home until after the hockey game. Probably as late as ten. I'll catch dinner there." I look at the clock. It's ten thirty. I have to be at the PEC Center at eleven. "Shit. I'd better go now."

A few years ago, if I'd said *shit* so casually in front of my mother, she might have scolded me about my language. Now she says nothing. I'm not even sure if she heard me over the dishwasher and the *ba-bang-ba-boom-ba-bang-ba-boom.*

"Leave your plate. I'll get it," she says. "Have a great day."

"Thanks. You too."

Isn't it sweet? Isn't it lovely what Nanny did for us? Eleven years ago, my mother was cleaning up my crap from that same table. Now she offers to clear my plate because she knows I have to get to work on time. How polite and thoughtful we all are! What acceptable *behay-vyah.*

5

THERE'S THIS GIRL.

She usually works register #1, and I like it that way because I always work #7 and she's far away from me and I don't have to nervously squeeze past her to get to the kids' meal boxes or the candy. We have to do a lot of squeezing in stand five because there's only about four feet between the counter and the hot tables where the cooks put all the food we have to serve up.

Anyway, for the matinee, she's at #4 because the stand is half-closed, and I have to squeeze past her twice to get stuff. She smells nice and her hair looks soft. I know...this is the shit I will think about when I'm locked up one day.

She's only been working here for a few weeks. Regular hours like me, but not always in my stand. She disappears a lot and I see her at break time in the smokers' alley, writing in a little book that she keeps in her pocket. She looks at me sometimes. She's caught me looking at her twice, but I've looked at her a lot more than that, because there's something about her. The way she wears her hair. The way she wears boys' combat pants to work even though Beth has asked her not to. The way she writes in that little book. She's beautiful—but not in that Nanny-starlet way where she cares about how she looks. She's the opposite. She doesn't care at all, which makes her even more beautiful. If I was a normal kid, I'd ask her out, I guess.

But Roger, my anger management coach, told me that dating and anger management don't go very well together. He told me that girls are infuriating. They always want to *know* so much. *Relationships make you think you deserve things, Gerald. Deserving leads to resentment. Girls think you should be doing things for them, too. The rules are blurry. You're doing so well.*

The matinee at PEC is some singing group for kids. By the time we open and the little kids come in, the only things we're really selling are pretzels, bottled water, and the occasional pack of red licorice. It's slow. Most of the parents are well dressed and make their children say thank you. Here's an example:

"What do you say to the nice man?" they say.

"Thank you," the kid says when I hand him his dollar in change.

"You should say it more nicely, Jordan," his mother says.

"Thank you," the kid says, no differently than before.

I hand him his pretzel and he sneers at me because he thinks I'm some sublevel adult who can't get a better job than concessions at the PEC Center. I hate parents like his. So concerned with appearances. I want to tell them that they're lucky the kid isn't taking dumps on their favorite couch. Or in their BMW.

After the preshow rush, I get to peek into the arena. Four guys dressed in different costumes—a cowboy, a railroad engineer, a suit, and a chef—play songs that use the same chords over and over again. The chef plays drums with cooking utensils. The cowboy occasionally drops the melody and takes off on a country music riff all by himself while the other guys roll their eyes. Then he hops on his guitar and rides it around the stage. The kids can't get enough of this. The high-pitched screaming makes my ears crackle.

"That's messed up," she says. It's the girl from register #1. "How can anyone even think that's funny?"

"I know, right?" I say. Then I walk away because she's irresistible, and I am on a mission to resist her.

I refill the cooler with bottled water and diet soda. I go to the bathroom to pee, and wash my hands exactly as an employee is supposed to. When I come out, she's nowhere to be found. Probably out writing about me in her little book. About how she tried to talk to the Crapper, but he walked away.

6

"GERALD?"

It's my manager, Beth. I look at her.

"Gerald, you've been standing there staring into space for five minutes."

I look at the clock. I see the well-dressed parents taking their overexcited kids to the souvenir stand for cowboy/ engineer/suit/chef costumes and kites and cups and T-shirts. We've closed our gate so we can count our drawers and switch up for the hockey crowd. I've already counted my drawer. I don't remember doing it, but it's done. I notice that Beth looks worried. As worried as Beth can look, anyway—she's so laid-back she's nearly horizontal. But still, she looks worried.

"Sorry," I say.

"You can take a break if you want," she says. "You've been here since we opened. And did you even eat lunch yet?" I'd like Beth to be my mother. She totally wouldn't let Tasha live in the basement with her rat-boyfriend sleepovers. "I have left-over chicken and fries if you want some," she adds, and points to the shallow stainless-steel tray under the heat lamp full of fried foods that never got sold.

As I reach in, Register #1 Girl reaches in, too, and our wrists brush against each other. I look at her and smile. She smiles back and takes her hand out to give me first pick. I do the same. Beth intervenes and fixes us each a paper dish of chicken fingers and fries, and we thank her. And then I go way back toward register #7 to eat, and Register #1 Girl goes to where everyone else is eating, over by the sinks beyond register #1.

I go back to my other day. The one I was living in my head when Beth snapped me out of it. My place-of-no-triggers. I invented it when I was little, thanks to Nanny. I call it Gers-day. It rhymes with pairsday or daresday. It's the extra day I get inside of a week that no one else knows about. I live it in little parts of those other, regular days like Monday and Tues-day and Wednesday, et cetera. While normal people who have seven days in their week may think I'm spacing out or "off in la-la land," as my asshole third-grade teacher used to say, I'm really living one more day than all of you. A good day.

All Gersdays are good days.

Let me repeat. All Gersdays are good days.

The postal abbreviation is GD. For Gersday. Or good day. Or anything you want to make it, as long as it's so good that all the bad goes away. The zip code is ☺☺☺☺☺.

And if I take a day in GD during every other FS 00000 or UF ????? week, then I get to have a longer life than everyone else. That's fifty-two extra days a year, which adds up.

Let me explain further.

A normal sixteen-year-old (nearly seventeen-year-old) would have lived about 6,191 days. I, Gerald "the Crapper" Faust, have lived 6,815. That's 624 days more than other near-seventeen-year-olds. Technically, if we go by days, I'm almost nineteen.

7

EPISODE 1, SCENE 12, TAKE 2

"GERALD, YOU CAN'T keep going off into your own world like that," Nanny said. "You need to stay here and listen to what I'm saying, do you *undah-stand*?"

I nodded because the director told me to nod. But I was still in Gersday, eating strawberry ice cream and walking down a happy street in a city neighborhood where none of the kids did things that made me want to beat them up.

Nanny must have noticed, because she grabbed me by the arms and put her face right in my face and said, "Gerald! You're needed here. You either listen or you spend time in the naughty chair."

I answered, "I'll take the naughty chair, please." Then I

got up and walked to it, sat down, and went back to Gersday and my ice-cream cone. One kid there wanted me to be on his kickball team. Another kid wanted me to go bike riding with him, and he didn't care that I still used training wheels. I finished my ice cream and thought it would be nice to have another one. And then Lisi was there and she handed me a vanilla cone with rainbow sprinkles. She had chocolate with chocolate sprinkles. We walked down a bunch of roads until we got to our house.

Mom was there and she hugged us when we got in and told us to finish our ice cream in the kitchen. When Lisi and I sat down at the table, Mom asked us how our day was and we told her how wonderful our day had been. When we were done, she said she had a surprise for us and took us to the hallway and showed us our new school pictures, framed and hung on the wall. Lisi looked like a little movie star. I looked like the cutest five-year-old who ever lived. There was one other picture—of Mom and Dad in that semi-embracing pose, her head leaned in on his chin a little. They looked so in love and happy. I stood back and looked at those three pictures and I cried happy tears. That's what Gersdays were all about. Happy tears. Ice cream. Mom not ignoring Lisi and me because she was too busy fussing over Tasha. That couldn't happen on a Gersday because on Gersday, Tasha didn't exist. Which means she didn't put plastic bags over Lisi's head or call me *gaytard*. She couldn't do those things because she wasn't there at all. As Nanny would say: *Simple as one, two, three*.

"Did you hear that?" Nanny asked.

"What?" I asked.

"The timer. It buzzed three minutes ago. You were off with the fairies for all that time. Smiling."

I checked to make sure I wasn't still smiling. "Sorry," I said.

"Gerald, you and I are trying to work on some very serious *behay-vyah* issues and I can't do it without your help."

"Yes." Close-up of me nodding. I could see the camera's lens swirling right into my face.

The boom camera panned left as Nanny hugged me. It was a fake hug, like we were onstage. Her rib cage stabbed me. "I can help you do it, but I can't do it for you. You *undah-stand* that?"

I nodded because the director nodded.

"Good. Now go tidy up your room and get ready for *suppah*. Your favorite tonight! Spaghetti and meatballs."

I I ◼ I I

Thirty minutes later, I was chasing Tasha down the upstairs hall with a plastic lightsaber. When I caught up with her, I hit her with it so hard that it finally broke. The sharp edge of the broken plastic scratched her arm a little. There was no blood or anything, but when Mom saw it, she acted like I was some kind of an ax murderer and gathered Tasha into her arms and yelled at me. I ran back down the hall and down the stairs and was about to run out the door when I felt the tight, skeletal grip of Nanny.

She dragged me to the *behay-vyah* chart in the kitchen. All my stickers for the day were removed and replaced with black dots and Nanny told me I'd be sent to bed with no spaghetti and meatballs. Tasha stood there and watched. She was pretend-crying—one of those noises that drove me to violence.

"See what you did?" Nanny said. "Only a few minutes away from your favorite *dinn-ah* and you ruin it by being mean to your *sist-ah*! Gerald, I don't *undah-stand* you at all." When the cameras panned to me crying, Nanny checked her hair and makeup in the oven door. She was wearing shiny pink lipstick, like pink mother-of-pearl.

"Cut!" the director yelled. After conferring with the other guys in charge and Real Nanny, he called Nanny over. Then he came over to me, Mom, and Tasha.

"Look, our guys didn't catch that fight with the lightsaber. I sent Tim out to buy a new one and if it's okay with you, we'd like to get Gerald and Tasha to reenact it so we can get it in the reel."

Mom looked at the guy like he was insane. "You want my daughter to get beat up again for the sake of your show?" she asked.

"We'd just like them to reenact it. If you don't mind. Tim will be back in a minute. There's a Toys"R"Us only a few minutes away. In the meantime, I'll explain to Gerald and Tasha exactly what I want them to do. No real hitting."

Real Nanny didn't look happy about this, either. She crossed her arms and said something to Fake Nanny, but Fake Nanny just shrugged.

Mom blinked back tears and gave her precious Tasha to

the director. I went willingly because this might be my chance to actually kill Tasha once and for all. On camera.

The director set us free until Tim came back with the new lightsaber. I went straight into Mom's walk-in closet and squatted over her favorite pair of penny loafers and left a hot, steaming turd inside each one.

▪ ▍ ▊ ▍ ▪

The reenacted fight was far lamer than the real fight because Tasha just sat there and cried and didn't scream or punch me the way she had before. Plus, my lightsaber didn't break, so I couldn't try to plunge the sharp end into her eye or brain. Afterward, the cameramen went back downstairs because we were going to have a one-on-one scene with me and Nanny before she sent me to bed with no dinner.

Then there was a scream from my parents' room. The cameramen raced in to see the fuss as it unfolded. They started wide, with a view of Mom's amazing closet and her impressive collection of shoes—from her dressy heels to her walking-sneaker collection—and then they zoomed in until the only things in the shot were her penny loafers and my turds.

While Tasha and Mom were freaking out on camera, I escaped back to the kitchen. I sneaked a Rice Krispies Treat and went back to Gersday to buy another ice cream. In Gersday, there's ice cream everywhere. Nobody's there to storm into your room and knee you in the stomach to make you chase them with a lightsaber. Nobody is drowning.

8

"CRAPPER!"

It's Nichols. He walks past our stand and gives me the finger up high so I can see it above the heads of the people waiting in line. After our short break to eat leftover chicken and fries from the matinee at the PEC Center, it's time to get ready for the five o'clock hockey game, and there are seventy people waiting in front of us.

The hour before the game starts is a blur of large Pepsis, five-dollar Molsons, pretzels, fries, hot dogs, and nachos. All the while, I'm eating ice cream in Gersday because I can live in two days at once. This is another advantage I have over lesser humans.

When Nichols comes back, he's still flipping me the bird as he approaches my register.

"Hey, Crapmeister. Can I have a Molson?" He throws down a five-dollar bill.

I stare at him. I imagine how easy it would be for me to pull him over the counter, drag him behind the fry table, and press his face into the hot dog rollers. How fun it would be to dunk his head into the deep-fat fryer.

"Dude. Did you hear me?" he yells, too loudly. I can feel Beth's attention from the other side of the stand, and I know there is no way Nichols is getting his Molson.

"I heard you. Sorry. My Molson is tapped," I say.

"I just saw her tap one a minute ago!" He points at Register #6 Lady. My hand reaches out toward him just a little and he sees it. His expression changes. I can't tell if it's fear or anger, but suddenly my heart rate goes up and I get ready to pounce. Everything goes silent in my head.

"Is there a problem here?" Beth asks.

Nichols smiles. "No. No problem. I was just asking this young man to get me a beer," he says. Like a bigger moron than the moron he already was.

"Can I see your ID?" Beth asks.

It's nice to see Nichols scurry off like a scared insect.

Beth says, "Do you know him?"

I say no, but she can tell I'm lying, and then she has to go over to #2 to check a hundred-dollar bill with her magic pen. I watch her walk away and catch myself staring at Register #1 Girl as she works. She even works beautiful.

I face the next customer. "Can I help you?"

"Can I have a pretzel?"

"Sure," I say. "That'll be four dollars."

The kid fumbles with a handful of quarters and hands me sixteen of them.

Nichols shows up at the side of my register, now with Todd. "Yo, Crapper. How about that Molson now?"

"Excuse me. We've been waiting for five minutes," the lady in front of me says to him. She's in her full hockey-fan outfit, complete with this year's new jersey, a pair of stone-washed jeans, and a pair of shit-kicker construction boots.

"Yeah, well, I waited, too, and now I'm back," Nichols says, leaning into my face, right over the counter. I lean into him—so close I can feel his breath. You can't bully a bully. I'm the Crapper.

I feel my right arm tense up. My fingers tingle. My adrenaline has already left the building. It's heading to my fist, which is ready to fire in three...two...one...

Hockey Lady grabs Nichols by the collar and says, "Little prick," and pulls him back to the end of the line. Then she returns and smiles at me.

"Thank you," I say. I flex my right fist to get the feeling back. My insides feel woozy from the rush.

"No problem," she answers. "They should know not to mess with hockey fans. We don't take any shit."

This makes me want to become a hockey fan. I would love to not take any shit.

She orders a bunch of stuff and while she's waiting on the

buffalo wings, she scoots over so the next person can go. While I'm filling that person's drink refill, the buffalo wings appear on the hot tray and I reach back and grab them. Then, as I'm handing them to the hockey lady, Nichols pops up in the back of the crowd. "I hope he crapped on those wings for you, bitch! That's what the Crapper does best!"

She looks at me and I can tell—she recognizes me. I avoid eye contact, but she doesn't go away. When I look back at her, she has this look on her face. I can't describe it.

I hand a soda to the customer in front of me and ignore her even though she's still staring at me. As I'm making nachos for the next guy, one of her kids comes up and says, "Mom? Are you coming?" and she leaves with the kid.

⸻ ▪ ⸻

During the first period, we get a chance to clean up our counter and refill the condiment stations. Because I'm brawny, I always take the big bottles of ketchup and mustard over to the stand and fill them. Plus, it gets me away from the other six cashiers, who tend to want to talk and get to know their coworkers. Most of the time, they talk about TV shows.

And I don't watch TV.

Ever.

As I'm filling the second container of ketchup, the hockey-fan lady in the shit-kicker boots from before comes up to me and puts her hand on my shoulder.

"You're Gerald, aren't you?"

I stop and look at her. I can feel my face drop, and I nod.

She has tears in her eyes. "You are?"

I nod again.

She squeezes my arm and says, "I am so sorry for what those people did to you."

I find myself paralyzed. It's been more than ten years since it first aired, and I've tried to make it part of someone else's childhood and move past it, like Roger says. I've tried to forget Network Nanny by not watching TV and by writing her pretend letters to tell her how I really felt. I've done all that. None of it made it go away. But this hockey lady is something brand-new. She just says it and I can't move. Can't speak.

"You okay?" she asks. "I know it's none of my business, but I couldn't help it."

All I can do is nod.

"I always wanted to find you and take you up into my arms and give you a hug. You poor boy," she says.

I nod again. I try to get back to my ketchup, but I can't see anything through the glaze on my eyeballs. Everything is blurry.

"Do you mind if I hug you?" she asks.

I shake my head no.

And when she hugs me, something really weird happens. Before I can even figure out what's going on, I'm crying. Like, *really* crying. It's like someone is twisting open a spigot. I'm facing the ketchup containers, so no one at stand five can see this. And the harder I cry, the more she hugs me and the softer she is. The longer I cry, the more I realize what's happening.

I am being hugged. In ten years, I have been recognized, scrutinized, analyzed, criticized, and even terrorized by a handful of the millions of *Network Nanny* viewers. Never was I hugged.

I am completely silent as I cry. She is completely silent as she hugs me. After a few moments, she reaches behind me and grabs a few napkins and hands them to me. Beth comes over and asks if everything's okay and when she sees I'm crying, she pats me on the back and tells me she'll take register #7 for the rest of the day if I need her to.

"No," I say. "I'm fine." I face the wall and the condiments and blow my nose and wipe my face. Beth goes back to the stand. I take a few deep breaths.

Hockey Lady squeezes my arm and says, "I'll stay in touch." Then she walks away.

I stand there for a minute and locate my invisible roll of plastic wrap and cover myself in it again—the barrier that keeps me from *them*. The armor that protects me from the whole fucking world. The polyethylene that keeps the tears in.

Register #1 Girl looks at me as I walk in the door and she has that look on her face like she wants to cry, too. I ignore her and go back to register #7. I make a pact with myself to never let anyone hug me again.

I'M STILL WEARING my brand-new hockey jersey when I get in the house. I bought it so I don't have to take any shit, just like the hug woman. I never got her name. I will never be able to see ketchup again without thinking about her.

Dinner is long over, but the house still smells of roast chicken and homemade gravy. Dad is in his man cave, doing whatever he does in there. Probably drinking. Tasha and her rat boy are downstairs blasting some awful country-and-western song and singing along.

Mom is at the kitchen table sawing off the bottoms of moisturizer bottles to use the inch and a half that never gets pumped up by the too-short pump straws.

She's wearing safety glasses, wielding an electric knife—like the kind you slice turkey with. There are eight moisturizer bottles on the table, and next to them is a tub. She's filling it with the lotion she gets out of the bottles that she's sawing.

This is the shit she cares about. Not what Real Nanny told her about being fair and equal to all of her children. Not the twenty-one-year-old daughter getting planked in her basement and becoming more dependent by the day. I admit, part of me wants to take the electric knife and, well, you know.

She waves. I wave back and go upstairs to my room, where I can unsee what I just saw.

GERALD'S HAPPY PLACE. That's what the sign on my door says. GERALD'S HAPPY PLACE. I've had that there since I was thirteen and got suspended the first time for fighting. I mauled this kid's face. Tom something.

Tom had it coming.

Back then, Tasha was still off pretending she was in college and Lisi was in high school while I was stuck in middle school with no one to protect me from all the assholes who called me the Crapper all day.

So I took a bite out of Tom What's-His-Name's face. Scarred forever. Mauled by a crazy, untamed warrior.

I mauled him so bad they sent me straight to Roger, the anger management guru. That first day, he asked me where I was happiest. I didn't tell him about Gersday. I just said, "My room." So we made this sign and I hung it on my door.

I guess I *am* happier here. I have my own bathroom with

a shower. I have a loud stereo. A computer. An Internet connection. Everything you need to separate yourself from everyone else.

Except: Tasha still lives in the basement. And Mom still never wanted me as much as she wanted that inch of moisturizer at the bottom of those bottles.

10

HERE'S HOW I handle Monday mornings. I put on my headphones and listen to a crazy playlist of tribal drumming from Native American powwows. Lisi got it for me at a powwow she went to with her stoner boyfriend last year.

I listen to it from the minute I pack my backpack to the minute I park in the school parking lot. If I'm early, I even sit there and listen until the very last minute. Then I put on imaginary war paint. Three red lines under my eyes. One black stripe across my face. The same red stripes down my arms. One red stripe from my bottom lip down my chin. I have already decided that if I ever graduate from this shithole, I will wear the real paint on graduation day.

When I go into school, I am a warrior. I'm noble. Fair. I'm the chief of my own tribe. I *could* scalp you. I *could* be dangerous. But I choose not to, which is why I'm the chief.

Up until this year, things were different. I wasn't choosing anything. I still had all Roger's bad anger words in my vocabulary—*should, have to, deserve*. I was still out of control.

It wasn't just Tom. There were others, too. The broken arm in freshman year. And nose. And that time I tried to crush a kid's neck last year. I memorized the walls of the middle school principal's office. I memorized every inch of the high school's in-school suspension room. I memorized every time they told me I had *one more chance*. That was five chances ago.

Roger was never impressed. Now he is, though. Because now I know about my triggers and how to block them all out. I put on my war paint and my feathers and I walk into high school and play chief.

"Hey, Gerald. I heard we won yesterday." That's the kid whose locker is next to mine. He's a cool kid, pretty much. Plays in the jazz band and smokes a lot of pot.

"Three to one," I say.

"Nice jersey," he says.

I look down at my jersey and remember the hockey lady and how this is my not-taking-any-shit jersey. It's like I've got a double layer of chief on today.

"Thanks."

He nods and goes to his homeroom. I get my books and head to Mr. Fletcher's room. That's the SPED room to everyone else.

"Hey, Gerald!"

"Hi, Gerald!"

I wave and look at the floor.

"Nice shirt, Gerald!"

All you dipshits who think the SPED room is full of half-wits are wrong. This is the best room in school because no one gives a shit about how bad you are or how dumb you are or how you limp or stutter or how you can't think right because you spent most of your childhood crying in your bedroom because you were dubbed *the Crapper* before you ever even got to first grade.

No one cares what clothes you wear, what brand name your shoes are, how rich your family is, or how many songs you've uploaded to your iPod. No one cares about my car. No one cares about my gated community. No one cares about my past. They know, I'm sure, but no one has ever mentioned it, and if someone did, I think Mr. Fletcher would probably shut them up faster than they could even say it.

Mr. Fletcher is a real chief. Compared to him, I'm like a chief in training, because he has patience that I will never have—dealing with violent little assholes like me, who don't need to be in his classroom, and then helping Deirdre do everything because she's got cerebral palsy. And some days Jenny starts having a fit and throwing shit around and he has to calm her and get her to the nurse for whatever the nurse does to make her normal again.

"Gerald, are you still working out in that gym?" Jenny asks me. "Because you're getting bigger every time I see you."

"Yeah. Man, you're buff," Karen says.

"Oh my god, you guys. Shut up!" That's Kelly—he's a guy but he's named Kelly, which is just messed up, considering he's been slow since birth. Seriously. If you have a slow kid, don't give him a girl's name. Right?

"Yeah," I say. "Shut up."

Deirdre aims her electric wheelchair toward me and then reaches over and squeezes my arm. "Soon you'll be too hot for us retards," she says, and laughs. Sometimes when Deirdre laughs, she spits a little. None of us laugh at her, because we're a family—which is something the school guidance counselor can't understand when I tell him this.

"If you had a chance to get out of the special education program, you wouldn't take it?" he asked me during our monthly meeting last month.

"No way. I love those guys."

"But it's not about them. It's about you. You don't need to be in the class, do you?"

"I don't know. Depends what you mean by *need*," I said.

I *need* to not be on my guard all the time. I *need* to not have people call me names. I *need* a place where I don't need war paint to survive. And that's the SPED room. The war paint I wear just to get from my car *to the SPED room*. It's for lunch. For the mainstream gym class I have to take. It's for just being here and not somewhere else where no one knows who I am...like South America.

Fletcher says, "Okay. Get your math books out. You're all going to be calculating linear equations before Friday or I'll get fired and have to live on the streets."

I knew how to calculate linear equations three years ago, but I open my book and follow instructions. I'm not playing stupid. I'm just safer here. Or everyone else is safer because I'm here. Or something.

I I ■ I I

They put that Tom kid in my lunch period. Which was their mistake, because all he's wanted to do since I ate a hole through his face in eighth grade is kill me. He sends me looks from FS all the time. I stamp them with RETURN TO SENDER and eat my food. But one day, the kid's gonna break. I can see it. Before I graduate, he's going to sneak up on me and whale on me hard and I'm going to have to defend myself and I'll be the one who ends up incarcerated.

Which I refuse to do. Which is why this war paint is so good. Because I know it will allow me to lie down and take it.

Even if he bites my face off.

Even if he kills me.

I can take it.

I'll just skip off into Gersday in my moccasins and feathers and I'll make my wild calls and dance my wild dances and eat Indian ice cream until I'm finally free. I almost wish he'd just fucking do it already. I'm pretty sure everyone would be happier.

No one talks to me here outside of SPED kids. No teachers. Not even the lunch ladies. I told Roger once that they all think I'm about to hop up on the table and do a shit.

"I doubt it," he said. "You haven't done that since you were little, right?"

"Yeah. But I can see it. They want me to."

"Huh," he said.

I'm right. They all want me to. And I want to entertain them again, just like when I was a kid. It would give them something to talk about. Something to text each other about. LOL! ROTFLMAO! WTF? GTFO!

The guidance counselor used to say that the only reason I didn't have friends was because I had a wall up. First, he's a moron. Second, who the fuck wouldn't have a wall up if they were me? My wall has war paint on it, too. It's a picture of a fearsome beast inside the outline of a television.

11

EPISODE 1, SCENES 20-29

I'D GRADUATED FROM behavior charts to chore charts—step two of the 1-2-3 program. Real Nanny kept smiling at me from the sidelines, but Fake Nanny was stricter. My crapping really put her off. Which is why I did it. But hey—I hadn't punched a wall in a month, so she'd solved *that* problem, right?

"Gerald, here's your chore chart," Nanny said. "If you do what Mum and Dad say and get a sticker on this chart for every day, you'll get to go to your circus."

Lisi and I had been begging Mom and Dad to take us to the circus since the signs went up around town.

I looked at the chart—a small grid with pictures of the

three things I had to do every day in order to go to the circus. The tasks were easy. A picture of a bed and a toy box. I had to make my bed and clean up my toy box in the playroom. The third chore was weird, though.

"What's that?" I asked.

It was a picture of our kitchen table with place settings on it. I'd never been made to set the table before and, in my mind, I shouldn't have to do it, because I was a boy. I know how sexist this sounds now, but I was five. Cut me a break.

"It's a new chore, but we think it will help you be part of this family and make it the best team it can be. Those other two chores are for you and only you, but this means you can participate in a whole new way because you're such a big boy."

I squinted at the picture. "You want me to set the table?"

"Very good! Yes! For *dinn-ah* only."

"I don't even know where the stuff is," I said.

"That's all right. We'll help you for the first few days," she answered.

And they did. They showed me where the plates were and Mom said *be careful* about a hundred times, but I didn't break anything. By midweek, I'd make my bed in the morning right after I got up and I'd arrive at four on the nose to set the table...before anyone else was even in the kitchen. Because that way it was easier to coat Tasha's plate in dirty toilet water. I did this every day for two weeks. Made my bed. Cleaned up my toys. Set the table. Toilet water.

The film crews left us alone those two weeks while Nanny

went and meddled in some other family's life, and then she came back to find all those perfect stickers on my chart and the news that I hadn't crapped anywhere but the toilet.

She high-fived me. "I *knew* you could do it. What a good boy." I saw Real Nanny giving her a thumbs-up when she did this. She still had all that weird actress drama—demanded a certain type of apple in her lunch salads and only drank her tea at certain temperatures—but she was turning into a real nanny. Or, at least, she was nailing the role.

She went to Lisi's chart then and saw that she'd missed a few days of room cleaning and doing dishes. Nanny said, "Lisi, you can do better than that."

Lisi just nodded because the director told her to nod.

Tasha's chores were more complicated because she was the oldest. She was supposed to clean the bathrooms on Saturdays and clean her own room and the upstairs hallway. She hadn't done any of it. Not even once. Nanny asked if she'd just forgotten to put the stickers on her chart, but Tasha shook her head no and smirked.

Mom said, "It's really too much to ask of a ten-year-old. I don't think she should be doing those sorts of chores. Especially the toilet."

Nanny said, "Cleaning a toilet is certainly not too big a job for a ten-year-old. She's nearly eleven. She's got to learn to take care of herself." Nanny looked over to Real Nanny to make sure she was on track. Thumbs-up.

Mom ignored the nodding director and said, "I disagree. I think cleaning toilets is a teenage job and, for now, she can help Lisi wash dishes and do other things around here to make sure the house is clean. Plus, isn't toilet cleaner poisonous?"

Nanny rolled her eyes at the camera. "You should have brought this to me when we made the chart, Jill. Tasha agreed to these chores two weeks ago. She should have been doing them."

"I told her not to," Mom answered, crossing her arms.

Then Tasha said, "It's his fault!" and she pointed to me.

I felt my body go numb. I remember it. I remember feeling numb and frightened at what she was going to say next. Because I knew that no matter what she said, my circus dreams were over.

"Oh?" Nanny said, hand on her hip, already in punishment mode. Camera one zoomed in. "How's that?"

"I hate the smell of bathrooms!" She burst into fake tears. "I can't even go into the bathroom at school if someone pooped in it because it reminds me of him! He's ruining my life!"

Nanny cocked her head to the right. "You can't clean bathrooms because you don't like the smell of poop?"

Tasha nodded because Mom nodded. Real Nanny glared at Tasha.

"And she told you this when?" Nanny asked Mom.

"This morning," Mom said. "The poor thing."

Nanny looked back at Tasha. Then she looked at Real Nanny, who was still glaring.

Fake Nanny clapped her hands together and swished her hair as if she was in a shampoo commercial. "Lisi, you lose two hours of screens this week, for a total of five hours, right, love? Next week, do *bett-ah* and you can have all seven hours."

Lisi smiled and nodded. Not sure why. Seven hours of screens per week was a stupid rule. Made us all have to talk to one another more...or find new ways to avoid one another.

Nanny looked at me next. "Gerald, you've just earned back your little *comput-ah*." My Game Boy. I hadn't seen it in a month. "And since you did every one of your chores for a whole two weeks, you get to go to your circus with Lisi and you can also have whatever you put in your reward box. Go get it, love."

I ran to my reward box and pulled out the piece of paper on which I'd scrawled *Ise Creem*. I handed it to her.

"Oh, ice cream! I do love ice cream myself. What's your favorite flavor?"

"Strawberry," I said.

"Brilliant. You go and sit on the couch while I deal with your *sist-ah*."

She looked at Tasha and pursed her lips. Mom stood close enough for Tasha to grab and sob into if she had to. "Tasha," Nanny said, "while I'm very sympathetic to your newly realized fear of the smell of poop, I must point out that you didn't do one single chore on your chart—not even the ones that had nothing to do with the bathroom—so you lose all screens for a week. No computer. No TV. No video games." Tasha clung to Mom then, as if someone had just hit her.

"Why do I get punished because he craps everywhere?" Tasha sobbed.

Nanny turned to Mom. "Has Gerald been pooping again?"

"He hasn't done it since my—uh—shoes," Mom answered.

That's right. And no holes in walls, either. I wished some-one would say that.

Nanny looked back at Tasha and continued. "We can make a new chart with different chores on it for you, and this time, if we put something on there that disturbs you, you have to speak up, all right?"

Tasha glared at me, then asked Mom, who looked scared, "How is this fair?"

"It's fair because you're learning to work as a family," Nanny said.

"Those charts are stupid," Tasha answered.

"Don't say 'stupid,'" I yelled from the couch. "You're not allowed to say 'stupid.'"

"Oh, shut up, you little crapper!" Tasha screamed. "I hope you choke on your stupid ice cream!" She ran to her room and locked the door.

After the crew left, Mom asked Dad to take me out for ice cream. We went to Blue Marsh Dairy and I got a big cone of strawberry and Dad talked on his cell phone to a client about a bi-level he was trying to sell. Then he joined me in eating my cone because I couldn't eat it all.

He said, "I'm proud of you, son."

"Thanks," I said.

Then we went back home and Tasha was sitting on the couch eating ice cream out of a bowl and watching TV.

I said, "Hey! I thought she wasn't allowed!"

Mom tried to say something from the kitchen, where she was making dinner, but Tasha talked over her and said, "Shut up, you little troll. You're the problem child. Not me."

So I went upstairs and I did two things.

I crapped in Tasha's pink-sheeted bed—right at the bottom, where her feet would hit it. After I was done, I pulled up the covers and sat on it, so it would be a big, nasty, sticky mess.

Lisi and I never got to go to the circus.

12

LET'S GET THIS out in the open: Lisi doesn't call home because Mom tried to talk her out of college. Not specifically, mind you, but in her own ignore-the-middle-child kind of way. She never urged Lisi to get college catalogs, never bought her SAT prep books. The guidance counselor even called her from school one day and asked why Lisi hadn't made college plans yet. Maybe the guidance counselor heard it in my mother's voice—the complete lack of giveashit—because after he talked to her, he started to get Lisi applications and interviews. After Lisi started getting offers from colleges, Mom said two things.

"College is such a hard place to fit in" and "Look at what happened to your sister."

Lisi doesn't call home even though she knows I need to talk to her.

Lisi is probably too stoned to care.

She proved Mom wrong and went to college.

I would very much like to follow her lead—not only in getting the hell out of here but also in going to college, maybe...though that's going to be hard, considering SPED class and all this trouble I get into. Mom and Dad could have helped me, but instead Mom just kept meeting with school officials with that same face she gave to Nanny. *What can I do with this boy?*

So I got to meet the first caring and nurturing people I ever met, thanks to the least caring and nurturing person I ever met.

SPED class is my mother.

◼◼◼◼◼

When I get back from gym class, Deirdre tells me I look even sexier sweaty.

"Jesus, Deirdre," I say. "You're killing me here."

She spins her wheelchair around and smiles her crooked smile. "That's only because you want me and you can't have me," she says.

I smile at her. Then I notice that her right foot is off her footrest, and I reach down to put it on for her.

"While you're down there..." she says as I go to stand.

I turn bright red.

"You made him blush, Deirdre!" Karen says.

"Dude, you're gonna have to wear baggy clothes from now on," Kelly boy says. "These chicks are crazy."

Fletcher says, "Okay, guys. Can we please stop concentrating on Gerald's deltoids for a minute and get back to linear equations?"

"Linear equations suck," Kelly boy says.

"Yes," Mr. Fletcher answers. "Linear equations *do* suck. However, you have to learn them or you can't graduate, and you guys want to graduate, don't you?"

I look around. Jenny is staring out the window. Deirdre and Karen are still giggling about my arms. Kelly is so far from understanding linear equations, I think it would take days on a camel to get him anywhere near it. The rest of the class is similarly distracted. By stuff. Anything. Taylor has ADHD or something like that and she has to rock back and forth to stay focused. That throws off Larry, who hates when she rocks and can't concentrate. None of them give a shit about linear equations.

"I don't really care if I graduate," someone says.

"Me, neither," Karen says. "Plenty of people who did great things didn't graduate from stupid high school."

"I want to," Deirdre says. "Just so I can make them put a fuckin' ramp up to the stage and watch me for all five minutes it takes to get up it and back down again. It will probably be the first time they ever realized that I was in the same fuckin' school as them." She drools a lot as she says this. Usually long series of sentences do this to her. She takes the back of her hand and wipes off her chin and laughs.

"Language, please," Fletcher says.

I picture myself in my chief makeup going up on that stage to accept my diploma. I watched Lisi get hers. It was only Dad and me there to watch because Tasha "broke her wrist" a half hour before we had to leave. It wasn't even swollen. Mom took her to the hospital for X-rays anyway.

Now that I think of it, I can't figure out if I even care about graduation. I don't think I do. I don't think it matters. To me or anyone else. I think all anyone really cares about is that I don't get locked up. And all I care about is getting out of here. I don't really think I could go to college anyway.

"Maybe we can finish linear equations tomorrow," Karen suggests.

"Yeah," rocking-Taylor agrees. "That would work."

The room bubbles into a chorus of light chatter. I stay quiet and watch Fletcher. He allows it for about one minute. Then he whistles. A two-finger whistle that hurts my ears.

"Here's the deal. We learn linear equations by the end of the week. You can all do them." He points to Larry. "Larry can already do them. He's been doing them for a whole year."

Larry nods.

Fletcher looks at me because he knows I've been doing linear equations since middle school, but he doesn't say anything about it. Instead, he says, "So if Larry can do them, so can you. And I'm going to make damn sure you don't just know them. I'm going to make sure you remember them. Now get up."

We sit there.

"I said get up," he says. Then he turns to Deirdre. "Deirdre, steer yourself over there." He points to the opposite side of the room.

As she does this, we all get up and stand at our desks.

"Let's shake things up a little," he says. "You can only sit down once you answer a question right."

"That's bullshit!" Karen says.

"Language, please. And no, it's not bullshit. I guarantee that you will all be sitting inside of ten minutes. Watch." He turns to me first. "Gerald, if I say that five plus six equals x, then what is the value of x?"

"Eleven," I say.

"You may sit down."

He turns to Karen. "If I say that x plus three equals twelve, then what is the value of x?"

"Nine," she says.

"You may sit down," he says again.

He turns to Taylor. "Say m equals ten. What would x equal in this equation? Four times m equals x."

"The x would equal forty."

"You may sit down."

As I watch Fletcher, I realize he loves this job. He loves his life. He's happy in the SPED room teaching all of us SPEDs. I don't think I know one other adult who's as happy as he is. Most of them just pretend all the time.

"You may sit down," he says to whoever just answered.

When the last person sits, he says, "Now—that wasn't so hard, was it? Tomorrow, we'll come back and do some more. For now, let's get you guys ready to go home."

SPED class takes a while to get ready at the end of the day. Taylor needs to gather up her coat and her book bag and anything else she needs and has to be reminded five times not to forget anything in her desk. Deirdre needs help with her jacket, and her foot has fallen off the footrest again, so Fletcher puts it back on and secures it there, giving it a loving, sturdy wiggle.

Have you ever seen *One Flew Over the Cuckoo's Nest* with Jack Nicholson in it? SPED class reminds me of it. We're not crazy or in some mental ward being psychologically abused by some sadist nurse, but we're an accidental family, the same way they are. I know from driving past the mental hospital a few miles away that people on the outside look in and just see mental patients. Not people. That's how people look at SPED, too. But we're all people. Real people. I'm like Jack Nicholson's character—once demanding, hard to handle, violent, and scary, but now electroshocked into brain toast by the golden rule of anger management: *Have no demands.*

13

JACKO WALKS RIGHT up to me when I get to the gym and says, "Okay, mon. I know you can't fight here, but how about outside here? How about you and me?"

"Dude. You're not Jamaican. Just give it up," I say.

"What you mean, I'm not Jamaican?" he says.

"I mean you've lived in the Black Hills development since you were three. Two developments down from me, remember? And you go to a private school that costs, like, thirty grand a year."

He pushes me. "You didn't answer my question, *bumbaclaat*." He says this in a really convincing Jamaican accent.

"Will I fight you?" I say. "No. Not even if you rip my head off and piss down my neck."

My anger management coach would have a field day with Jacko. He has all the physical cues. *Clenched jaw. Shaking all over.* I walk past him to the speed bag and drop all my stuff on the floor, in the corner. I take off my shirt and start on the bag.

Jacko says something to me, but I don't hear him.

I stop the bag with my left hand and ask, "So why do you call yourself Jacko, anyway?"

He doesn't answer me, and after looking at me for a few seconds, he just walks away. *Fists tight. Muscles tensed.* I go back to the bag and superimpose faces on it. Tasha. Nanny. Tasha. Mom. Tasha. Nanny. Tasha. Nichols. Tasha. The cameraman from the first episode who said, "Look at his little pecker!" Tasha. Mom. Nanny. Dad. Nanny. Tasha. Mom.

I start to sweat. I feel the war paint dripping off my face and arms. The chief rolls down my back and onto the gym floor. Now I'm just Gerald. My arms burn. My neck burns. The bag hypnotizes me, and I'm mesmerized by how it seems to know when my hand is coming toward it. How it knows me. Saves me every day from going to jail. *Fuck jail.*

There is a rough push from the side into my rib cage. My first reaction is to pull my right back and let it fly. I stop mid-punch and see it's Jacko. He's saying some shit I can't keep up with. I start to back up. I make him dance with me. His two friends are behind him. They walk me around the gym, weaving in and out of the equipment.

He throws a slow punch and I dodge it. He throws a faster one and I dodge that, too. I feel the gym watching us. All other sounds have ceased except the drums in my head. I hop from foot to foot. I feel at one with the universe doing this dance with Jacko. Like I'm on one of the chief's peyote trips.

Jacko keeps throwing punches. I keep escaping them. I know how to catch his fist and flip him. I know how to knock him right out. I know how to kill him with my bare hands and eat his face, if I want. Instead, I make him dance. And dance. And dance. He's starting to get tired. He's getting slower. He's sweating. I can see his American fat jiggling on the surface of his furious Jamaican muscles.

"Okay! Enough!" A trainer steps in. "You! Back to the bag," he says to me. "And you—come with me," he says to Jacko the middle-class fake Jamaican.

I go back to the bag, but instead of working out, I just pick up my things, put my shirt back on, and head out the door toward my car.

14

I AVOID THE boxing gym for the rest of the week. I don't want that Jacko asshole sending me away. I bet they already have a reality TV show for that. *Teen Jail. Pubescent Prison.* I bet I'd get paid a packet to get in there. I am the original reality TV fuckup. What better way to follow my downfall than to air it on national TV?

On Wednesday, I want to go work out because I miss it, but instead I buy a speed bag and when Dad gets home from work, we mount it on the wall in the garage, near my old rusty pull-up bar. He tries it but can't keep up. When I show him how to do it, he smiles. And then he frowns.

And then the banging sound starts down in the basement

and we both leave the garage. He gets a drink and goes into his man cave. Mom throws random fruits and vegetables into the food processor in the kitchen and pretends she's making a random fruit-and-vegetable puree, when we all know she's just trying to be louder than the banging below her. I wonder, for the first time, if she does it to block out the sound not for our sake but for hers. I wonder, and then get instantly grossed out, if she and Dad even do it anymore. *You know how your mother is.* I go to my happy place and spend an hour in Gersday before I fall asleep.

It's a nice night in Gersday. Dad and I play Ping-Pong in the basement. In Gersday, the basement is still Dad's home gym, and I lift weights and he runs on the treadmill and then I hit the new speed bag a little and then we play Ping-Pong again and he beats me. When we go upstairs, he doesn't offer me a drink, and he doesn't pour himself one. Instead we eat oranges at the kitchen table while Mom tells us funny stories about what happened to her at work today. Because in Gersday, Mom has a job. She doesn't just turn pages in magazines, make pretend fruit puree, and fast-walk to meditate, and there are no handmade centerpieces.

Then the phone rings and it's Lisi and she wants to talk to me, because in Gersday, Lisi calls home and talks to me. We talk for an hour about how college is going and what it's like in Glasgow. After I hang up, we play a family game of Scrabble and I win. Dad and Mom both high-five me. My score is 233.

I I ▪ I I

I have this dream and it wakes me up at four in the morning on Friday. I can't fall back to sleep because I can't figure out what the dream means, but I know it means something important. The dream goes like this: I have something in my nose. In my left nostril. So I go to a mirror and I look up my nose and I see this big thing in there, like a huge booger, and so I reach in and I pull out a perfectly wrapped Hershey's Kiss chocolate candy. It even has the little paper Kiss flag sticking out of the top. And in the dream, I think, *I wonder why this hasn't melted yet*. And then I think, *Since it's wrapped, I might as well eat it*. And then I unwrap the Hershey's Kiss and I eat it.

I think this dream is about how messed up I am. I think it's about eating the crap that comes out of my nose and pretending that it's a perfectly wrapped Hershey's Kiss.

I I ■ I I

On Friday, the last hour of SPED is awesome. More games with linear equations, this time with two variables. More of Deirdre's sarcastic flirting. More of Fletcher's happiness and encouragement as if he doesn't know who I am. As if he thinks his time spent on me is worth it. Can't he see the permanent boom mike suspended in front of me? The reflectors? The spots? Can't he see the cameramen following me around the halls? The *behay-vyah* chart with all the black spots that I wear on my chest?

I I ■ I I

I have to go straight to work after school. Beth has me on register #5 and I tell her I can't work #5.

"I have to work number seven. You know that," I say.

She sighs.

"But it's closer to the cooler and everything," she says.

I shrug. "I really have to work on number seven."

She gives me a nod and tells the woman on #7 to move to #5. She switches the money drawers even though we're not even open and there's $150 in both of them. Then she sighs again.

"You okay?" I ask.

"Yeah. Tough day."

She's never a downer like this. Beth is awesome. Like—always awesome. I would totally be into her if she wasn't, like, fifty. She's the perfect opposite of me—she lives in her own sunshine state. Postal abbreviation SS. It is on an entirely different coast from FS. Her coast has beaches and seventy-five-degree waves, and mine has cliffs and the water is too cold to swim in.

"Can I do anything to help?" I ask.

She shakes her head and smiles a little. "You can make sure everyone has enough ice."

So I make sure everyone has enough ice and I start wrapping hot dogs and I do as much as I can to make Beth stop sighing. It's not right, her being like this.

"Yo, Crapper!" Nichols says from the walkway. "You gonna be cool tonight or am I going to have to sic Todd on you?" Todd looks mortified. Not just because Nichols is an idiot, but because he knows I could take him with my eyes closed. I keep wrapping hot dogs and hear nothing but the blood in my ears and my heartbeat.

And then she's here.

She's here saying, "Can I help you with those, Gerald?" and I'm so scared of what I'll say or do that I just nod and we wrap hot dogs together silently. She gets the jumbo dogs and wraps them in silver. I wrap the regular ones in blue. The other five cashiers do other stuff. I don't care. She smells like berries.

"How come you're always at register number seven?" she asks.

"Dunno," I say.

"Really?" she asks. "You don't know?"

"Not as busy. And no credit card machine."

"Ugh. I hate that thing," she says. She crinkles her nose up when she says it.

"Yeah."

"Yeah," she says.

I think about this for a minute, and then I ask, "So why don't you switch registers? Two and five don't do credit."

She answers, "I can't do two because"—she lowers her voice to a whisper—"I'm not eighteen."

"And five?"

"I—uh—I just like number one. It's, like, my place." When I don't say anything, she adds, "You probably think I'm a freak now or something." I watch her expression turn pained.

"No. I'm—uh. I'm always on seven for the same reason," I

say. "I like it there." I don't add that I like it there because she's on #1 and I'm in love with her, even though I don't even know her.

I don't add that.

"Oh," she says. "I guess we all have our quirks, eh?"

15

I CATCH HER looking at me a few times across the distance. When it's busy, there's a lot of space between register #1 and register #7. I counted on my way to fill the ice bucket. It's nineteen paces.

I don't think I'm too dangerous to date anymore. I mean, I know Roger thinks girls are infuriating and that I shouldn't be opening myself up to that shit, but she's cute. She's funny. We're both weird. She's weird because she writes in that little book. I'm weird because I used to crap on stuff. And because I wear war paint to school. And because I ate part of some kid's face once when I was thirteen.

I should clear that last part up.

Tom What's-His-Name was asking for it. I mean that in a strictly pre–anger management way. Now, I know that Tom was just being a douche, and I was to blame for eating his face. *Tom did not deserve a hole in his face. I did not deserve justice.* But anyway. He called me Crapper all the time. Like—never called me Gerald, ever. Just Crapper. And in middle school, we were stuck in the same class two years in a row, for seventh and eighth grades. As if middle school wasn't hard enough.

From the time Nanny left to the time I ate Tom What's-His-Name's face, I fell behind in school because no one helped me. Sometimes Lisi would, but I felt stupid a lot, so I didn't always ask her. By middle school, Mom had petitioned to get me into SPED again. This was her mission in life, I guess. The elementary school wouldn't let her do it, because they said I did fine in regular classes. But middle school was middle school. And the first quarter of eighth grade was just that Tom kid calling me Crapper all the time again and all the teachers letting him. It distracted me. I got mostly Ds and Fs on my report card.

Then one day—it was a normal day—he didn't do anything over the top. Just called me Crapper the way he would. Casual. "Hey, Crapper, can you pass me that book?" And I just turned into a hungry tiger. I think people tried to pull me off him, but before they could, I'd bitten him on the arm and the shoulder, and finally my teeth sank into his cheek. I took a bite, like he was an apple. I spat it out. He screamed.

I don't know. Something snapped, I guess. After five years of locking myself in my room with no one remotely concerned about that fact, and then a year and a half of being called the Crapper, I ate a kid's face. Sometimes these things happen.

I I ■ I I

Nichols doesn't show up until the end of the second period of the hockey game, and when I see him approach, I look over at Beth and give her the *come here* motion with my head. She recognizes him from last time and pretends to be annoyed so Nichols thinks she's the bitch.

"ID?" she asks.

Todd Kemp is already walking away, but Nichols just stands there staring at her. She could totally take him. She stares back. He gets that sarcastic smirk he has all the time, like he's better than us.

Nichols walks away and Beth nods, then motions toward the mob of people coming at us for food. "Here comes the rush," she says.

I look up and see Tasha standing right in front of me.

This sends me to Gersday, where a bowl of ice cream awaits, and two tickets to the circus for me and Lisi.

Tasha's drumming her fingers on the counter. "Pretzel and a jumbo hot dog and a Pepsi."

"No," I say. Beth stays by me when she hears me say this. I am in Gersday, so I don't give a shit what either of them thinks, because Tasha doesn't exist, so Tasha obviously *can't* have a pretzel, a jumbo dog, or a Pepsi. Things that don't exist can't buy, eat, or carry things that do exist. That's just a simple fact.

"Dude, get me it," Tasha says.

I don't say anything. In Gersday, the trapeze act is stunning. Lisi and I *ooh* and *aah* between bites of creamy goodness.

"You're a dick," Tasha says.

I don't say anything, because saying something to someone who doesn't exist would mean I'd be talking to myself, right?

"Forget it," she says, and walks away to get a pretzel somewhere else.

Once she sees I'm fine with the next customer, Beth goes back to acting as runner for the busier side of the stand, where Register #1 Girl is working.

Register #1 Girl has a name, but I don't use it, because all girls fall into one of two categories and she has a 50 percent chance of falling into the bad one. And if she falls into the bad category and I use her name, then I will have another trigger, and I don't want another trigger.

After we close, clean, and mop, I go outside and she's there, waiting for her ride. I want more than anything to offer her one, but I'm not allowed to offer beautiful girls a ride. That could put me in danger. Instead, I stop and talk to her while the two of us watch the next night's crew unpack their stuff at the loading dock. It's the circus, which seems like Gersday kismet. I wonder if there's a trapeze act.

"My dad is always fucking late," she says.

"So's mine," I say. "I think that's why my parents bought me a car when I turned sixteen. Just so they wouldn't have to taxi me around anymore."

I'm glad she doesn't ask me about my car. I get embarrassed about it. Like I'm some rich kid because a bunch of people used to watch me crap on TV. I don't have anything more to say, but I stand with her anyway. The PEC Center borders the bad side of town. During the day it's fine, but at night I wouldn't want Lisi standing around waiting by herself, so I'll stay with Register #1 Girl until her dad gets here.

"What do you think that is?" she asks, pointing toward something the circus guys are pulling out of a truck.

"No idea. Maybe a trampoline? Or some kind of platform?"

"I vote for trampoline." She squints. "Looks like those legs fold out."

A horn beeps. She turns toward the road and says goodbye. I watch the circus unload for a few more minutes before I go home. When I get there, Tasha and the naked mole rat are already in the basement making barnyard noises and Mom is already asleep, so she can't start mowing grass that isn't long or blowing leaves that aren't there, to block out the sound and act like our life is normal.

16

EPISODE 1, SCENE 36, TAKE 1

NANNY LEFT US alone for the last week but left her little spy cameras all around the house. It was creepy. I started to put a towel over myself in the bathroom. I looked down most of the time. I stopped picking my nose.

One night we were watching TV in the living room, and Mom and Dad were somewhere else in the house doing Mom-and-Dad things. Tasha sat with her back to a camera and did what she'd do—called me names and poked me and wiped spit in my face—and then, when I didn't react to any of those things, she pinched my nose and mouth closed until I turned pale. When I started to cry, Lisi said, "Tasha, just leave him alone." This made Tasha punch me. She did it low down, so the camera couldn't see it. Right in the balls.

When I could catch my breath, I came at her like a train and I hit her over and over while she screamed and swore at me until I eventually pushed her right off the couch. I picked up the nearest thing I could find—a wood carving of a giant mahogany fish that Mom and Dad bought on their honeymoon—and was about to slam it into her face, but Dad got there just in time and pulled me off her.

The cameras saw all of that.

Mom and Dad knew they were on camera, so they tried to discipline me the way 1-2-3 Fake Nanny had instructed. As they doled out punishments, I felt like I was floating through the deepest parts of the sea, holding my breath. A whale swam by and brushed against my back. A school of fish swam around me in a fish-cyclone and then swam away again. I could see the surface and the vague brightness of life above the water, but I was tied to something by my ankle.

I was five years old and I already knew it—that the day I inhaled would kill me.

17

SATURDAY MORNING I have to get to the PEC Center by eleven for the circus. I'm at the kitchen table with Mom and Dad at nine. It's very civilized. Mom is reading an issue of *Walker's World* and Dad is talking about this great deal across town with an indoor swimming pool and three decks.

"It's the perfect house at a quarter of what it's worth. I'd buy it now if I could." He puts printed pictures on the table and Mom stops to take a look at them. Downstairs, it starts quietly at first. A few squeaks and then small sounds like a washing machine. Then *ba-bang-ba-boom-ba-bang-ba-boom-ba-bang*.

I look at the picture on the MLS real estate listing. The pool looks warm and one of the decks looks high enough to push Tasha off and make it look like an accident. Or frame Mr. Trailer-Park Whiskers.

"Why don't you buy it?" I ask.

Mom makes a chuckle through her nose in that cynical way she does.

I reach over and grab the other pictures. It's a really great house. Even in this market, we'd make money selling this place and moving. More acreage. Different school district. New start. Maybe we can move one day when Tasha is out and forget to tell her where we went. *Ba-bang-ba-boom-ba-bang-ba-boom.*

"This place would sell for a lot, right?" I ask.

Dad nods. "At least four hundred. At *least.*"

"We're not moving," Mom says. She gets up and opens the lower cabinet next to the sink and retrieves the blender. "I'm not leaving a gated community for some house in the woods. I feel safe here," she says. Then she opens the fridge and pours some apple juice and yogurt into the blender and starts it.

Dad yells, "We'd save in community fees. And taxes."

Mom hits a higher speed on the blender. We can all still hear the *ba-bang-ba-boom-ba-bang-ba-boom.*

I say, "Yeah. And we wouldn't have rats in our basement."

Dad gathers the pictures and the MLS papers and stuffs them into his briefcase. Mom stands there pretending like she's making a smoothie, but we all know she's not. I get up and walk over to the basement door and kick it before I open it and scream, "Jesus, will you two just *stop it* already? Grow up! Move out! Just shut the hell *up*, will you?" I slam the door.

Mom turns off her blender and we all look at one another.

They look at me like I just shot a bear in the leg or something. Like the bear is about to come at us. I look at them like maybe I'm okay with the bear coming at us. *I can take the fucking bear.*

Seconds later, it starts up again and it's really loud and she's moaning extra-vulgar on purpose and Dad gets up and washes off his plate and puts it in the sink and Mom just stands there with her left hand on the blender's lid and her right hand hovering over the LIQUEFY button and we hear them both—uh—you know—*arrive*—and then, inside of fifteen seconds, Tasha's in the kitchen in her bathrobe.

Dad, Mom, and I stand there looking at her for a second: freshly inseminated, hair standing straight up, cheeks pink, last night's mascara chipped around her eyes.

"What the hell is your problem, you little prude?" she says to me.

"Hey," Dad says. This is his attempt to what? Defend my prudeness? What?

She walks over to me and shoves me in the chest. She says, "Dick."

I stand there and take it. I breathe in. I breathe out. I do not react. I enjoy every millisecond of being *her* trigger instead of her being mine.

She shoves me again. Mom puts her hand on Tasha's shoulder.

"This is my house as much as it's your house," Tasha says. "I can do what I want in my room."

"Fine," Dad says firmly—as a sort of gut reaction to make her just go burrow again.

"It's not *fine*. He's messed up," Tasha says.

"You make too much noise," Dad says. "He's right."

"Doug, we offered her a pla—" Mom starts.

Tasha turns to me. "Why are you so hung up on sex anyway, Gerald?" She stands inches in front of me with her arms crossed. "Can't get a girlfriend?" I imagine how bad the screams would be if I grabbed her now and stuck her palm on the burner Mom used to make her tea. I picture the perfectly circular ring burns on her fingers. Breathe in, breathe out.

"Tasha," Mom says.

Tasha taunts, "No one wants our fucked-up little crapper."

I'm chief all the way. Not a word. Not even a rise in blood pressure.

She stares at me.

I stare at her.

Mom and Dad are frozen for a second and then they say "Hey" or "Whoa" or "Enough."

When she sees she isn't getting a rise out of me, she leans down to my face and puts me in the patented Tasha grip: my nose pinched between her index- and middle-finger knuckles and my mouth held shut by her thumb. She pinches my nose hard and it hurts. She says, "I always knew you swung the other way. That would explain a lot, wouldn't it?"

Mom and Dad just disintegrate into two piles of incapable, lifeless flesh. My chief dissolves. My joy is gone. I am brought back. I am drowning right here in the kitchen, surrounded by people who don't care if I drown. They just stand there, watching. Home snuff movies, reality TV.

As I start to run out of air, I panic. I remember I have arms. And teeth. So I grab her hand and I bite it. Hard. Like a tiger would bite a hand—the same tiger that bit Tom What's-His-Name in eighth grade. I am not myself. I can only see me from the angle of the camera that was once mounted on the kitchen wall. My stripes are magnificent. Nothing else in the world is that shade of orange.

I watch myself wipe Tasha's blood on Mom's sparkling white tea towel and leave for work. Then I turn off the show.

■ ■ ■ ■

I am eating ice cream in Gersday and driving down the highway at about 234 miles per hour. I may have run red lights. I can't be sure. I could be driving on the wrong side of the road.

I am four. Tasha calls me gay and holds my head under the bathwater. I don't know how to drive a car, but I like to sit in the driver's seat and pretend.

I am six. Tasha calls me gay and holds her hand over my mouth and nose while I sleep. I love to ride the shiny, coin-operated race-car ride outside the supermarket.

I am seven. Tasha calls me gay and tries to suffocate me with a living room pillow. I am driving bumper cars at a country fair.

I am almost seventeen. Tasha says I swing the other way and puts me in the Tasha grip in the middle of the kitchen in front of our parents. I am driving through a watery black hole, never to return.

PART
TWO

18

THE HIGHWAY IS made of ice cream. The bridges are made of waffle cones. There are smiling, waving Walt Disney characters as mile markers. Each one says, "Hello, Gerald!" I take the butter pecan exit. The road is bumpy from pecans. I bounce into the backseat, where Snow White sits with her hands on her lap and says, "Good boy, Gerald! You've made us all very proud."

Snow White looks out the window and waves to her friends as we pass each one. Goofy. Pluto. Mickey. Donald. They blow kisses to her.

She says, "Would you like a regular cone or sugar?"

"Regular, please," I answer. She hands me a chunky cherry regular cone, and I begin to eat it.

The limousine driver asks, "How's the weather back there? Are you too hot? Too cold? I can adjust it if you want."

"I'm fine," I say.

Snow White says she's cold, so he turns up the heat. "Ladies first," the limo driver says. "You have to make them happy or else we all suffer, right, Gerald?"

"Right," I say, but I don't mean it. I can't see why ladies have to come first. Not in Gersday.

When I look out the window, I see we're driving to Disney World. There are signs that say ONLY 100 MILES TO THE MOUSE! or BE OUR GUEST! I eat my ice cream and try to ignore the stifling heat. Snow White doesn't seem bothered. She just keeps waving to her friends.

"Gerald," the limo driver says, "do you want to go to the circus before or after we drop Snow White at home?"

I don't know how to answer this question.

Then Snow White hands me an inflatable hammer. It's the same one I won at the fair when I was five. I wondered where it went. I hug it even though I am nearly seventeen and there is no reason for me to hug an inflatable hammer. Then she hands me a Ziploc bag of Game Boy games. When I look closely, I see they are all the games I ever asked for. The ones I never got. Before I can hug those, she hands me a puppy. And a hamster. And then she hands me a card that says *Happy 8th Birthday!* On the inside, she has forged Mom's and Dad's signatures perfectly. I realize that Snow White is a lot craftier than she seems. I'd never have pegged her as a forger. She always seemed so sweet.

Suddenly I don't want to be in the backseat with crafty Snow White, but I'm covered in all the things she's given me. A shoe box full of baseball cards. A pair of in-line roller skates. A little ball for my hamster to run around in. And it's hot back here. And the puppy is thirsty—he makes that thirsty breathing noise with his tongue out. Snow White looks at me and smiles, but I don't trust her anymore. She knows too much.

I am driving again.

I look in my rearview mirror and see there is no one in my backseat. I glance around the car and there is no inflatable hammer, no puppy. I am not driving to Disney World. The road is made of tarmacadam. I am Gerald. I am Gerald and there is no way I can ever be anyone but Gerald.

19

EPISODE 2, PRESHOW MEETING

A YEAR AFTER Nanny left us alone, Mom wrote another letter.

I couldn't stop myself from crapping on stuff all the time because it was the only method of communication that worked to remind them that I was still alive and still angry. Nanny hadn't fixed us. She hadn't fixed Tasha, who now, at age eleven, had started to hump pillows on the couch while we were all in the room. Dad would just leave. Lisi would go to her room and read. Mom just turned the volume up on the TV and pretended that humping couch pillows was normal—that her daughter making those weird, erotic faces while watching a Kraft Macaroni and Cheese commercial was totally okay. I was too young to understand any of it.

But just old enough to get yelled at for picking my nose.

So, the rules were: I couldn't pick my nose, but my sex-fiend sister could hump stuff in plain view of the entire family with no problems.

And so crapping became how I got my point across. *We are not okay. Fake Nanny messed us up worse. Mom isn't doing anything different.* Maybe if other people saw it and she had to clean up dressing rooms at the mall or drive home barefoot from her friend's house because I dropped one in her sneaker, she would have to make so many excuses and apologies that she would get the message. But she didn't get the message.

She wrote the letter, and Nanny agreed to come back.

The ratings had been good, the producers said. *Network Nanny* had competed with the other established nanny shows on TV and won. Elizabeth Harriet Smallpiece had finally found her fame in being a nanny who wasn't really a nanny. She was so good, they let Real Nanny go, which was a bummer because I was pretty sure Real Nanny had Tasha figured out.

They negotiated for more money. I overheard Mom and Dad's conversation about the whole thing. Dad sighed a lot. Mom talked about the one thing that really worried her.

"I think we should get the kitchen redone," Mom said. "It's so outdated."

"We can't afford that."

"But we're getting money for the show and all," she said. "And the kitchen is getting old."

"It's only fifteen years old. What's wrong with it? Everything works," Dad argued.

"But what will people think when it's on TV? They'll think we don't *care* and that we don't take care of our house," she said. "They'll judge."

Dad made a grunting noise in his throat but didn't say anything else.

We had two months until filming. Mom had some guy come and measure the place up and he had a kitchen installed in less than six weeks. He was a cool guy, too. Talked to me like I was normal. Let me help him and gave me my own little screw gun so I could play with offcut pieces of wood. I didn't crap in his toolbox once.

And then Nanny came back—first for the initial visit, which was mostly reintroductions. I tried to find her purse so I could crap in it on the first day, but she put it up high on the new fridge and I didn't have a chance to get it. I planned on doing that at least once, though.

But then the weirdest thing happened.

She pulled me aside.

"Gerald, I know things are very unfair for you *he-ah*," she said. "I'm going to try to get your mother to see that this time 'round."

I didn't trust her, but I nodded even though no one was telling me to nod, because there were no cameras yet.

"Did you hear me?" she asked. Her hair was even bigger now, as if it was inflating to keep up with her idea of herself.

"Yes."

"And what do you think?" she asked.

"I think that's good," I said.

"So you'll help me sort things out, then, will you? And be good?"

I nodded.

"Where's Real Nanny?" I asked.

She looked a little hurt but then smiled. "She's taught me everything I need to know. I'm flying solo this time 'round. So you'll be good, yeah?"

"Sure. I'll be good," I said.

Nanny didn't say much to anyone else before she left. The producer and director had talked to Mom and Dad and said they'd be back the next day for the usual setup. I looked forward to it.

After Nanny left, Mom and Dad sat the three of us down and promised us that we would go to Disney World if we could show TV viewers that we were cured. All four of them looked at me when they said this. Lisi and Dad smiled and did encouraging things. Mom and Tasha frowned and squinted at me.

Afterward, while I was brushing my teeth, Tasha came into my bathroom and slammed me up against the wall with her hand around my throat. As I swallowed a mouthful of toothpaste out of fear, she said, "I've wanted to go to Disney World my whole life. Everyone else in my class has gone. So if you mess this up for me, I'll kill you."

I couldn't sleep that night. I was too full of thoughts about my promise to Nanny-Big-Hair and about how Tasha was going to kill me. These two facts duked it out in my head for hours. And then I realized I didn't want to go to Disney World, because Tasha was going to Disney World.

So at two in the morning, I got up and sneaked into her room and got her Barbie Princess Cinderella's Carriage and laid a turd in it. In the morning, without a word to me or anyone else, Mom put the horse and carriage and turd in the trash. Before the camera crew arrived at nine in the morning, she went to Toys"R"Us to replace it.

20

I AM HUGGING the ketchup. To everyone else, I am simply filling the condiment containers. But in Gersday in my head, I am hugging the enormous industrial bottle of ketchup that is really the anonymous hockey lady who cares about me. I need her in my life. I want to find her at the next hockey game and ask her if I can come over for dinner. No one at her house would say I *swing the other way* just because I don't like to eat my breakfast to the sound track of my sister getting laid. No one would try to cut off my air supply. They probably don't care about the inch of moisturizer at the bottom of the bottle.

I somehow manage to fill all the ketchup containers

without spilling a drop. I somehow manage not to disappear into thin air. I somehow manage not to finally die of embarrassment on the spot.

That could happen any minute. I might be the only person who ever actually died of embarrassment...if the cops don't come and arrest me for biting Tasha first. The courtroom scene in my head is so disappointing. Mom sits over in the prosecution's area. Dad stands hesitantly in the aisle. No one sits in my area. Lisi never finds out I'm in jail until I write her a letter. *Why didn't you call me?*

I go back behind the counter and shuffle sideways down to register #7. Register #1 Girl smiles at me and I smile at her and I get this feeling as if I'm an idiot. *Like a beautiful girl would ever like you, Gerald. Seriously.*

Saturday at the circus. Little kids and their parents who grip their little hands too tightly. Little kids and parents who don't grip their little hands at all. Little kids screaming and crying and squealing and laughing. I watch one. Her laughter is so pure. It's like electricity. I wish I could plug into it and be her laughter. I watch her cheeks turn into perfect, round plums. Her hair is in pigtails and she's holding a souvenir stuffed toy.

I can tell she hasn't seen anything bad yet.

No one has used her as entertainment.

No one has done anything to her but love her.

"Pretzel."

I look up and there's this guy. He's in a suit. He's short. He's saying it in that way like I'm a machine. Like I'm a *Star Trek* replicator.

"Pretzel," he says again.

I stare at him. I want to say Snarky-Nanny things. *Yes. Pretzel. That's a noun. Very good.*

"You deaf?" he asks.

I keep staring at him. I think about jail. I think of Roger and my anger management knowledge. *You can't demand that other people have manners. You can* hope *it, though. You can wish.*

I look at the guy. I wish he had manners.

"Pretzel?" he says, with his hands out like he's now exasperated with my lack of giveashit about his pretzel. I look at his outstretched hands and think of a thing Dad says. *Wish in one hand and shit in the other. See which one piles up first.*

The guy stands there for a few more seconds, and then I walk away. That's the only option because I'm not getting him a pretzel and I've already been a tiger once today, so I'm not sure I can stop myself from being a tiger again. I walk right out of stand five and into the arena. I pause at a main door and watch the circus.

There's a clown in the center ring and he's pretending to pull his own tooth. The audience is laughing hysterically. I have no idea why this is funny. Pulling one's own tooth seems like a bad thing to do. I figure I must have missed something. He has a cartoon-dentist outfit on. Next to him is an oversize pair of pliers. They are as big as a bicycle.

An usher motions for me to come all the way in and close the curtain, so I do. As I stand in the darkened doorway, I breathe in. Breathe out. Breathe in. Breathe out.

I am eating ice cream on the trapeze. Strawberry. I put it down and begin to swing on the bar, and then I jump and I catch the next bar and swing high and flip and am caught at my wrists by Lisi, who is swinging on the other bar. As we swing and do tricks, she talks to me.

"After this, do you want to move to Glasgow with me?"

"Yes, please."

"We can talk then."

"Yes, please," I say again.

Because in real time, we've never talked about it. Not as adults. Or whatever we are. We hinted about it. We dealt with it in whatever ways we could. But never the drowning. We never talked about that.

The day she left, she locked her eyes with mine. She has green eyes like I do. She said, "Take care of yourself."

"I'll have to," I answered.

"Call me if you need me."

"I will."

She hugged me—the only one in my family who ever did that—and she kissed me on the cheek. "Stay out of trouble," she said. "We'll talk soon."

But we never did talk. And she never calls. It's been more than three months. I've stayed out of trouble. Until today. Until the tiger.

On a high swing, I let go of Lisi's wrists and fly through the domed ceiling at the PEC Center and become a bird. I'm a pigeon. I'm an escaped canary. I'm a bald eagle. I soar to the mountain to the east of town and I sit atop the tallest tree and I look at all the people. Lisi the bald eagle perches next to me. She asks me, "Gerald, what are you doing?"

I say, "I don't know."

"Come back and do the trapeze with me," she says.

After a few more swings, we're doing our synchronized double flip. We do it twice. Three times. The crowd is awed. They think we are the two most talented people on earth right now. They want to be us. They want to fly, too.

They toss flowers at us. They give us a standing ovation. This?

This is entertainment. If anyone had asked, this is what I would have answered.

ANYONE:	Do you want to be on TV?
ME:	Yes.
ANYONE:	Would you like to play the part of the naughty boy who craps on his parents' kitchen table?
ME:	No.
ANYONE:	Well, what do you want to be, then?
ME:	I want to fly on the trapeze.
ANYONE:	You're too little. We can't let you do that.
ME:	Well then, I want to be a bald eagle.
ANYONE:	This is why we don't ask five-year-olds questions like this.
ME:	How is a kid crapping on his parents' kitchen table entertaining?
ANYONE:	I don't know. But people seem to like it.

ME: You haven't noticed that it's a little
           perverted? Watching a kid poop on TV?
ANYONE: That's ridiculous. Why would you say
           something like that?
ME: Because it's true. Isn't that the only reason
           to ever say anything?

21

I HAVE NO idea how I got back to register #7. I don't remember leaving the arena. I don't remember knocking to get back in. I don't remember squeezing by irresistible Register #1 Girl. I don't remember counting out my drawer, but my money is in the zippered bag and my tally sheet is filled out and signed. By me. I have no idea where I was for the last hour. Last thing I remember is watching the circus.

We have an hour break before the next show. Half the cashiers go out to smoke or call their loved ones. I think about my loved ones. I think about what happened in real life this morning. So I decide to go out and call Dad.

"Hey, Ger, how's work?" he says.

"Fine," I say.

"Great," he says.

"Are you with clients?" I ask. He's always with clients.

"Nope. Driving to that place with the indoor swimming pool. Our secret, okay?"

"Sure," I say. Then I don't say anything because I want him to talk first.

"So...that was crazy this morning, wasn't it?" he says.

"Yeah. It was. My whole life's been crazy, though, you know?" I say. "I mean, when it comes to—uh—Tasha."

"Yeah," he says uncomfortably. "She exaggerates." Not *She totally had it coming because she was trying to suffocate you.* Nothing like that.

"I like girls," I say. "So she's wrong."

"You don't have to tell me that," he says. "Anyway, we'd love you no matter what."

I feel that's code for something else. Like he believes her. Like he believes that I swing the other way.

"So, did they call the police?" I ask.

"The what?" he says, distracted by his GPS telling him to turn. "No. Of course not. It's all fine."

I bit my sister in self-defense because she was trying to kill me in front of our parents. It's fine. Clearly.

I hear his door *bing*ing when he opens it and I hear him close it and mutter to himself about some key code. "Look, we should talk about this at home. Over drinks. Tonight? After work?" he says. "When do you get off?"

"I'm not coming home," I say. I surprise myself when I say

this. I check the concrete where I'm standing to make sure it's not made of ice cream. Nope. Still cement.

"Of course you're coming home," he says. "You're sixteen. You live there. And we'll work this out. I promise."

A puppy. A hamster, Rollerblades, baseball cards. I promise, I promise, I promise.

I hear his shoes taking each step to the front porch and I hear him breathe more heavily as he gets to the top.

"I'm not coming home," I say. "Not while she lives there." I feel a rush when I say this. Panic and fear and tiger all at once.

"Look, we can talk later," he says as he swings the front door open with a creak. "I'll make sure this works out right, okay?"

"I'm not coming home," I say.

I hang up and wander through the skinny smokers' alley to the back of the PEC Center, where there's a huge parking lot and loading bay. I hear yelling, so I walk until I can see who's saying what. There's this tall, round, bald guy and two skinny guys up against him. A woman sits behind them on a suitcase. The two skinny guys get right in the bald guy's face.

"We're fuckin' out of here, Joe," one guy says.

"This is such bullshit," the other one says.

"Tomorrow we're in Philly. You can leave after that," (assumed) Joe says. He rubs his bald head. "I just paid you! How can you fuck me over like this?"

"Fuck Philly and fuck you," the first guy says, and the three begin to walk away from Joe. I'm tense because, as much as this sounds crazy coming from a face-eating, neck-crushing, sister-biting table-crapper, I'm not a big fan of confrontation.

"Well, fuck you, too!" Joe says. He stands there for a minute, furious. "Good luck finding a way out of this shitty little town!"

I watch the three of them walking, and once they get across the railroad tracks, one of them pulls out a smartphone and they get their bearings and start to walk in the direction of the bus station that's ten blocks away.

Joe, the tall, bald guy, stands outside for a minute, and I hear his last words echo in my head. *Good luck finding a way out of this shitty little town.*

I turn around and run right into Register #1 Girl and another cashier.

"Sorry," I say. "I didn't know you were here."

"We heard the yelling," she says.

"It's over now," I say.

It's over now, Gerald. Good luck finding a way out of this shitty little town.

22

REGISTER #1 GIRL and her cashier friend turn around and go back toward the side door. (Have I mentioned that she has the cutest ass in the universe? I probably haven't. The boys' combat pants work. That's all I'll say.) I walk back to the edge of the parking lot and sit down on a step and watch people. It's pretty quiet. The security guards are wandering around doing security-guard things. *Maybe I can be a security guard. I'm big enough. Beats counting hot dogs.*

I feel like I just fucked up by telling Dad that I'm not coming home. At the same time, I really don't want to go home. At the same time, I pretty much have to go home.

A kid appears at the bottom of the steps—he's about my

age. He's tall and his hair is just long enough to fit into a pony-tail. As he climbs the steps toward me, he looks over his shoulder to the loading bay, and when he gets out of sight he reaches into his pocket, pulls out a box of cigarettes, and lights one. Then he screams, "FUCK THIS SHIT!"

I admit this makes me jump. He sees me and moves his head to acknowledge that I'm sitting here. I scream back, not nearly as loud but loud enough, "FUCK THIS SHIT!"

We look at each other for a second. I have my usual Gerald-thoughts. *He recognizes me. He can see the behavior chart and all the black marks. Any second now, he's going to say, "Hey! You're the Crapper!"*

He walks up a few more steps and sits where he can talk to me—about three steps down.

"Fuck this shit, you know?" he says.

"Dude. I know. Seriously. Fuck. This. Shit."

Then we laugh. Really laugh. He has to wipe his nose because he snots from laughing so hard. I can't tell if my laughter is real. I think it is.

After he stops laughing he asks, "You work here?"

I nod.

"Good money?" he asks, taking a long, hard drag on the cigarette.

"Better than none at all, I guess."

"I don't make shit. Not until I'm older."

"Oh," I say. We sit in silence for a minute and I try to place his accent. He's not from here. He's got a Southern accent, I think. But not all the way. "How old do you have to be?" I ask.

He drags on his cigarette and says, "We work as hard as anyone else on the show, you know?"

Now he has a New Jersey accent. Or New York.

I ask, "You're with the circus?"

He laughs again and smoke comes out his nose. "I *am* the fuckin' circus, man. Every fuckin' day of my fuckin' life."

Down by the loading bay I can hear big, bald Joe yelling. *"Where the hell is that kid? I told him to get that bus cleared out before matinee! Useless son of a bitch!"*

"Huh," I say, because I don't know what else to say. Then I add, "What's with the clown-dentist thing? How come that's funny?"

"I don't know," he says. "I never understood clowns."

"You're the circus and you don't understand clowns?"

"Nope. I think they're totally stupid," he says, taking a pull from his cigarette. "But the kids like them."

"Huh. A clown pulling his own tooth doesn't seem like kids would like it," I say. "I guess that proves I'm not a kid."

"What do they pay you? Seven, eight bucks an hour?" he asks.

"Seven fifty."

"You cook?"

"Nah. I work the register. It's okay. Keeps me out of the house," I say.

He laughs at this.

"What?" I ask.

"I sure as shit wish I could get myself out of *my* house." He takes a last drag on his smoke and crushes it under his boot while it's still only half smoked. Then he points to the circus buses in the parking lot. "I've wanted to blow it up for years," he says. "I know how, too. I could do it. Blow the whole thing up. End this shit for good. For all of us."

"Shit," I say. Because I feel like I've just met myself. *Hello, other Gerald. Nice to meet you. Would you like to blow up the world with me? The whole fucking world?*

"Can't blow up your own family, though, you know? I got sisters. Nieces and nephews. And a grandmother..." He trails off because Joe is yelling again. *"Find that little shit for me and get him into that fuckin' bus. It has to be clean in an hour."*

"True," I say. "You can't blow up your whole family. Been there."

"Really?" he asks.

"Yeah," I say.

"We should be friends. I don't have any friends, so why not be friends with another psycho like me?" When he says this, my heart aches a little for being a psycho like him. But I can't deny it.

"We should," I say. "What's your number?" I give him mine.

He enters the number into his phone and sends me a text. It says *I'm Joe Jr.* While I enter his number into my contact list, I text back *I'm Gerald* and I half expect him to look at me and point and say something about Nanny-Fuck-This-Shit, but he doesn't.

"I'd kill to come with you," I say. "Everything sucks here."

"Trust me, nothing sucks more than my life. Anyway, you make seven fifty at your job, and you'll never make that with us. Big Joe is a cheapskate." On cue, Big Joe starts to yell again. "Shit. I'd better go. My dad is pissed," he says.

As he walks down the steps and out into the open lot, his father screams stuff at him and he ignores it as he goes to one of the buses and stands out of sight and lights another cigarette. I realize that I want to be him, even though I've only known him for five minutes.

"Fuck this shit!" I yell after him.

He nods and I can hear him as I walk away. "Fuck this shit!"

23

THE GIRL AT register #1 has told me her name again, but I still won't use it. I just smile at her and feel scared of her and want to smell her hair. Which sounds creepy, but I don't mean it in a creepy way at all.

When I look over at her during the preshow rush, I see that she's not happy today. I think back to when I saw her in the smokers' alley between shows. How she had a quiet conversation on her phone. How she wasn't her usual smiling self. At the time, I thought she was mad at me because of what I said when she and her friend came over to see what the yelling was about, but now I'm thinking this has nothing to do with me.

So when I see her on my way to refill her drawer with hot

dogs, I say, "Hey," and she says, "Hey," and she makes it really clear that she's not going to smile and so I smile at her but she still won't smile.

Fact: Being in a five-foot radius of her makes me not want to kill anyone.

Once the circus starts and the crowd dies down, I walk to register #1, where she's leaning on the counter writing something in her tiny book. I don't want her to think that I'm reading it, so I stand back and wait until she's done.

"Whoa. Gerald. Way to sneak up on me."

I ask, "You okay?"

"No." She sighs.

I nod, and I want to hug her because I can tell a hug would make her feel better. But Roger told me that I need to stop thinking that I know what other people need or want. He said, "Because of your childhood—uh—*situation* you have a larger sense of self than many."

I remember that frustrated look he gave me when I didn't understand this.

He translated. "You think the world revolves around you."

"No I don't," I said. What does Roger know anyway? He's just another guy like me who graduated from lame anger management class. I hate when he talks like he's some sort of headshrinker.

Thinking about him makes me mad, so I look back at sad Register #1 Girl and I say, "Can I help?"

She laughs a little. "Only if you have a magical time machine."

"And if I had a magical time machine?" I ask.

"Then I'd want to be in the future, two years from now. Preferably with some money and going somewhere exciting. Like Morocco. Or India."

"Wow," I say, because I've never known anyone who wanted to go to either place before. I don't think, in nearly seventeen years, I've ever even heard a person use the word *Morocco* in a sentence.

"Would you come with me?" she asks.

I want to make her smile, so I say, "Yes." But I don't want to go to India or Morocco.

"Really?" she asks. "You'd want to come with me?"

"Sure," I say. "I mean, I guess. I don't know anything about India."

"I can't figure you out," she says. "One minute I think you might be nice and then the next minute, you're—uh—just hard to figure out."

"A puzzle." That's what the guidance counselor calls me.

"A puzzle," she says. And then she smiles. This makes me smile. And then Beth shows up. She's in manager mode, which I guess is how I will always know her. But she seems like she'd be fun outside of the PEC Center. Sometimes she sees her friends here and they talk about what they're doing on the weekend. One time a guy mentioned skinny-dipping. It made me think about how I will probably never go skinny-dipping.

Beth says, "Gerald, can you do a dog count for me?"

I leave to count hot dogs.

Once we close the gate after intermission, I move slowly. Everyone else rushes to get home. Registers #4 and #5 had to leave right away to pick up their kids from babysitters. Beth asks me if I can clean the hot dog rollers and I say yes, and I tell her I'll mop, too, because if I mop, then I'm the last one out.

"Hannah already called mopping," Beth says. That's Register #1 Girl's name. Hannah.

I clean the hot dog rollers and take all the dishes back to the sink where #2 is washing. Beth asks the remaining cashiers if we want any of the leftover food and I realize I haven't eaten all day and I'm really hungry. She gives me a little tray of chicken fingers and fries, and when I get to the condiment counter, I take a napkin and put my chicken fingers on it and fill the rest of the tray with ketchup. I coat the fries in it. I dip the chicken in it. I think of the hugging hockey lady the whole time. I coat my food in her so I can be hugged from the inside.

As I eat my ketchup-covered food and watch Register #1 Girl mop the floor behind stand five, I rethink my ideas about India. No one there would know me. No one would call me the Crapper. Tasha doesn't live there.

India would be great.

I wish I could fly there right now so I can keep my word. *I'm not coming home.*

A half hour later, I'm sitting in my car in the parking lot. Not the garage I parked in, but the PEC Center parking lot, where the circus workers are busy loading their trucks to move on to Philly. I've texted Joe Jr., my new friend, and I haven't heard back. I don't want to leave the lot until I get to say good-bye or something. (A psycho's good-bye: *Fuck this shit!*)

As I look around for Joe, his father points and yells a lot. Yells *a lot*. He swears in almost every sentence. I rolled down my window a little and I've been listening. They're $%#*ing driving tonight. They $%#*ing start setup at the next place at three in the $%#*ing morning. The $%#*ing $%%holes who quit today were supposed to be driving the $%#*ing talent bus so they could get there early and $%#*ing sleep before matinee tomorrow.

"And if that isn't $%#*ing bad enough, I've got $%#*ing gas," he says into his cell phone.

I like him. He's the opposite of Dad. Dad, who has called four times in the last hour and left two messages. *Gerald, I hope you weren't serious about not coming home today. We'll talk about everything later.* Message number two was more serious. *Gerald, call me when you get this.*

Joe's dad would leave a far more straightforward message. I know this from watching him for a half hour. He'd say something like this: *Get your $%#*ing ass home and don't be $%#*ing late.*

Then I see Register #1 Girl. She's walking across the alley and talking on the phone. It's dangerous here at night. Especially on a Saturday. Especially for a pretty girl who smells like berries. I leave my car and I try to follow her on foot, but she's gone, so I go back to my car and start driving around the block. After two circles, I start to panic a little. I want to roll down my window and yell her name. Instead, I widen my search area and I find her four blocks away already. Heading for a worse part of town.

"Hey," I say. "Let me drive you to wherever you're going."

She stops and crosses her arms. Sighs.

When she gets into the car, I can tell she's been crying. I still want to hug her, but I know not to. Instead I ask, "Where are you going?"

"Nowhere."

"Oh," I say. "You seemed to be going somewhere."

"I was."

"So tell me where and I'll drive you."

"I was going nowhere," she says.

"Oh," I say again. "Can I come with you?"

She laughs at this and it breaks the tension in the car, which was getting pretty high because she is the first girl I have ever had in my car. And all I can think about is all the things ever said to me about girls. It's like girl-talk soup in my head.

Don't go out with girls.

Don't even walk with girls.

Girls lie about stuff.

Girls need more than you can give, Gerald.

One wrong move and you're arrested.

Girls aren't worth the trouble at your age, anyway.

Maybe you swing the other way. That would explain a lot.

24

I DON'T TELL Register #1 Girl that I have a plan tonight, but I have one. I texted Joe Jr. again and told him, but he still hasn't replied. We drive around for a while, and when she asks me when I have to be home, I say, "Never."

"What's that mean?"

"I don't know," I say. "I guess I'm not going home."

"So where are you going?"

"Nowhere," I say. "Just like you."

She nods and asks if she can put on some music. I say sure and she plugs her phone into my stereo and blasts out some old punk rock. I don't know who or what kind, but it's not bad.

After two songs, I start to feel like this is wrong. I don't trust her. Maybe she'll tell someone that I picked her up and tried something that I didn't. Maybe this is all a big joke and her girlfriends are waiting for her somewhere so they can all laugh about how she made the Crapper think he had a friend.

Wouldn't be the first time someone did that.

We drive around aimlessly for almost a half hour. Register #1 Girl talks about work mostly. Small talk. I say some stuff, but I think I'm mumbling. She looks out the window a lot. When I look at the clock and see it's nearly eleven, I turn down the music. "So what are we really doing?" I ask. "We can't just drive around forever. Do you want me to take you home?"

"How old are you?" she asks.

"Almost seventeen," I say. "Ten more days."

She's surprised. "You look older."

"Yeah. I know."

"I'm sixteen, too. Not sweet, though."

At first I don't get it. I think she's teasing me about something I don't understand.

"You know—sweet sixteen?"

"Oh," I say. "Right. You're not sweet. I get it."

The clock hits 11:04.

"Look," she says. "I kinda lied."

I hate lying girls, so I just shrug until she tells me the punch line. *The joke's on you, Gerald.*

"I was going to a friend's house. Well, two friends. But then we started talking, you know? And I—uh—I always wanted to know what you were like," she says. When I don't respond because I'm too busy trying to figure out what that means, she adds, "They live over on Franklin. You can come, too, I guess. They're nice."

Franklin Street, depending on which block you're talking about, is a mess of crack houses and dive bars. I can't imagine Register #1 Girl has friends there.

I can feel her looking at me, waiting for an answer. I say, "Do you want me to take you there?"

"Don't you want to come in with me?" she asks.

I can't tell her that I'm afraid my car will get stolen on Franklin Street. I can't tell her I don't like meeting new people. I can't tell her I am wrapped in plastic wrap so tightly sometimes I can't breathe. So I say, "Sure."

She directs me to the house and there's a parking spot about a half block away. In the summer on a Saturday night the street would be busy, but now it's not. We just pass a few guys walking down the sidewalk. They don't say anything, but as they approach I remember that I was a tiger earlier today and that I can be one anytime I want. I'm not scared of anyone. Except Register #1 Girl and her friends I haven't met yet.

She walks up the steps and I follow her. It's a house, not an apartment. It's a row house attached to about twenty other houses. The porch light is on and I can see the door knocker is a set of brass testicles.

Register #1 Girl doesn't knock. She just walks right in and I follow her. I don't know if it's the invisible plastic wrap or my nerves, but I think I'm sweating.

"Hey!" someone says. "It's Hannah!"

Register #1 Girl says, "Hey! It's Ashley!"

She walks in from the kitchen and is gorgeous. Red hair in a braid. Tank top and a half sleeve of colorful tattoos. Barefoot. Wedding ring. She hugs Register #1 Girl and then shakes my hand as I'm introduced, and smiles at me.

"Nice to meet you, Gerald." She doesn't look twice to see if I'm *that* Gerald. She just says, "Nice to meet you, Gerald," and goes back into the kitchen. "I'm baking." We follow her into the kitchen and Register #1 Girl goes to the fridge and grabs a bottle of water as if she lives here.

"You want something to drink?" she asks.

"No thanks," I say.

She shrugs and walks through the kitchen into the back room, where Ashley's husband is sitting. Register #1 Girl tells me his name is Nathan. He is as handsome as Ashley is gorgeous. They are the beautiful people. I had no idea the beautiful people could live on Franklin Street. You'd think it wouldn't be safe for them. Especially since they don't lock their front door.

"Nice to meet you, man," Nathan says. "Sit. Relax. Grab a beer."

"I don't drink." That's what I say through the plastic wrap. To me, it's sound waves bouncing off polyethylene—like a kazoo just said something.

I am suddenly distracted by the fish tanks in here. There are eight of them. I realize I am sweating because they make the room hot and Ashley is baking. Cookies, I think. It's hard to smell through the layer between me and the rest of the world. But I think it's chocolate chip cookies.

Register #1 Girl sits in a chair that's surrounded by three of the aquariums. She watches the fish and says, "Gerald, come here." She pats the chair next to her leg as if I could fit in that space—or as if I'd want to.

I stay on the small couch next to Nathan, who is watching a documentary about Jacques Cousteau. Register #1 Girl doesn't ask me a second time. She just sits there and stares at the fish. She's totally relaxed—I can see it in her face. I am the opposite of totally relaxed. I look at Nathan and I envy his beard. I decide when I'm older I'm going to grow a kick-ass beard.

Fuck this shit. Let's grow beards.

"Ashley! Beer me!" he says. Not in a bad way. "Bring one for Gerald, too!"

When she brings us both a beer, she kisses him on the lips right there in front of us. A big, loving kiss. I've never seen people act like this. It must show.

"We're newlyweds," Ashley says. "Have a cookie." She points to a plate of chocolate chip cookies.

"Congratulations," my kazoo-self says.

"Has Hannah told you all the names she's given the fish?" she asks.

"No."

We both look at Register #1 Girl. She is lost in the fish. This makes me wonder what might be in the cookies. These people are too mellow. Their house is too relaxing. The fish are too colorful.

So I open my beer.

25

"AREN'T THEY AMAZING?" she asks.

I'm busy worrying about if I'm sitting too close or if she can tell that I'm sweating too hard to answer.

"That's Lola. I named her that because she's yellow and just looks like a Lola, you know?" She points to the bigger, blue fish. "He's Drake. He's always biting everyone."

I look around to all of the fish tanks and try to estimate how many fish are in the room with us. I'd say there are about a hundred. We're outnumbered.

"Get it? Drake? Dracula?"

I pretend to look at the fish, but really I'm looking at Register #1 Girl's face. Her skin reflects the fluorescent lighting of the tanks, and she looks translucent.

"One day, I'm going to get fish," she says. "I'm going to get a huge tank like that one." She points to the long tank at the end of the room. "It'll be cool. No more parents. No more rules. No more anything except a job and a house and my fish."

Nathan scratches his beard. "You rock, Hannah." Then he bends his head toward the kitchen and yells, "Ash! You're gonna miss the best part of this documentary if you don't come in now!"

Ashley comes in and sits on the love seat next to him and they hold hands. Register #1 Girl cares about nothing except the fish. I sit here, nervous. I never realized how uncomfortable I am around happy people before. I feel like one of those fish—behind glass.

When I finish my beer, I figure I've been here for about an hour. I've learned a lot about Jacques Cousteau and underwater life. My clothing has absorbed about a pint of sweat. Register #1 Girl has had two bottles of water and three cookies and has rotated from tank to tank so that she's acknowledged every fish in the room. Then she just gets up and says good-bye. Just like that.

"See ya." She waves, and Ashley and Nathan wave from the love seat and keep watching the documentary.

"Later," Nathan says. "Hope to see you again, Gerald."

"Take some cookies for the road," Ashley says. "I'll eat them all."

Register #1 Girl grabs a half dozen cookies and we walk through the kitchen and out the front door. I lock it behind me out of habit. Or maybe because I liked Ashley and Nathan so much I don't want anything bad to happen to them before I can go back.

As I walk toward the car, I realize I want to go back almost immediately.

I want to live there.

I can tell by Register #1 Girl's sad face that she feels the exact same way. She wants to live there, too.

We don't say anything until we're five minutes out of town. I check my phone, and there's still no reply from my new friend Joe-Psycho-Jr. Even after my second text. *I'm coming with you to Philly. Don't leave without me.*

"They're really nice," I say.

"Yeah. They're awesome." She says it like she couldn't care less about them—like she's only using them for their fish. I can't describe her right now. It's like when we were there on Franklin Street she was herself, but now she's wrapping herself in my plastic wrap. *Probably because she's stuck in the car with you, loser.*

"Are we just going to drive around now?" I ask.

"I don't know. You're in charge. Where do you live?"

I think about what I said to Dad today. I think about Tasha. "I guess I don't live anywhere. But I have an idea. I just don't know if it's a good idea," I say as I drive back over the bridge toward the PEC Center.

"I'm open to ideas. Except that we run off and get married," she says. "I'll never get married."

I feel myself blush when she says this. *Dear Register #1 Girl: Marry me right now.*

"Kidding," she says. "I don't think you want to run off and get married." When I don't say anything, she adds, "Wow.

Sorry. I hope that didn't make you mad. Sometimes I don't know when to shut up."

"Nah. I don't get mad," I say. Breathe in. Breathe out. "I think I probably want to get married one day, though. I mean, when I'm old. Not now."

"So what's your idea?" she asks.

"It's not Morocco," I say. I turn into the PEC Center parking lot and drive to the back where I won't be in the way of any of the circus trucks. I stare at the crew loading the trucks.

After three minutes of us watching them together, she says, "You're going to run away with the circus?"

I figure I can lie to Big Joe. I'll tell him I'm eighteen and he won't ask me for $%#*ing ID. He'll tell me, *This isn't some $%#*ing picnic, boy. It's $%#*ing work. Hardest work you'll ever $%#*ing do.*

That's how I see it in my head.

"Am I allowed to talk you out of it?" she asks. "I mean— would that even work?"

Gerald, be real. There is no way this beautiful girl likes you. She only wants to talk you out of it because it's a crazy idea. "I don't want to count hot dogs all my life, you know?" I say. "And I'm not going home."

She senses it in my voice. Register #1 Girl is very observant like that. "Did something happen? Are they bad to you?" She cuts that sentence short. I can see her rewinding the tapes in her brain. I can see her picturing the five-year-old me squatting on the kitchen table.

"Do you want my car?" I ask.

"Seriously?" As she says this, her phone buzzes again and she presses the IGNORE button. I saw it said *Home* on the screen, though. I check my phone. No more messages from Dad. Still nothing from Joe Jr. "Aren't your parents going to want it back?" she asks. "You're only sixteen. You'll be, like, a missing person. I'll be driving around in evidence. Shit. I'll have to lie," she says. Then she punches me lightly on the arm. "Way to put me in a bad spot, Gerald."

"Sorry," I say. "I can just abandon the car downtown. Someone'll steal it. It's the perfect alibi."

"I'll still have to lie," she says. "Or, you know…I could go with you."

"I don't want to get you into trouble," I say. "You should go home. I can drop you there. Then you can say that you thought I was just going home."

"Or…not. Life is *boring* here. India, remember? Morocco?"

I want to tell her that being bored is not a reason to run away. I want to tell her that she's got a chance at a decent existence. No crapping videos to haunt her. No rodent-planking siblings. No anger management. No SPED class. No crazy fake Jamaicans out to kill her. Instead, I don't say anything because it feels right, her coming with me. And then the back driver's-side door opens, and my new friend Joe Jr. is sitting in my backseat.

"Are you $%#*ing crazy?" he asks.

26

"DIDN'T YOU HEAR anything I $%#*ing said on the steps today? My life sucks. Why the $%#* would you want my life?"

"I—uh—don't know," I answer.

"Hi," Register #1 Girl says. "I'm Hannah."

Joe Jr. nods at her. "And you have a $%#*ing girlfriend? Gerald, as your friend, I have to talk you out of this. It's a shitty life with shitty pay, and while it may look good to you because of some shit at home or whatever your problem is, it's not as cool as you $%#*ing think it is."

"I think it's cool," Register #1 Girl says.

"You're just a kid," Joe Jr. says. To both of us.

"You're just a kid, too," I say.

"Yeah, but I'm a circus kid. It's different. I don't have any $%#*ing choice, dude." He looks into my eyes. "Fuck this shit, remember?"

Register #1 Girl is getting edgy. I can tell because she's frowning at Joe Jr.

"I don't have a choice, either, man. If I stay here, I'll end up in jail. And I don't want to work counting $%#*ing hot dogs my whole life."

Joe Jr. sighs. Register #1 Girl is still frowning at him. "Look," he says. "You go to school, right? You have a girl. You have a house. You have a job. You even have this $%#*ing awesome car."

"It *is* awesome," I say.

"What does that have to do with shit?" Register #1 Girl says. "If Gerald wants to work for the circus, who the $%#* are you to say he can't?"

Joe Jr. ignores her. He looks at me in the rearview mirror. "Don't make me tell my dad that you're not eighteen. I don't want to bust on you like that."

In my head, there is a series of explosions—like Joe Jr. and I just blew up all the circus buses and the trucks and my house and the school and the whole $%#*ing PEC Center. But really, it's not an explosion. It's an implosion.

Because he's right. About everything.

And why hasn't Register #1 Girl told him that she's not my girlfriend? What's her deal? And why am I so especially pissed off about Tasha today, anyway? Hasn't she been calling me gay since before I ever knew what *gay* meant? Hasn't she been drowning me in plain view since I was born?

27

EPISODE 2, SCENES 7-15

CAMERA NUMBER ONE was on Nanny. "I think we should have one day that's all for Gerald. He gets his favorite foods, plays his favorite games, and can do whatever he wants so long as his *behay-vyah* is good."

Camera number two panned to Mom and Dad. They nodded.

Camera number three was set for a wide shot of all of them at the kitchen table. "I think his 'outbursts' are his way of trying to get your attention and because you're working so much, Doug, and you're his male role model, he needs to spend more time with you. Not a lot. Just a bit of boy time, you know?"

Camera number two focused on Dad trying not to look

pissed off. During this time, Nanny fluffed her hair in a mirror she'd propped against the wall. She took it to all her scenes with her. She had somehow become bonier since the last time she was here, so her cheekbones were jutting more than usual.

Camera number one again. "And Jill, sometimes you're so busy telling him to hush up you forget to listen to him. I think he feels that. I think he feels like he's in the way. I think he may even feel like you don't want him around. You spend so much time with Tasha that the others feel like you don't want them," she said. "We need to have a better attitude."

Mom looked stunned that this had been said aloud. Stunned. She excused herself from the table and went to the bathroom for five minutes.

After a short coffee break, Nanny clapped her hands and clasped them together. Then she got on one knee—which she often did to talk to me—and said, "Well. Today is *your* day, Gerald. What would you like for breakfast?" Camera one came in close.

I asked for waffles and Mom fixed me waffles. I asked for more maple syrup and Mom gave me more maple syrup. Mom asked me what I wanted in my lunch for all-day kindergarten and I said I wanted a peanut butter and marshmallow crème sandwich, potato chips, and Jell-O.

"We don't have any Jell-O," Mom said. "But I have pudding. Will that do?"

"Yes, please," I said.

Such acceptable behay-vyah. I could tell that Nanny, on the sidelines, was pleased. She kept winking at me the way Real

Nanny used to. Camera number two caught my smile, I think. They wanted as many angles of me smiling as they could get during episode two.

I ate all my waffles and I asked for more, and Mom gave me more even though it was against her nature. When I was done, I was allowed to go to my room, not make my bed if I didn't want to, and get dressed in whatever I wanted to wear. I made my bed anyway, and I wore my favorite camouflage pants and a long-sleeved T-shirt under a cool short-sleeved T-shirt of two T. rexes with boxing gloves on.

Mom hated those pants. She grimaced when she saw I was wearing them, but that was the point. I showed her my perfectly brushed teeth and my unsticky, lemon-fresh washed hands. She acted impressed, but by then she was too busy doing a homework sheet for Tasha to really care.

Nanny stepped in, motioning for a camera to follow her. "Jill? What are you doing?"

"Tasha forgot to do her homework last night," Mom said.

"Yes," Nanny said. "But what does that have to do with you?"

Mom looked at her and scowled.

Nanny sat at the table, gently reached over for the paper, and pulled it toward herself. Then she slid it across the table to where Tasha usually sat, and left it there.

"What are you doing?" Mom asked.

"I'm making Tasha do her own *home-wehk*," Nanny said. "That's how we do things now, yeah?"

Mom looked mad. "She just forgot, that's all."

"Do you know what my mum used to call it when I'd forget to do my lessons?"

Mom didn't answer.

"She'd call it hard knocks," Nanny said. She knocked on the table two times. "Hard knocks for me at school that day, right? Because it's my job to get my own work done, isn't it, Jill?"

"I don't do it all the time. Besides, you don't understand. This is America, not England. It reflects on me," Mom said.

"I *undah-stand* completely," Nanny answered. "And it only reflects on you because you let it. We'll talk about it *lay-tah*."

■ ■ ▓ ■ ■

My school day was good. I came home to spaghetti and meatballs. I could smell it from the minute I opened the door, and I felt like something had changed.

I was so happy about my dinner, I ignored Tasha humping the couch arm while I watched an after-school cartoon. I was so happy about my dinner, I ignored how she shoved me in the upstairs hallway for no reason. As the garlic bread went into the oven, I was so extra-happy, I stuck close to Mom and the kitchen so Tasha couldn't do anything crazy to me. Dad came home. We went out and played ball because he asked me what I wanted to do and that's what I wanted to do. The cameras ate it up.

And as we all sat down to eat dinner, I almost cried about how great this was. The happiest day of my life. The spaghetti was perfect. The meatballs were fried just right. The garlic bread was crunchy.

Cameras one and two caught the whole dinner from every angle. Then they caught Dad tiptoeing over to the counter and grabbing a box of something called fresh cannoli and bringing the box to me for first pick.

"What's a cannoli?" I asked.

"Try it," Dad said. "I bet you'll love it."

A fresh cannoli was one of the nicest things I'd ever eaten. It was almost better than ice cream.

Nanny came in at the end of my day and gave me a big, bony hug.

"You had a fantastic day, didn't you, Gerald?"

I nodded because I wanted to nod.

"What was your favorite part?" she asked.

I pretended to think about it awhile, but I knew the answer already. "Playing ball with Dad. And the dessert Dad brought home."

Nanny looked at Dad and smiled. From the way she flipped her hair, it almost seemed like she was flirting with him. "Isn't that the best feeling in the whole world?"

Dad nodded, even though he could see from Mom's face that she wasn't feeling very good about my answer. Or about Naughty Nanny's hair-flipping.

When I was on my way upstairs for the night—to change into my pajamas and pick two stories—Tasha came bounding down the steps. She pushed me hard and I fell down the stairs backward. When I landed at the bottom of the stairs headfirst, I cried, but not out of pain as much as out of fear. No one came to me but Nanny. The rest of the family just stood in the hall, staring. Nanny checked my head and said it wasn't bleeding. I told her Tasha had pushed me.

"I caught him trying to take a dump at the top of the landing," Tasha said.

None of them believed her. Not even Mom. I could see it. So Tasha started that high-pitched wailing she did, and she latched on to Mom's side and begged, "Please believe me! Why would I lie? Please believe me!"

Mom switched sides and muttered something about how I was impossible. The rest of us knew the truth. My pants weren't even unzipped.

"Go *upstay-yas* and get those jams on, Gerald," Nanny said after inspecting my head again. "Who do you want to read you stories tonight?"

"Lisi and Daddy," I said.

"Very well," she said. "You and Lisi brush those teeth and do your bathroom business, and Daddy'll be up in a minute."

I nodded, but once I had my pajamas on and Lisi was in the bathroom, I sneaked halfway down the stairs and listened.

Mom was crying.

"I'd never push Gerald down the steps on purpose. I love that kid," Tasha said.

Nanny had her stern voice on. "I do not believe Gerald was trying to defecate at the top of the stairs, Tasha. He'd just had a brilliant day, and I can't see why he'd do that. Can you?"

Tasha answered, "He's retarded, right? Isn't that the answer to everything?"

This was the first time I'd heard it.

28

I DON'T THINK life can be *boring* at Register #1 Girl's house. Boring to me always spelled middle-class venetian-blind window treatments, perfectly mowed lawns, and white picket fences. Her house is not any of these things.

As we drive down the quarter-mile driveway, I can feel her cringing. She told me I could drop her at the mailbox, but I wouldn't do it. She insisted, but I refused. When you take a girl home, you take her to her door and make sure she gets in safely. That's what you do.

I've never done this before, but I still know that's what you $%#*ing do.

But now she's wincing as we drive through a tunnel of

junk that started about ten yards back. Mostly scrapped cars and tractors. Some farm equipment. And then a bunch of stuff I can't ID in the dark. Cardboard boxes that have been outside so long they've melted into each other, plastic children's toys that used to belong to Register #1 Girl, I'll bet—a seesaw and a faded-pink pretend car.

Things are organized, though. It's not like those hoarder reality TV shows kids talk about at school. It's—a job site. It's a business. To my left, there's a barn and there's something spelled out on it in hubcaps. There is some sort of order to the cars and how they're parked and where.

"What does your dad do?" I ask.

"Isn't it obvious? He's a—a—" she says.

"He sells scrap metal? And parts?" I try.

"Yeah. That. Whatever. He's a freak."

We reach the house, which is a modified ranch house with nice flower beds and no junk around the front, and she gets out of the car before I can say anything, so I call her back.

"Hey!"

She stops and comes to the driver's-side door.

"If I was going to run off to the circus with anyone, I'd pick you," I say.

She smiles. "We totally should have done it. Just for something to do."

"Maybe next time," I say.

"You working the hockey game?" she asks.

"Yeah."

"See you then," she says. She flops her arm in a halfhearted wave and then goes toward the back-door carport, which is a tunnel of small machinery. A band saw. A lawn mower. As I watch her go through the back door, I realize that I just spent the evening with the girl of my dreams. It's like having a winning lottery ticket in my hand and having to climb $%#*ing Mount Everest to pick up the prize.

But I have the ticket.

I have the ticket.

Except seriously, Crapper. There is no way in hell you're ever winning that lottery.

At the end of the driveway, I pull out my phone. Another message from Dad. *I don't want to call the police. Mom's worried. Let us know you're okay.* And a text from Joe Jr. *You have no idea how good you have it, Gerald.*

As I drive back to the house, I think about this. About how lucky I have it. Sure, Joe Jr. doesn't know I'm the Crapper, so he thinks my life is roses and rainbows. He doesn't know about the infestation in my basement or the fact that I will never get anywhere if the starting line is SPED class, where I don't even belong.

My phone buzzes. *And your girl is cute.*

Somehow this fact—that he thinks she's my girl and that she's cute—makes it okay to go home and face the planking gerbils.

Is this all it would have taken for me not to have been the world's biggest asshole for the last four years? A girl? I don't know. I don't think Register #1 Girl is just any girl. She smells nice. She's beautiful because she doesn't try to be beautiful.

She has that little book. She is at one with the fish in the tanks—like me. We are both looking out into a distorted world and we are stuck, maybe. Stuck between feeling safe in the tank and feeling confined.

And she likes me, no matter how impossible that may seem.

Roger would say I'm just thinking about myself again.

Somehow, tonight, I don't think there's anything so wrong with that.

Maybe sometimes it's okay to think about myself.

29

DAD IS WAITING for me in the living room with the light on. It's 1:50 by the time I walk in the door because I took the long way home from Register #1 Girl's house. Dad is probably drunk.

"I thought you weren't coming home," he says.

"I wasn't."

"Shit. I was all ready to rent out your room, too," he says. Definitely drunk. "Can I fix you one?" He holds up his glass.

"Nah," I say. "I'm beat. Long night."

"Hockey game?"

"Circus, remember?" I say.

"Ah yes! The circus. No animals, I hope. Nothing sadder

than poor circus animals, as your mother would say." *Wasn't she the one in charge of making our whole family circus animals?* I want to ask that, but I don't.

"No animals," I say.

He shuffles the ice in his empty glass around and then sighs. "Shit, Ger. What do I say to you?"

"Don't know, Dad. I don't know."

"I can't kick Tasha out," he says. "But I don't want her living here, either."

"Why can't you kick her out?"

He sighs again.

"If she stays, I can't stay," I say.

He laughs. "You know, I saw that place today—the one with the pool and the decks? It'd make a perfect bachelor pad for us."

I stare at him. What the hell is he talking about now? Leaving Mom? Us moving out? Just drunk banter? "Are you serious?" I ask.

"About which part?"

"All of it. Any of it," I say.

"I don't know, kid," he says. "Lisi is gone. You're about to go. The only reasons I stayed. I mean, don't get me wrong, I love Tasha and she's my firstborn daughter and all, but she fucked up my marriage, man. I mean—completely fucked up my marriage." He sits there trying to remember what he was going to say, but he's so drunk he can't grasp it.

"I can't stay here if she stays here. That's all I know," I say.

"Well, Ger, then we're in the same creek on the same boat

with the same shitty paddle. Because there's no way your mom will let us sell this place and she's not going to make Tasha move out."

"We could rent," I say.

He makes an index-finger cross. "Jesus Christ! I'm a real estate agent! Are you trying to kill me?"

"Well, can you buy the place with the pool? Can you afford it?"

He shakes his head.

"What about with my money from the PEC?"

"You're a kid," he says.

"Who cares? I make money."

"Can't do it," he slurs.

"Well, unless you want me to run away and never come back, it's time to have a talk about this with Mom. And maybe Roger ... because he agrees that Tasha is a problem."

"Who the hell is Roger?"

"The anger management coach you pay every other week," I say.

On cue, the banging in the basement starts. Dad looks at me and I raise my eyebrows. *Good luck rowing your way out of this creek with that shitty paddle.*

I look at Dad and I know he's resigned. He's almost fifty, I guess. Maybe that's when you resign. He disappoints me. It's like he's willingly staying in jail after he found the key to his cell.

When I go to bed, I stop thinking about Tasha the trigger rodent. I think about Register #1 Girl and how big her eyes are and how they seem to be saying something to me, but it's like I don't speak big-eye language. I look forward to tomorrow's hockey game, even though it's Boy Scout Day and the place will be insanely busy.

And then I think about how close I came to running away tonight with Joe Jr. and the circus. The $%#*ing circus. If I'd done it, I'd be halfway to Philly by now. Wheels ditched. Talking to Register #1 Girl in a bus full of strangers. Ready to set up a circus before tomorrow's matinee. Ready for a new life, crazy as it might have been.

But what's crazy and what's sane when everything is possible and yet nothing ever happens?

30

WHEN I GET into Fletcher's SPED room on Monday, war paint applied, Deirdre is telling a story about her new heated wheelchair cushion.

"I didn't mean to make them mad. It was a nice gift," she says. "But it makes my ass sweat."

Kelly boy and Karen are cracking up. So is Mr. Fletcher. I take my seat and look at Deirdre. She's got this delicate skin that's really soft. You can tell just by looking at it. Her head is always cocked a bit to the left and her hair sticks up in spots no matter how much her aide brushes it. She's smarter than all of us. Maybe even Fletcher. Thing is, her body doesn't work so great, so she's here, stuck with us.

I still have the tribal drumming in my head from my drive to school. It feels silly today. I'm no chief. If I was a chief, I'd have gone to Philly with the circus on Saturday night. If I was a chief, I'd kiss Register #1 Girl. I'd get out of SPED class. I'd kick Tasha out myself. This morning she was up early and she said, "Have a nice day, loser," as I walked out the door. Mom was standing right there. What amount of war paint can cover that up? How loud do the buffalo drums have to be to drown out the sound of *that*?

I ■ ■ I I

After second block, the SPED room splits up. Some go to other classes, some go to early lunch. I pack up my backpack and head toward the locker room for gym. Nothing stupid happens in the locker room, and gym is bearable because Nichols has started ignoring me on account of having a new kid to talk to. The new kid just moved here from New Mexico, I heard. He's really good at indoor soccer.

We play with what looks like an oversize tennis ball. It's fun because the ball moves fast on the smooth, varnished wood floor. I take defense. I always take defense because offense is too much like trying to pick a fight. If I was up there by the goal right now, I'd probably put the ball in the net, but I'd probably accidentally punch someone to do it. And then jail. And then teen-jail TV. *Young Jailbirds. Boys Behind Bars.*

So I play fullback. Luckily, my job is easy because the teams are unevenly matched and our offense keeps scoring and there's barely any action back here by the net.

When gym's over, we go back to the locker room and New Kid says, "Hey, Crapper. I remember you from TV."

Nichols laughs.

"You were one sick motherfucker, man," New Kid says.

I don't say anything. I go to my locker and start to change. But New Kid doesn't stop. "Do you still do it?" he asks. "Shit on stuff?"

I don't say anything.

"Just so you know, you can't take me, okay? I might be crazier than you." He pokes me to get me to look at him. "Just so you know, okay?"

We have a crazy-eyes stare-off. He stares. I stare. He makes crazy eyes. I make crazy eyes. Eventually I win, and he walks off.

I finish getting dressed and I go out into the hall and aim myself for the cafeteria.

"Gerald!" I hear as I'm coming out of the locker room door.

I look up and see Register #1 Girl. "Oh, hey," I say.

"Hi," she says.

"Hi."

She tips her head to the side and frowns at me a little. "You okay?"

"Yeah. Sure. Gym sucks, that's all."

"Mightily," she says. "Indeed."

Who else would say that? *Gym sucks mightily indeed.* I love her.

"Uh—you still here?"

"Yeah," I say. "Going to lunch. You?"

"Lunch also. Shall we sit together and make all the freaks talk about us?"

I have so many answers to this. The first that comes to mind is: *Are you sure you want to do that?* The second is: *Are you sure you want to do that?* Why is she acting like I'm not Gerald "the Crapper" Faust?

"Okay," she says. "I'll take that as a no."

"No no no," I say. "Yes. Take it as a yes. I just—uh—never sat with anyone at lunch before. And you know, I'm—uh—well, you know."

"No. What? You're what?" she asks.

"I'm, well. I'm," I try. "I'm not very popular."

She smiles. "Welcome to the club, Gerald. I'm also not popular. I'd go one step further and say I am rather *un*popular. I'm okay with that. Aren't you?"

By this time, we are in the cafeteria and Register #1 Girl is walking toward a small booth at the side of the caf. Booths are cool. Makes the lunch experience feel less like school and more like a diner. Plus, there is only so much space in a booth. No one can intrude. She tosses her two backpacks into the seat first and then sits and I do the same.

We both pull out our packed lunches and she says, "Do you know my name?"

"Sure," I answer.

"So how come you never use it?"

"Hannah," I say. In my head I say *Hannah Hannah Hannah Hannah.*

She looks relieved. "Oh, good. So now we're on a first-name basis. What you got there?" She points at my lunch. Mom packed my favorite for me today. Chicken salad sandwich.

"Chicken salad," I say.

"And an apple," she adds. "And what's that? Soup?"

"Protein shake," I say, holding up my thermos. "My mother believes in the power of protein."

"Ah. I see." She empties her brown bag onto the table. There are two packs of Reese's Peanut Butter Cups, a small bag of Doritos, a Ziploc bag of Girl Scout cookies, and a Coke. "As you can tell by my lunch, my mother believes in nothing."

I nod and smile because she's hilarious. "I'll trade you half my sandwich for one of those Reese's," I say.

"Deal." She puts her hand out and I give her half of the diagonally cut sandwich and snag an orange packet. She bites into the sandwich and talks with her mouth full. "Jesus! Is that apple in there?"

"And grapes."

"Fuckin' A," she says, as if she's never eaten anything but what's spilled out in front of her.

We eat for a while. She asks to taste the protein shake, and I warn her that it's vanilla, which tastes like nothing, and she says she still wants to taste it and then complains that it tastes like nothing. I drink it anyway while she slurps down her can of Coke.

I save the Reese's for last because it was always my favorite candy before Nanny told Mom we should all give up sugar.

"I really liked your friends," I say.

"Nathan and Ashley? Yeah. They're the shit."

"Where do you know them from?"

"Ashley worked at my last job. She was a waitress. I was a busgirl. Our boss was an asshole. We bonded and lived happily ever after."

"Cool," I say. I think about bonding. I don't think it's something I can do inside all this polyethylene.

And then I realize that for twenty whole minutes, I haven't felt the need to kill anyone. Maybe longer. Maybe all day. I don't know. I didn't feel like killing New Kid in the locker room even though he was being a douche bag. I didn't feel the need to kill Nichols, either.

After five minutes, the silence at the table is killing us. I can tell it's driving her nuts, and I can't come up with anything clever to say, so I don't say anything. I chew everything maybe fifty times. I start to sweat from the pressure.

She finally says, "So you know my name and we almost ran off with the circus together, but I can't tell if you're my friend or not."

"Sure," I say. "I'm your friend."

"You don't say much."

"I'm not used to having to say anything, I guess."

"But you're my friend?"

I want to tell her that she's my girl, but it seems wrong. Roger would not approve. So I nod.

"If you're my friend, then you need to know that I carry this with me all the time and you're never allowed to look at it," she says, pulling her little notebook from her back pocket.

"I've seen you write in it before. At work, remember?"

"And?"

"I don't want to look at it. I mean, if that's what you were asking," I say.

"I wasn't asking you anything. I was telling you that if we're friends, that's part of the deal," she says. "And some of my old so-called friends had a problem with it, so I figured I'd get that part out of the way."

"Oh," I say. "Why'd they have a problem with it?"

She's already got it balanced on her knee and is writing. "They thought I was writing about them," she says.

"Oh," I say.

"And I was. But it's still none of their business," she adds. "And before you ask, yes, I have written in it about you, too. So you've been warned and if you're friends with me, you're friends with me *and* the book, okay?" She looks down again and continues writing.

"Fine with me," I say. *That's all fine with the Crapper, Hannah.* I have a minute to think while she writes. I figure since we're making deals and putting it all out there, I should say something. Anything. Because she's treating me like a normal person and she must know by now that I am Gerald. Youngest of three. Reality Boy.

"Hannah?" I ask. She looks up. "So, if you come with the book and we're still friends, I have to make sure of something."

She gestures for me to continue.

"So you know that whole shit that happened when I was a kid, right? Like, the TV show and what people call me and why I'm a freak and all that? You're okay with that? I mean, not with me being like that, because I'm not—like, not for a long time—but I mean, you know—you're okay that that was me once? And stuff?"

She smiles at me but doesn't say anything. So I allow my nerves to say, "I mean, I'm not supposed to trust girls or go out with them because my anger management coach says that girls are probably not a good idea and I'm thinking that that might even mean as friends. I mean, it's cool and it's not like I'm going to hurt anybody but—I—uh—oh, shit. None of this is coming out right."

She leans forward. "I know who you are. And I don't care. You're a nice guy," she says. "I have a shrink, too, and mine says I should dress more like I care, but I'm not sure what she means by 'care.' Dress like I care? About what? You know? Care about what?"

"You have a shrink?" I ask.

"Doesn't everyone?" she says.

"I don't think so," I say. Roger isn't exactly a shrink. But I guess it's kinda the same thing.

"Well, I do and you do, so that makes two of us, and that's all the friends I got, so as far as I'm concerned, yes. Everyone has a shrink," she says.

Hannah looks at the big clock on the wall and goes back to writing in her book. Up until now I thought I was the only kid in Blue Marsh with enough problems to see a shrink—or Roger, who acts like a shrink. When I look around the caf, I can't see anyone else who is remotely as messed up as I am.

Not even Hannah. But maybe I'm wrong. Maybe most other people are messed up, too. It just wasn't aired on TV or, you know, aired on Tom What's-His-Name's face.

My phone vibrates in my pocket and it's a text from Joe Jr. A picture. It's the clown dentist with the huge pliers in the ring, pretending to pull his own tooth. I enlarge it and show it to Hannah.

She says, "I'm telling you, dude. We made the wrong choice."

"I don't know," I say.

"Now we have to think of another plan to get us the hell out of here," she says, then goes back to writing in the book.

"Is that what you're writing about?"

"Yes."

"You're writing a plan to get us out of here?"

"Yes," she says. "We're going to kidnap ourselves."

I laugh a little because I think she's joking.

"I'm not kidding," she says. "I'm writing my list of demands as we speak."

31

THANKFULLY, HANNAH'S NEXT class is upstairs, because I really don't want her to see me going into the SPED room. And I think about that feeling through last block while we do more linear equations.

I am not retarded.

I learned to read late, yes, because nobody taught me, but I can read fast now. I read all the time.

I used to love math until third grade and that stupid asshole teacher who yelled all the time and made me so nervous I started eating paper and other bizarre things like chalk and erasers. Because that's what you get when you're famous, right? Even if you're eight?

I used to love school until everybody got old enough to point and laugh.

That's when Mom started to push for special ed. "Face it, Doug. I'm pretty sure he's developmentally delayed in some way." Not *I'm calling the principal about that teacher.* Not *Let's pull him out of public school* or *Let's move away to a place where no teachers will pick on him.* No talk about Tasha, who was trying her best to flunk out of her first year of high school. Just this shit about how I had to be retarded.

As Kelly boy fights linear equations one by one, I think about the doctors we went to and the school psychologists. I think about how my mother ordered medications, as if little pills could make our past go away. As if little pills could make me go away.

As I zone out in Fletcher's class I try to think of my own list of demands. I picture a note made of cutout magazine letters:

DeaR FAuSTs, We HAVE YoUR SoN. HeRE are OUR DeMANdS:

But I can't fill in the demands.
I doodle in my math notebook. I write: *Freedom.*
Duh.
I write: *A second chance.*
Shit. That's not a demand, it's a pipe dream. I can't get it, so I can't demand it.

I write: *Shit*. Then I scribble over the doodles so no one can read them.

I don't have any demands. I don't know how to demand. Demanding isn't something I do. What I do is: I want. And so far, all I want is stuff I can't have. Like someone murdering Tasha, or having a mother who might buy Reese's Peanut Butter Cups for my lunch instead of protein shakes. Or Hannah. I want Hannah.

"You, you, you, Gerald. That's all you ever think about," Roger used to say. "You see yourself through a Gerald lens. What about other people? Can you care about other people without it relating to you?"

I look around the SPED room and I know I care about other people. I've known Deirdre for two years and I care about her. I've known Karen and Jenny for that long, too, and I care about both of them. Last time Jenny had a fit the size of Utah, I was the one who made sure her head didn't splatter on the floor when she slipped out of her chair.

And I care about Hannah now. But I don't think I should. She probably thinks I'm a loser for not running away. She will probably just turn into another Tasha in my life. I will always be drowning in my own pathetic inability to breathe underwater.

"Yes, Gerald?"

Only when Fletcher calls on me do I realize my hand is up. I don't know why my hand is up.

"Can I have a lav pass, please?"

He points to his desk and I get a lav pass and walk to the

nearest bathroom. I look at myself in the mirror and ask, "What are your demands, Reality Boy?"

My reflection doesn't have any demands.

All demands have been removed from my reflection. Roger, my professional demand-remover, has done a spotless job.

Should *is a dirty word. No one* should *do anything for you. You deserve nothing more than what you earn.* Reality Boy is still angry, though. Because Reality Boy knows he deserves all kinds of shit he never got.

The longer I stare at myself in the mirror, the more I want to punch myself. Right in the face. I want to break my nose. Split my lip. Bite a hole in my cheek. I want to beat some sense into me. Instead, I punch the toilet stall door. It swings in and slams into the toilet-paper holder. My hand is numb. But not as numb as the rest of me.

32

EPISODE 2, SCENE 15, TAKE 2

WE WERE SUPPOSED to be making chicken Parmesan for Mom and Dad's anniversary dinner, but Nanny didn't really seem prepared for cooking. She was agitated. As we sloppily prepped food she kept saying *Mind my shoes! Don't splash on my dress!*

She handed me a Ziploc bag full of bread crumbs and cornflake crumbs and flecks of seasoning that Tasha had mixed together. She said I would shake the fillets of chicken around in there. She called them *fill-its*.

Tasha corrected her. "Fill-ays," she said.

Nanny gave her a look. "Don't be cheeky," she said. Then she plunged a chicken fillet into the bag I was holding and secured it.

"Now give it a good shake!" she said. And I shook it because she and the director acted out how to shake a chicken fillet in a bag.

Then Lisi took charge of the cheese-and-sauce part, and laying the fillets into a shallow ceramic dish, and Tasha, who'd preheated the oven to exactly 350 degrees, put the whole thing in and set the timer.

I still had the lump on my head from two nights earlier, when Tasha had pushed me down the stairs.

Mom and Dad were at a movie. We'd gone shopping that afternoon, and Nanny would be taking care of us while Mom and Dad ate a romantic dinner and did stuff parents do when they're alone. Hold hands, presumably.

At least for the cameras.

Because I don't think Mom and Dad held hands. Or kissed.

In fact, it was that afternoon when I realized that Mom and Dad didn't seem to like each other very much. They'd fought a lot while the kitchen was being remodeled. And before that. And before that, too. I vaguely remembered them fighting when I was really little. I vaguely remembered Dad once saying he was leaving.

Part of me—the six-year-old me—still daydreamed about that. I daydreamed that he'd take me with him. I wasn't sure if I'd made it up in my own head or if Dad had really said it. It would be one of those things I'd ask Lisi when we finally talked.

If we ever talked.

When Mom and Dad came in from their movie, they acted

so surprised about the chicken Parmesan. Nanny and Tasha had checked it in the oven a few times to make sure it was perfect. We'd chilled a side salad. We'd made garlic bread. We served it all up to them and I even pulled Mom's chair out for her.

We kids went upstairs with Nanny, who said it was time to get ready for school in the morning and to get ourselves ready for the week. She told Tasha to go into her room and gather her homework and make sure she had her laundry put away and organized. Then Nanny took Lisi and me into my room along with a cameraman. She looked at her watch. "We have an hour to play any game you want," she said. "Then Nanny has a hot date." She kicked off her very un-nanny high heels and loosened the belt on her dress and sat down on the floor at the end of my bed.

Without a word, Lisi went into her room and brought back Clue. Nanny called it *Cluedo*, which made Lisi and me laugh. Lisi did the cards-in-the-secret-envelope part because she never cheated, and I sometimes couldn't help myself.

We played three games in that hour.

Nanny said, "You two are little dotes, you know that?" When we looked at her like we didn't know what *dote* meant, she explained. "It means you don't cause any trouble."

Lisi stayed quiet. In my head I counted the times I'd caused trouble. I certainly counted crapping on stuff around the house as causing trouble. I concluded Nanny must be drunk. Maybe that's what a hot date was.

Nanny looked at Lisi. "Did Tasha ever play Cluedo with you like this?"

Lisi shook her head. "Tasha hates us."

"Tasha doesn't hate you," Nanny said.

"She tells us all the time," Lisi said. "She calls us names and hits us."

I reached and felt the lump on my head from two nights before. "She pushed me down the steps because she hates me."

"I'll look into that," Nanny said. "Would that make you feel better?"

Lisi's face was red now. "It won't change anything."

I added, "Yeah."

"Mom and Dad never care what Tasha does to us."

For a split second Nanny looked like she understood. Like maybe she knew—like maybe she remembered her promise, on the first day she came this time, to make things in the house fair for me. Then she said, "Let's change things up, will we? I want to be Mrs. Peacock this time!"

The cameraman got the entire hour on tape until Tasha started screaming in her room like someone had stabbed her.

Nanny got up and ran to Tasha's room and knocked on the door, telling the cameraman to stay in the hall.

By this time, Mom was halfway up the steps. "What are they doing to her?"

"I've got it," Nanny said. "Go down and enjoy your meal."

"How could you let this happen?" Mom asked.

"Tasha's in there on her own," Nanny said.

Mom clearly didn't believe it. "Where's Gerald?"

"He's been with me for the last hour," Nanny said. She pressed her mouth to the crack of the door. "Tasha! Open up the door!"

Tasha screamed, "I need Mom! I need Mom!"

"I'm here!" Mom called.

Tasha slowly opened the door and Mom gently pushed Nanny out of the way and went in.

Nanny, Lisi, Dad, and I stood in the hall until Mom opened the door and demanded that we come into Tasha's room to see what was going on. There was a giant turd in her bathroom sink. Allegedly. I didn't get to see it, but I admit I was curious because I'd only ever seen my own turds and I wondered what other people's turds would look like.

Nanny said, "Gerald didn't do that. He was with me for the last hour. We were playing a board game. On camera." She seemed completely pissed off that Mom was somehow blaming her for this.

"Well, he somehow *magically* got in here and did this," Mom said.

"Yeah," Tasha said.

Nanny and Tasha stared at each other. Then Nanny took me and Lisi to our rooms and told us to stay in there with the doors closed.

She took Mom, Dad, and Tasha downstairs, and after that I didn't hear anything because I did what I was told and stayed in my room.

But when I saw episode two when it aired, they'd cut the whole thing out. The whole day—the chicken Parmesan, the side salad, the garlic bread, the hour of Clue, Nanny's fancy blue dress and hot date, and even the mystery turd.

They cut it all out as if the day had never happened.

33

DURING THE LAST half hour of SPED, I sat there think-ing about what had happened in the bathroom and how much I had wanted to punch myself in the face. I wished I could just split into two and have the other me beat me to death and then that half of me could go to prison. *Homicidal Half Boy*: tonight at eight.

I text Joe Jr. once I get in my car in the school parking lot. *Fuck this shit*. I erase it. *Do you ever hate yourself?* I erase that, too. *Why do we take it?* I erase that and roll my eyes for being so dramatic. I finally type: *Still can't figure out why the clown dentist is so fckn funny*.

I drive to the boxing gym. When I get there, it's pretty

empty, and I go straight to the big bag and grab a pair of gloves and I start working it. It's amazing how out of shape my hands feel after a weeklong break. And after punching the dumb bathroom stall today, my right hurts when I hit the bag. I try to superimpose faces on the bag. *Have a nice day, loser.* Tasha. Mom. Tasha. Mom. Tasha. But then it's just me. Me. Me. Me. Me. Me. Me. Me. Me. Me. Me. Me.

After a little while, Bob the trainer walks over and watches me.

"Your left is weak," he says. "Here." He shows me how my left isn't punching straight, and moves his left the way he wants me to move my left. Then he says, "Keep that blocking hand up."

I pull my right close to my chin and hit the bag with my left a few times. He nods in approval and stands behind the bag to steady it. My hands still hurt, but I keep going until I sweat through my shirt. Then I move to the speed bag.

"Did you work out your shit with the Jamaican?" he asks.

"He's not Jamaican."

He nods. "You know who I mean, though, right?"

"Yeah."

"He's a great little boxer," he says. "I think he could go all the way."

I stop and look at him. "He couldn't take me last week. Too slow."

"He's lazy," Bob the trainer says.

I've been coming to this gym for over three years now, and if Bob thinks Jacko the fake Jamaican could go all the way, then I assume he knows if I could, too.

"Could I go all the way?" I ask.

"If you were allowed in the ring, I think you probably could," he says.

Then I start on the speed bag and Bob the trainer goes back to his office and I'm left wondering if I even like boxing anymore.

Now that there's an *all the way* and I can't get there, boxing seems stupid. It's like learning how to be a clown but never getting to perform your stupid dentist act in the ring. It's like learning how to drive while you're spending life in prison.

I stop hitting the bag and stand there. I stare at it as it swings back and forth and eventually comes to a stop.

The bag is me. I can't explain why the bag is me, but the bag is me. I have been swinging and I have come to a complete stop. I have no idea why. I have no idea why *anything*. Like, why I'm here. Or why I stopped. Or why I was swinging. I have no idea why my tribal music didn't work this morning. No idea why I don't feel like the chief. No idea why I felt like the chief in the first place. No idea why I ever started boxing. Or nonboxing. No idea why I wrap myself in plastic wrap and no idea how not to or what it really means. I just can't breathe. I feel like I'm going to spontaneously combust, so I pick up my keys and my sweatshirt and I leave.

I sit in the parking lot with the heater blasting until I get warm enough in my sweat-soaked shirt. Then I punch the dashboard. It leaves my knuckles stinging, like what happens when I punch the drywall.

A car parks in the lot, and it's Jacko the fake Jamaican. He gets out and walks into the gym. As I watch him, I am a snow-ball of rage that's reached the bottom of a very steep hill. I turn off the car and follow him in.

I grab a fresh mouth guard from the cabinet and put on headgear. He sees me and smiles and I nod at him in that way that can only mean I'm ready, and he finds headgear and puts his mouth guard in, too.

We find a random guy to lace us up and I fly into the ring.

No one rings a bell or referees us. We just start going at it. I go for his face, mostly. He goes for my ribs. There is blood inside of a minute—no idea whose blood, but who cares? That's the point. Blood is the point.

B-L-O-O-D I-S T-H-E P-O-I-N-T.

If I could bleed out the Crapper into the ring, I'd do it.

If I could bleed out everything that's wrong with my life, I'd bleed until I was empty.

I hit him in the face over and over again and his nose is pouring. He is a fountain of blood, and yet he won't keep his hand up to block, and I keep hitting the open target. *He is me. Me. Me. Me. He is too dumb to block his face, so I will punch it.*

Have a nice day, loser.

Minutes go by—it's impossible to tell how many. I try to maintain a rhythm, but he's clumsy and slow and he won't dance with me like he did last week. When I dodge his head shots, he slams me in the guts again. When he does that, I take the opportunity to pound his nose further into oblivion.

At first he said stuff. I don't know what. Stuff to egg me on, all garbled in the fight. Now he says nothing. He's breathing through his mouth. He's wishing for the bell, I think. But there is no bell and I keep punching the fountain of blood.

My ribs are cracking. I can feel the snap. It feels good. Ribs are like prison bars for my insides. Jacko is snapping all the bars. All the bars. Jacko is setting me free, rib by rib.

This thought distracts me. This thought makes me see that I am failing.

Roger will be so disappointed.

Just as I start to wonder if Hannah will visit me in jail, the fake Jamaican catches me on the side of my head—on my cheek, I think—and makes my neck twist. I nearly lose my footing, but I pull up my left to block and dance backward a little and take a short breather. It feels like we've been doing this for an hour.

He's hunched over now, still spurting blood. He's tired. He tries to aim for my head a few times, but I dodge and block and slam him one in the gut and one in the chest that knocks the wind out of him and he doubles in half and while he's bent over, I take my knee and jam it into his face and his head and he backs away and I kick at him like I'm an animal.

I am an animal. Jacko has just broken me out of my cage.

"Whoa! Whoa!" someone says. It's Bob the trainer. "Jesus, guys! What the hell?"

Before now, nothing existed outside of this ring. Now there's Bob. And Jacko is bleeding a river.

"What the hell, kid?" Bob says again. I'm breathing fast, my mouth forced open by the mouth guard, and then I realize he's talking to me.

What the hell, kid?

Jacko isn't saying anything, either, as Bob shoves shit up his nose and takes a soaking sponge to his face to see where the cuts are. I'm still dancing. Hopping. Waiting. My body is in destroy mode. Bob walks over to me and motions for me to hold out my gloves. He pulls them off and my hands are like clubs.

"You didn't even tape up?" he asks.

It echoes. *You didn't even tape up?*

It's a dumb question, asked by someone who thinks we *thought* about this. Like Bob hasn't met angry, impulsive teenage boys before today.

He makes me sit on a stool in the corner of the ring with my hands in a bucket of ice water. He takes Jacko to the office and as I sit there, I wonder again if Hannah will visit me in jail.

"I'll visit," Snow White says.

"I will, too," Lisi says.

"I'd really like to talk about it now," I say.

They disappear and it echoes. *I'd really like to talk about it now.*

34

I AM IN my happy place, surfing the Internet with ice on my cheek and ribs and hands and anywhere else I can put it. Mom asked me what the ice was for. I told her I'd been at the gym and that my hands hurt. That didn't surprise her at all.

She's going to see my cheek, though, if it bruises. And so will Roger, at tomorrow's appointment. It's not like I came out looking as bad as the fake Jamaican, though. He was so messed up, I'm checking my window for the cops every five minutes.

The Internet helps me forget. Some guys watch music videos. Some guys watch porn. I watch circus videos because I really think I'm going to do it. I really think Joe Jr. is wrong about how great I have it. He doesn't live in a cage, you know?

As I play the same trapeze video over and over and stare at the monitor, I try to will myself into Gersday, with no luck. It's as if Gersday has been hacked and someone changed my password.

The trapeze artists are like magic. It's a circus in Monaco, where no one has heard of the Crapper. These three Asian women and three Asian men do this act. It's like nothing I've ever seen in my life—so many spins and twists, and then they manage to catch each other in midair. How do they do that? I half think about trying it—trapeze—but then I remember that everything is pointless, like boxing. Learning trapeze would only mean I would never be able to actually perform on a trapeze.

I click on a different video and I watch a guy do a double flip and miss his catch and land in the net. The audience applauds anyway.

I hear Mom call my name, but I ignore it. Then she calls again. "Gerald! Phone!"

I go into my parents' bedroom to pick up the cordless and I can't figure out who would call me at home. I think maybe it's Lisi and she got my mental message that I needed to talk. Or maybe it's the police.

"Hey," Hannah says. Then Mom hangs up.

My heart stops for a second when I realize it's her.

"You there?" she asks.

"Yeah," I say. "Hi. How'd you—uh—I mean, wow. I was pretty sure our number was unlisted."

"It is," she says.

"Oh." I walk to my room quickly so Mom can't hear me, and I close the door.

"Beth gave it to me," she explains.

I'm pretty sure Beth only had my cell number, but whatever. It really doesn't matter now, does it? "So hey. You working on Wednesday?" I ask. "Dollar Night. Should be a riot."

"I didn't call to talk about work," she says. "I called to talk about you."

"Me?"

"You."

"What about me? I mean—yeah. What about me?" I say.

"I like you. I want to go out on a date or something. Together," she says. "And before you tell me again that you're not allowed, you should know that I'm not allowed, either, and that my parents can't know and my brother sure as hell can't know."

I'm in Gersday. My desk is made of waffle cone. I am ice cream. Peach soft-serve ice cream.

"Gerald?" she says.

"Yeah."

"And just so you know, this isn't some defiant shit I'm doing. I mean—I've liked you for a while and I was too shy to say anything because, well, you're Gerald."

I say, "Wow. I had no idea." And then after an uncomfortable second of searching for something else to say, I say, "I'd love to take you on a date. . . . God. That sounds so retarded."

"Don't say that," she says.

"What?"

"Going on a date doesn't sound retarded. Plus, that word bugs me. So there's rule number one. No saying *retarded*."

"Huh," I say. "I hear it a lot, so I guess it doesn't really bug me anymore. But if we're making rules, I have one."

"Yes, we're making rules. What's yours?"

I have no idea what my rule is, so I blurt out, "No musicals. I really hate musicals. Movies, stage, any musicals, forget it," I say. This is a joke, but she doesn't laugh. She sounds nervous. *You don't seriously believe she likes you, right? You're probably on speakerphone right now, her friends huddled around with their hands over their mouths, giggling.*

"That's easy. I hate musicals, too," she says. "And no chick flicks. I hate that shit."

"Deal," I say. I reach up to my face with my sore right hand and feel my smile. I trace it with my index finger.

"How can being called retarded not bug you?" she asks. "I mean, you know. I know everyone in your class has been called something at least once, but still."

So she knows I go to SPED class. Good. "I guess being Gerald 'the Crapper' Faust has its benefits," I say. "Plus, there's a lot you don't know."

"Then we'll have to schedule long walks to talk about it," she says.

I don't know what to say. *I give it a week, tops, before you fuck it up completely.*

"Gerald?"

"Yeah?"

"So—uh—you're not just saying yes out of pity, are you?"

"What did you mean when you said you were shy because I'm Gerald?" I ask.

"Uh—you're Gerald. Famous. A local celeb. Generally untouchable by any reality TV star who came after you."

"Shit," I say.

"Sorry."

"I'm not famous. I'm infamous," I say. "There's a big difference."

"I don't know. I think you're famous," she says. "And I should know. I even remember when the paper ran a story about your family and my mom cut it out for me so I could keep it."

"You watched that crap?"

"Yeah. Didn't you?"

"You don't seem very shy to me," I say.

"I'm shy until you get to know me. Then I'm just Hannah." She laughs a little. "And, Gerald?"

"Yeah?"

"Tomorrow in school—you'll be okay and stuff? Like—to me? This isn't a big joke or anything, is it?"

I had no idea other people could be as paranoid as I am. Especially not Hannah. She seems so confident. Maybe that's why she sees a shrink. Maybe she's paranoid. Maybe she's bipolar—up and down like Tasha. Shit.

"What?" I say. "Of course I'll be okay to you in school. We're friends. Like, even if this dating thing doesn't work out. We're friends." I say this like I'm in some Charlie Brown movie. Like I'm Linus and she's a girl Linus.

"That's cute," she says. "Probably impossible, but cute. Now go explain to your mom that I'm not a weirdo. She acted like I was some stalker or something when I asked for you. I'm guessing you guys might get that a lot." She laughs like it's funny, but we did get stalkers a lot, once.

"Okay," I say.

"I'm going to watch last night's episode of *Dumb Campers* that I recorded. Can't wait to see who got voted off. Bye, Gerald."

"Bye."

I think, *Rule number three: No talking about reality TV. Ever.*

I sit there for a minute and smile.

When I open my door to return the phone to my parents' bedroom, Mom is at the top of the steps.

"Who was that?" she asks.

"Just a girl from school," I say.

"That's what she told me. But how'd she get our number? I thought we only gave out cell numbers, remember?"

"Yeah. Sorry. I think I gave it to her by accident. We were in a rush," I say.

"A rush?"

"Yeah. She needed help with linear equations," I lie. "It was the end of class. The old number just came out, I think."

I walk through her bedroom and return the handset. She's still at the top of the stairs when I get back. "Linear equations?" she asks.

"Yeah. Who knew?" I say. Then I go back to my room

and close the door. I lie on my bed and close my eyes and I jump back into Gersday, where I want to tell Lisi about how I have a girlfriend. I want to be on the trapeze, catching her as she catches me. I want to be the joint that she smokes so that we can finally talk about everything without having to use words, because I will be a drug in her brain. I want peach soft-serve ice cream. I want to *be* peach soft-serve ice cream.

I whisper, "I demand to be peach soft-serve ice cream."

35

EPISODE 2, SCENE 0, TAKE 0

"DON'T YOU DARE say a word," Tasha said in my ear.

She had her knee pinned right in the middle of my back. The neighbor kid, Mike, was still naked in her bed, lying there smiling.

"I'm twelve now and I can do what I want," Tasha said. "And you're gay anyway, so you should just get out of here and go dream of wieners or whatever gay little retards dream about."

Before I could run, she grabbed me by the collar of my polo shirt, and I could feel the button against my throat. "If you tell them, I'll kill you."

Then she let me go and I ran to my room and locked the door behind me.

Five minutes later, I could hear their noises from my room, so I sneaked downstairs to where Lisi was reading a book. This was the one day Mom trusted Tasha to babysit us while she went and trained for that weekend's walk for multiple sclerosis or cancer or whatever the reason. She would only be gone an hour and a half, she'd said. Mike was in the house five minutes after Mom left. He lived two doors down.

This was our week off from cameras and Nanny. It was the perfect week for Tasha to bring a boy into the house through the back door. A perfect week for Mom to leave her in charge in the first place. We were all sneaking now.

I asked Lisi, "What does *gay* mean?"

She looked over her book and sighed. "You're not gay. Tasha's just mean."

"But what does it mean?" I asked. I was six now. Lisi was eight. Tasha had had her twelfth birthday a few days after the chicken Parmesan night with Mom and Dad. She had wanted a sleepover party and invited ten of her friends, but only one came. Lisi said that was because she was a bitch to her friends, too.

Lisi sighed again. "*Gay* means two things. Technically, it means boys who like boys or girls who like girls. But a lot of people say it and mean *stupid*."

"So, Tasha's just calling me stupid?" I asked.

"Tasha is calling you both, I think. She says it to me, too."

"Huh," I said.

"She's just being nasty. Six more years and she'll be gone," Lisi said.

"Six?" I asked. I did the math on my fingers. It meant that when I was twelve, I'd be free of Tasha.

"Yep. She'll be at college or something. Which will be good for us."

"Yeah."

"Do you want me to read you some *Harry Potter*?" she asked.

I snuggled up next to her and she read until Mom came home. Mike sneaked out the back door while Mom showered, and Tasha said she had to shower, too. Back then, I had no idea what she and Mike had been doing. I didn't know anything about sex, and I didn't understand that twelve was probably way too young to be doing it.

So far, Tasha's Disney World dream was close to coming true. I'd stopped crapping anywhere but the bathroom. We all did our chores. Sometimes Tasha was even nice to us. She'd offer to play a board game or do something fun. But then she'd go back to her usual self and haul off and hit me or half suffocate me and call us names. Lisi told me that Tasha was *hormonal*. I had no idea what that meant, but Lisi said it made Tasha worse than she already was, so we should just try to keep to ourselves.

That day when freshly showered Tasha and freshly showered Mom had a huge screaming match upstairs about something, we crept up the steps and peeked into Tasha's bedroom and saw what Tasha was doing.

I remember my eyes going so wide I couldn't blink. Lisi's jaw dropped.

Tasha had Mom pinned up against the wall, her hands around Mom's neck. She shouted, "Bitch! I hate you! I wish you never had me!"

Mom tried to say something, but Tasha was squeezing too hard. Then she realized she was squeezing too hard and let Mom go. Then Tasha slapped her roughly, right across the face. I lived that scene over and over in my head for years. I thought about how I should have saved Mom. How I should have stopped it somehow. But I knew I couldn't, because I didn't fully understand it. I didn't know the word *psychopath* when I was six. But it would have been helpful.

I could still see the mark on Mom's face when we all sat down to dinner that night. Lisi pointed at it to remind me. Dad didn't come home until later, when Mom was already in bed.

36

I WAKE TO find that my facial bruise from Jacko's lucky right hook didn't surface. It's just a little red. My ribs? My ribs are another story. They're purple and blue and yellow and black.

If my ribs were my face, I'd be in serious trouble.

But no one is going to see my ribs, so I just take a few headache pills and go to school. I get to my car without seeing anyone. No Mom. No Tasha. I skip the drums and the war paint. After beating the fake Jamaican in the ring yesterday, I feel like it would be disingenuous.

At lunch, Hannah finds me at the door to the caf and we walk in together and we sit in a booth and stuff the other half of our seats full of our books. She pours out the contents of her bag and I give her half my ham and cheese sandwich in trade for a pack of Oreos from her mountain of weird junk food. She even has Pop Rocks. I didn't think they made them anymore.

"Rule number three," I blurt. "No talking about TV. Especially reality TV."

She stares at me. "But that's all I do." Then she can see I'm hurt or concerned or whatever I am and she says, "I mean, I have to watch what my parents are watching because we only have one TV, and that's all *they* watch. But it's not all bad, Gerald."

"I'm not telling you what to watch or what not to watch, but just don't talk about it with me. I don't watch TV. At all."

"Wow," she says.

"It's not as hard as you'd think," I say. "There are plenty of other things to do, you know."

She pulls out her notebook and flips to the blank back page. "So rule number one was no saying *retarded*," she says, then looks at me. "I still can't believe you're okay with that word."

"You'll understand one day, I promise," I say. Shit. I'm not sure I even understand it, so I have no idea how I'll explain it to her. Maybe a letter. *Dear Hannah, I'm not really retarded. My mom just insisted that I be retarded for some reason I can't figure out yet. Love, Gerald.*

"What was rule number two?" she asks.

"No musicals."

"Right," she says, and scribbles. "And rule number three is no talking about TV or reality TV."

"Right."

"Like, can I mention that I watched it?"

"Nope."

"And I can't share a funny part?"

"To me, there *are* no funny parts," I say.

She nods. "I get it." She stares at the list. "So, I guess rule number four is that our parents can't know and my brother can't know."

"Or my sister. Ugh."

"Right. Or your sister," she says. "Didn't she go back to college or something?"

"She lives in our basement. And I'd rather not talk about it," I say. "But that's not a rule. I will want to talk about it, I guess. Just not now." She nods. "And what's with your brother? Will he come after me and chop my dick off?"

She chuckles through her nose. "He's in Afghanistan. But he's very protective of me, and my parents are, too." She sighs. "They seem to think that I'll become a statistic."

"Oh," I say. "So that works with my next rule. Number five. No physical contact for two months."

She looks at me. "What the fuck? Seriously?"

"You think that's too long?"

"Um—yes?" she says. "Two months is, like, sixty days."

I shrug. "I have trust issues. You do, too. We see shrinks and shit. I think we should take it slow."

"But two months? You're on crack," she says. Then she

leans in close to me. "I was hoping to kiss you later. Or maybe on our date. Or maybe at work on Wednesday. Dollar Night, right? Who couldn't use a kiss on Dollar Night?"

"I still stand by rule number five," I say. I just don't want this to go wrong. I want it to be real. Not sure how to express this to Hannah. *Dear Hannah, Up until now, my only choices were jail or death. Love, Gerald.*

"Look," she says. "I'll write it in, but I think it's excessive. And I think it's a rule we can break. Deal?"

"Deal."

She closes her book. "Can I ask you a question?"

"Sure."

"Is reality TV real?"

"Are you seriously asking me that?" I ask while simultaneously thinking, *I can't believe she just asked me that.*

She nods innocently and I look at her for a minute, feeling my broken ribs throb underneath my shirt. Have I told you yet about her freckles? "It's so far from real, you have no idea," I say.

"So, you weren't anything like the kid I saw on TV?" she says awkwardly. "Like, you didn't do those things or you did?"

I take a deep breath. "I did those things. But you guys never saw the real us. You only saw what they chose to show you to make it more entertaining. The nanny wasn't even a real nanny. She was just some actress. Did you know that?"

"Did you really punch her?"

That episode was widely publicized. "Yes," I say. "And I'd do it again, too."

"I've seen it on YouTube. The punch scene. Man, it's funny," she says. "Like, six million views so far."

I shrug.

She says, "For a six-year-old kid, you had a hell of a right hook."

"This is breaking rule number three," I say.

"Oh, come on. Have a sense of humor," she says.

I give her a stern look and feel my face go hot with anger. *And there it goes, asshole. Didn't even last twenty-four hours. Told you so.*

37

AFTER SCHOOL, HANNAH finds me at my locker and asks for a ride home. I'm still mad at her about saying that thing after lunch. *Have a sense of humor.* Just thinking about it makes my face heat up again.

"Sure," I say. I don't say anything else.

When we get outside, it's colder than it was this morning and I'm suddenly freezing without a coat on. As I wait for the heater to come on, Hannah sits in the passenger's seat, reading texts on her phone. I open my phone and check my texts, too. There's one from Lisi, which is a first. *What do u want 4 ur bday? Shld I just get u a gift card?*

And one from Joe Jr. *We leave today for SC. Then FL. Dentist clown still not funny.*

I text Joe Jr. back: *See you soon. Send me your FL address.*

Then I text Lisi back. *Send shovel for bd. Digging tunnel to Scotland.*

That's the best I can do for Lisi. Joking. I know she knows I miss her. I don't think she knows how much I need her, though. I know it's selfish, but sometimes I don't know how it was so easy for her to leave me here with these people. How could she do that and then not even call me?

I ask Hannah, "What's your number?"

She tells me and smiles at me when she says the numbers and I feel my anger subside. *Maybe I do need a sense of humor.* I add her number to my contacts and I write her a text. *Just because I made rule #5 doesn't mean I don't want to.*

Her phone jingles and she reads it and adds me to her contacts and then texts back. *I know.*

"So, you remember how to get to my house?" she asks me once we're free of the school parking lot.

"Yep."

"Not an easy place to forget, I guess," she says. "Nor is the fact that you are now dating the junkman's daughter."

"You aren't the junkman's daughter," I say.

"I know who I am. You don't have to break it to me, you know. I've lived there my whole life," she says. "It's a huge pain in the ass."

I nod.

She adds, "Do you know how many parents send their girls to the junkman's daughter's house for a sleepover party? None. Do you know how many parents send their kids over to play? Yeah. None. And how many come trick-or-treating? That would be...none."

"Trick-or-treaters are a pain in the ass, anyway," I say.

She nods her head and asks if I want to hear her punk rock song about being a junkman's daughter and then she sings it to me without my saying yes. I'm not sure it can qualify as a song because all it is, is yelling and some screaming in the middle and then more yelling and a lot of swearing in the middle and then a big scream—like a death scream—at the end.

"Very cool," I say.

"You should hear it with a guitar. It's way better," she answers.

"You play guitar?"

She fiddles with her hair. "Uh, no. Uh—my ex did."

"Oh."

"Sorry."

"It's cool," I say. "It's not like neither of us had lives before now."

Although when I say that, I realize that I haven't had a life before now. Well, I guess I did have a life but—uh—*Have a sense of humor, Gerald.*

Once we're on the road Hannah asks me, "Are you sure you don't want to stop at the baseball park and make out?"

"I really don't think we should break a rule on the day we made it," I say. "That would just kill the viability of all future rules." Truth: I can't imagine the pain of making out right now. My chest feels like it's going to collapse and I can't wait to get home to Mom's medicine cabinet. I plan on hitting her prescriptions for this pain.

"Do you want to park and just talk?" she asks. "Because I don't feel like going home yet. My to-do list is way too long today. I'll be up all night, I bet."

"Really?" I ask as I pull into the baseball field's parking lot. "I forget regular classes get so much homework."

"I already did my homework," she says. "The to-do list is the usual Tuesday-night bullshit. Wash, mostly. Then dinner. Then dishes. Then folding wash, some leftover review homework, then cleaning. Then bed. Before midnight if I'm lucky."

"You do your own wash?" The idea of it makes me feel babied. My mom still washes everything of mine. She folds my boxer shorts into perfect little squares.

"I do everybody's wash," she says. Then she laughs. "Fuck. I do everybody's *everything*. I'm a full-service junkman's daughter."

I smile at her while feeling like a mama's boy for the boxer-shorts squares.

"Except the junk," she says. "I don't sell junk, deal in junk, stack junk, buy junk, or have any fucking thing to do with junk. But everything else, I do."

"Huh." I think back to Nanny's 1-2-3 lectures about responsibility and how chores make you independent, but this seems excessive. "Why?" I ask.

"They're too busy watching TV and waiting for the phone call that never comes about my brother being dead."

"Wow."

"Yeah," she says.

A minute slips by. "Is that why you see a shrink?"

She shrugs. "Nah. My mom thinks the shrink will help me be—uh—less weird."

"You're not weird."

"We're both weird," she corrects. "What you mean is, *There's nothing wrong with being different.*"

"Totally."

"Yeah, my shrink doesn't buy it. She's, like, the Martha Stewart of shrinks or something. She'll have me dressed right and scrapbooking in no time."

I laugh. "No scrapbooking. We should make a rule about that," I say. "And don't listen to your shrink. You're perfect just like this." I look at her for a second too long and she gets self-conscious and looks at her lap.

"I guess we should go," she says. "Or we could go to Ashley's house and I could say hi to the fish," she adds.

I really want to do this, but I can't skip my meeting with Roger. I tell her, "I have my shrink appointment in an hour. Maybe tomorrow?"

I pull out of the baseball parking lot and drive down her road. When we get to her mailbox, she says, "Just drop me here."

She leans in as if to give me a quick good-bye kiss, then pulls away and says, "Psych." Then she slams the car door shut.

I blast the heat and take off for my meeting with Roger. I don't know why I'm so cold. Then I look at the passenger's seat and there's Snow White holding an industrial-size tub of peach ice cream.

"Jesus," I say. "You scared me."

"Scared you?" Snow White laughs. "Why, I don't think I've ever scared anyone in my whole life, Gerald."

"Shit," I say. Then I look at her and she's smiling at me and I feel bad for cursing in front of Snow White.

Christ, Gerald. Have a sense of humor.

38

"HOW'S YOUR ANGER?" Roger says.

"It's angry, I guess. I wouldn't know. I haven't seen it," I say.

We look at each other.

"None at all?"

"Nope."

We look at each other again.

"Seriously?"

"Seriously," I say. Truth: I'm a little high on the pain pills I took out of Mom's medicine cabinet.

"Proud of you, man." He pats me on the arm and I can feel it vibrate all the way to my bruised, semi-numb ribs. "Last meeting you were still working on the feelings you had about your sister."

"She's a douche," I say.

"Anger level?"

"Maybe a three or four," I answer. "Nothing too bad. She called me a loser yesterday and I didn't care," I lie.

He looks at me like he knows I'm lying. "You on mellow pills or something?"

"No."

"You know," Snow White says. "You should probably tell him the truth."

"Anything going on at school?" Roger asks.

Shut up, Snow White. "I'm good at algebra," I say.

"Algebra? Huh. Good for you, man."

"Thanks." *Yeah. Thanks for not noticing that most high school students are good at algebra two years ago and I've been purposely retarded by my own mother.*

Mental note: *Shit. You really need to think on that, Gerald.*

Why would my mother want me to be retarded?

And, more important, has her inherent need for me to be in SPED class made me the face-eating, Jacko-beating asshole I am today?

Snow White pipes up. "You can make it sound like you and that boy were just fighting in the ring. That's not bad, is it? He couldn't have expected you to last this long without getting into the ring."

I shoot her a dirty look.

"Is something wrong?" Roger asks.

Everything is wrong. Everything is always wrong. Everything will always be wrong. But Roger doesn't need to know any of this. Roger just needs me to get better. His supervisor needs to see annual improvement on my anger-survey scores and a decrease in incidents. That's all Roger needs.

"Did something happen?" Roger asks.

"Nope."

He squints at me as if to say *Come on*.

"I met a girl," I say.

I half expect a slap on the back and raucous laughter, even after his warnings. Men talking about girls. Girls: the answer to all of our problems.

Instead, Roger winces. "Dude. Be careful."

"She's cool," I say.

"I get it. You're, like, seventeen and you like girls. I really get it," he says. He taps his fingers together and looks for something else to say. "Just be careful. As much as you like her now, she's going to drive you over the edge one day. I mean, this calm you have . . . it's temporary."

Snow White makes that annoying giggle in her throat. "Temporary. Oh my. We didn't expect that, did we?"

"Gerald?"

"Yeah?" It's like he's the Crapper and he just crapped right on my joy.

"Did you hear me?" Roger asks.

"Yeah." *I am so fucking sick of people crapping on my joy.*

"Is something wrong?"

I look at him and I can hear the blood rushing through my ears.

I look at Snow White and then at Roger. "How could any-one expect me to train in a gym full of aggressive assholes and not end up in the ring fighting one of them? I mean, shit. What were you guys thinking? Why didn't you suggest tennis or some shit like that? Why boxing? I was already beating people up, right?" I say.

Roger nods.

"I mean, am I wrong to think that was one of the stupidest ideas you ever had? And where were my parents when I came home and told them that I'd be doing this? Are they that fucking stupid? Boxing? Seriously?"

I'm watching him and I realize that he doesn't even look disappointed. He almost looks happy that I'm saying this. Snow White is smiling so big I want to smack her. *Have a sense of humor, Gerald.*

I look at Roger's entertained expression and I say, "Hold on. Was this some kind of a test or something?"

"Back up," he says. "To the fight." He cocks his head a lit-tle and smiles. "Did you win?"

I remind myself that Roger was once an angry little jerk-off like the rest of us in FS. He's been *saved* and wants to save me. Or maybe not. Asshole.

And yet I can't hold back my smirk. *You're an asshole, too, Gerald.*

Snow White looks disappointed in both of us.

"Show me your hands," he says.

I do. He inspects the cracks and bruises and swellings. I lift my shirt without him having to ask, and show him my ribs. When I stretch my head downward, I see my skin has gone that deep purple-red color in spots and I wonder if I'm bleeding internally.

And then I see us from the outside—from Snow White's perspective. I see a dumb kid lifting his shirt to show a dumb grown man his bruised torso. I see them both celebrating the win over Jacko the fake Jamaican. It's like they enjoy pain. It's like they *want* to be angry and bruised. It's like they're proud of it.

When I see it that way, I know it's true. I *am* proud of it. I *was* proud the day I chewed that hole in What's-His-Name's cheek. I *was* proud on Saturday when I bit Tasha's hand until it bled. I *was* proud every time I crapped on the kitchen table.

I am addicted to anger.

This makes me smile.

Snow White says, "Gerald, why on earth are you happy about *that*?"

What else do I have to be happy about?

"I could name a thousand things," she says.

"So what's the other kid look like today?" Roger asks.

I let my shirt drop down, and I answer, "Roadkill."

We look at each other, two FS refugees. I want to ask him why he's so concerned about me dating a girl. Was Roger some wife beater? Did he smack his kids around? Does he really think that girls can only lead to trouble?

"Roadkill. Awesome. I'd put my money on you any day," Roger says.

Snow White and I stare at him. It's like we just witnessed a butterfly emerge from its chrysalis. Except that the butterfly isn't quite what we expected it to be, because the whole world is full of shit.

39

I SPEND A half hour watching the Monaco trapeze video before I get ready for school. I'm late to the breakfast table and as I eat my breakfast and think about how Roger seemed to get off on seeing my bruises last night, Tasha comes upstairs in her bathrobe and says some stuff to Mom while I pretend she's not there. Then she turns to me. "I hear you have yourself a girlfriend, big guy. You gonna bite her, too?"

I ignore the bite comment and say, "What are you talking about? I don't have a freakin' girlfriend."

"Not what I heard," Tasha says.

"Aren't you, like, twenty-one? Why are you hanging around here and gossiping about high school kids? Are you retarded or something?"

I get up and walk out of the kitchen, and Tasha says, "I'm not the one in special ed."

I turn around and face the two of them. "Yeah, well, I'm not the loser living in my mom's basement because I'm so stupid no college will take me after dropping out three times."

"Stop it," Mom says.

"I'll make sure your new girlfriend gets the message that you don't like girls," Tasha says. "Danny knows her brother."

I shake my head and shrug. "I don't know what you're talking about, but whatever it is, it sure as hell won't get you a fuckin' job, will it?"

At this, I walk out the door to the garage. Danny is in the garage. I want to just jump on him and punch him until he becomes the garage floor—a big, huge, sticky red spot on the perfect concrete that Mom makes Dad power wash twice a year as if garages should be clean places where oil doesn't leak and mice don't pee.

"Hey," Danny says to me.

"Hey," I say, walking through the garage toward my car, which is in the driveway.

"Can I use your speed bag?" he asks.

"No," I say.

I get into my car and turn the ignition to warm it up and then I go back into the garage and Danny is still there, standing in the exact same spot as he was a minute ago when I said no. I think he's trying to decide whether to use the speed bag while I'm at school. I realize that he belongs here in the Faust family. He is the half-wit son they always wanted. He can take my place.

I go inside. I say to Mom, who is now standing in the kitchen by herself, "Mom, I figured out what I want for my birthday."

"Oh?" she says.

"How about a gas card? You know—the kind that's pre-paid, so I can save some money this year before college."

She chuckles a little. "College?"

I pick up my lunch, and when I get back into the garage, Danny is still standing there.

"You can totally use the speed bag," I say. "Just don't sweat up my gloves, okay?"

He's still staring at me with the rodent stare as I close the garage door behind me.

■ ■ ■ ■ ■

I don't turn on any tribal music on my drive to school. I check twice to make sure I have my work pants in the backseat. Today I chose khakis. I think they make my ass look firmer and now I care about shit like this when I'm serving hockey fans from register #7.

I'm so early, the student parking lot is empty. I open my backpack and pull out my library copy of *Romeo and Juliet*, the kind with plain English on one side and real Shakespeare on the other, which I started reading last night.

As I read, I'm surprised by how it doesn't go over my head, and angry that I thought it would.

I am not retarded.

My mother has a screw loose.

She needs me to be dumb so Tasha will be happy.

She wanted Lisi to not go to college so Tasha would be happy.

Fuck.

Have a sense of humor, Gerald.

I try to have a sense of humor about this. *Isn't it funny how messed up this all is? It's not you! It's her! It's them! That's funny, right?*

⠀⠀⠀⠀■ ■ ■ ■

When Hannah gets to our lunch booth, I'm still reading *Romeo and Juliet* and I'm just getting to the part where Romeo says *"Ay, mine own fortune in my misery"* and I read it twice—and I check the other page, in plain twenty-first-century English to be sure, and I laugh.

"What's so funny?"

I can't tell Hannah that I'm happy to not be retarded. So I say, "Oh, nothing. Just Shakespeare. Funny guy."

She nods and slips into the booth. "No lie. Have you read *A Midsummer Night's Dream* yet?"

"No."

"It's hilarious," she says.

I suddenly feel dumb again. It's so easy to feel dumb. There is no pressure there, in Dumbville. When you're expected to be dumb, then crapping on stuff and never having read *A Midsummer Night's Dream* is all the same big zero in your life.

"Gerald?" Hannah says.

I look at her, but I'm still thinking about how it's more comfortable being dumb.

"God," she says, and sighs. "Sometimes you are so hard to talk to."

I say, "What?" like I'm irked, because I don't want her to say that.

"I said: You're hard to talk to," she says. "Because you go off in your own little world." She leafs through a textbook while she says this, as if she's not angry. Or maybe she isn't angry. I can't tell. She adds, "You always did, too."

"What's that supposed to mean?" I say. "I always did? You mean like since last week?"

"No, Gerald, I mean like since you were a kid. On TV. You used to do it then, too," she says.

And I realize why dating is not a good idea for Gerald Faust.

Dating isn't good for Gerald Faust because everyone knows his secrets.

And everyone has psychoanalyzed him.

And everyone knows what his problem is.

And everyone knows he has baggage.

And everyone thinks they know how to help him.

Because everyone believes what they see on TV.

Because no one has realized yet that it's all full of shit.

"You don't know shit about me when I was a kid, and not only did that break rule number three, but it was a stupid-ass thing to say and you're completely fucking wrong."

She stares at me. She seems surprised.

"I want an apology," I say. I stand and gather my things from the booth.

"But you did, Gerald. You did used to go off into your own world," she says. "And you still do it."

"You don't know anything about anything," I say. "You're just a fucking brainwashed moron like the rest of them," I say—okay, I mutter—on my way past her toward the cafeteria door.

I eat my lunch in the hallway outside Fletcher's room, where Deirdre and Jenny are eating and talking about TV shows.

Mom packed her famous chicken salad today and it doesn't taste anything like it tasted last week. That's probably because I'm realizing that her needing me to be learning disabled could compare to her wanting me to be in a wheelchair...all so Tasha could run faster.

It would take a lot of kick-ass chicken salad to make me un-realize that.

40

"YOU CALLED ME a brainless moron," Hannah says.

She's walking me to my car and I haven't offered her a ride, so I'm about to tell her not to get in when she gets in. Mental note: *Lock car from now on.*

"Well? Didn't you?" she yells.

"No," I say, now trapped in a cold car with a screeching teenage girl. I am thankful for rule #5. I am thankful this hasn't gone far. "And who invited you into my car?"

"You called me a brainless moron," she says again.

I look at her. "No, I didn't. I called you a brain*washed* moron like the rest of TV viewers who think they know Gerald Faust but who don't know *anything* about Gerald Faust.

And no, I'm not apologizing. You broke rule number three in a big way. Using some bullshit you once saw on the TV against me is way out of line, Hannah."

I get out the driver's-side door, I walk around the back of my car, and I open the passenger's-side door like a gentleman. I stand there until she gets out, and once she walks toward the buses, I walk around to the driver's side of my car and get in.

And that's when I see she's written ASSHOLE on my dashboard in silver Sharpie marker.

My drive to work is fast.

When I get there, Beth, who is hovering over a full hot dog roller, says, "It's Dollar Night. I have to make four hundred of these before we open. And I haven't even started anything else." At this moment, I try to imagine her skinny-dipping and drinking beer with her friends and I can't see it. I can't see anything but the wrinkles of Dollar Night worry on her forehead.

My phone buzzes in my pocket and I don't want to look, because I'm sure it's Hannah playing some ASSHOLE game with me. "I'll get everything else," I say. And I do. I fill the ice, count my cash, set up the condiment stand, fix the cheese dispenser for the trillions of Dollar Nachos to come.

By the time I'm done, Hannah has been at register #1 counting her cash for ten minutes. Each of us pretends the other isn't there. It's perfect until Beth asks her to come over and help her wrap hot dogs. I'm already wrapping hot dogs, so we stand there and wrap silently and I give her a few dirty looks and she gives me dirty looks and then we go back to not looking at each other.

After a minute, Beth says, "Shit. The tension here is intense." When neither of us answers, she laughs to herself and answers for us. "Yes, Beth, it is. It's because we're teenagers and can't figure out how to talk to each other."

"Hey!" Hannah says. "I'm not some idiot just because of my age."

"Yeah," I say.

"So what's the problem?" Beth asks.

I shrug.

Hannah says, "I asked Gerald today to stop going off into his little dreamworld because it's hard to deal with him when he does that and he freaked out on me and called me a brainless moron."

"I did not call you a brainless moron. I called you a brain-*washed* moron because you brought up the bullshit you saw on the TV from when I was five. Jesus! How the fuck would you feel if I had twenty-four-seven movies of your house when you were five and said something like *Hannah, stop being so emotional. You've always been emotional—don't you remember that time when you were five?*" I take a breath. "Anyway, if you believe that's really what my house was like, you're wrong. And so making judgments from those bullshit shows...or even bringing it the hell up is just out of line, man."

"But you do space out," Hannah presses.

"Yeah, I do. So fuckin' what? Who doesn't need a minute to themselves every now and then, okay? I space out. I go on a journey. I zone. Whatever. Who cares? And why does that give you the right to psychoanalyze me?" I say.

Hannah sighs. She has tears in her eyes. "Look. At lunch, I was just trying to say that sometimes you're hard to talk to. And you've proven that I'm right in every possible way. Whatever. Be immature if you want. I don't care."

She walks away from the hot dog–wrapping table and leaves me and Beth here, wrapping. My phone buzzes in my pocket again and I can see it's not Hannah texting me, so I stop and take off my plastic glove to check the message.

It's from Joe Jr. *Can you talk?* That's the first text, from earlier.

Dude. Can you talk? That's the second text.

I tell Beth that I have to go to the bathroom and I find my way to the smokers' alley, where I first met Joe. I dial his number, but he doesn't answer. I leave a voice mail.

"Hey, Joe. It's Gerald. I just got your texts and wanted to talk. I'm working, though, so I have to go back now, but I'll call you again on break." Oh shit. I remember it's Dollar Night and there are no breaks. Okay. "Or I'll call you when I'm off work. Hey, I was serious about me coming to see you. I want to do it. My birthday's in a week, and I asked my mom for a gas card."

I hang up and instantly regret nearly all of that voice mail. Voice mail was invented by confident people to make unconfident people say stupid shit that gets taped and haunts us forever.

As I walk by Hannah on my way to register #7, I say, "Oh, and nice touch writing *asshole* on my dashboard. Your maturity is oozing. Maybe you need to spend less time analyzing me and more time asking why you'd vandalize my car."

"Because you were being an asshole," she says.

I turn around at register #3. "All depends how you look at it. Because from my side, it was the person *writing on my car* who was being the asshole. All I did was tell you the truth," I say. "It's not my fault if you can't handle it."

"Dude, that's what *I* was doing. Telling you the truth," she says. More tears in her eyes.

"You don't know anything about me, Hannah. Nothing," I say, and I walk to #7. As luck would have it, the employees come to buy their pregame food and I ring them up and get busy while Hannah gets some time to sulk. If nothing else, I hope she's learned that playing head games with a kid whose whole life is a hellacious head game is a bad idea.

⸻

I always forget how bad Dollar Night sucks. We sell out of our four hundred hot dogs before third period. Before we do, we have this crotchety old man telling us that the hot dog is cold and we tell him no, just the bun is cold and he says that the cold bun is making the hot dog cold and that we should steam our rolls and that he'd like to return a half-eaten hot dog for his dollar back.

Roger has a name for this kind of thing when he's in therapy mode. He calls it priority confusion. This guy is so worked up over the temperature of his hot dog that he can't see how unreasonable he's being about returning a half-eaten hot dog.

We all have priority confusion throughout the day. Some have it more than others, I guess.

This brings me to Roger's lessons about the high road. Not only did I have to give up the words of anger—*should, deserve,* etc.—but also I had to start owning my shit. So, for example, I have no trouble admitting that I bit Tasha's hand last Saturday. I'm not sorry about it. Frankly, in the case of calling Hannah a brainwashed moron today, I'm also not sorry about it. *But* as Roger so cleverly points out, just appearing to be on the high road puts you on it. And so I know that part of my head game with Hannah will be to apologize first. That way it's her problem and no longer my problem. Roger calls that *cleaning the slate.*

There is a lull before we start closing down the stand and I go to Hannah and she looks at me with her mean face and I say, "I know I'm hard to talk to sometimes. I know I go off into my own world. I do that on purpose." I shift in my shoes a little because her expression hasn't changed. "Because I don't trust anyone because—uh—you know. People aren't really trustworthy and they bring up my past and shit and it's not very comfortable."

She doesn't say anything.

"So I'm sorry I said that at lunch, but there are a lot of people who believe what they saw on TV and I don't want you to be one of them, okay? And at some point, whenever it hits you that you were wrong, you can feel free to apologize for vandalizing my car," I say. Then I go out to the condiment stand and start to haul over the big containers of ketchup, mustard, and barbecue sauce.

Dollar Night crowds are slobs. I had to come out here

twice tonight and clear off their mess, and now it's filled again—mostly with hot dog wrappers. There are trash cans in every direction, but they just leave them here like this is acceptable behavior.

And if anyone knows about acceptable behavior, it's me.

41

SCRUBBING THE HOT dog roller tonight is a long job made for someone with a lot of upper-body strength. That's me. By the time I'm finished and taking the grease tray to the sink, everything else has been done and Register #4 Guy is about to start mopping. Hannah has taken off her PEC Center Food Service shirt and is standing there in her punk rock black sleeveless T-shirt that says UP YOURS on the front.

As I walk by her with the clean and dry tray for the roller, I say, "You want a ride home tonight or is your dad coming to pick you up?"

"What's that supposed to mean?" she asks.

I keep walking. I'm the clean one now. I made my apology

and owned my shit. So I replace the tray, grab my coat from the little cubby next to register #7, and go out the door to the bathroom, where I pee, wash my hands, and check my face for any stray grease or barbecue sauce.

On my way out of the bathroom, I bump right into someone familiar and I can't place her until she smiles and holds out her arms for a hug and then I flinch because of my ribs. She looks at me and asks me how I am.

"I'm good," I say. I say this loud enough so that Hannah can hear, because I can feel her watching me.

"Good," Hockey Lady says. "I worry about you."

"I'll be seventeen in a week. Only one more year until I'm out of that house," I say.

She nods. "What did you ask for, for your birthday?"

"I asked for a gas card. That way I can save for college instead of putting all my money from this job into my gas tank."

"Practical," she says. "You take after your father."

If staying married to a neglectful, magazine-page-turning nutcase is practical, sure, I think.

She hugs me again. "Well, if I don't see you before next week, happy birthday, Gerald. Seventeen," she says, and shakes her head. "I'm so glad you made it."

"Me, too," I say.

"I had my doubts," she says. And that's what's left echoing in my head as she walks away. *I had my doubts.*

I take off my PEC Center T-shirt as I walk toward the door of stand five and I can feel my other shirt go up with it, which means Hannah is getting a full view of my very muscular and bruised upper body and I take my time straightening myself out.

I find Beth and ask her if she needs any more help closing the stand.

"Nope," she says.

"You sure?" We smile at each other. I'm pretty sure she knows what I'm doing.

"Everything okay?" she asks.

"Totally."

She smiles. "Don't look now, but Hannah is waiting for you at the door," she says. "Want me to put you on register number two tomorrow?"

"Seven," I say. Very seriously. "I'm always on seven."

I say good night and tiptoe over the mopped parts of the floor and head toward the door and there's Hannah, just like Beth said.

"Hey," I say, as if she didn't write ASSHOLE on my dashboard.

"Hey," she says, as if she didn't write ASSHOLE on my dashboard.

Then, before we can talk, my phone buzzes again and I say, "Sorry, Hannah. I have to get this really quick. Do you mind?"

I look at the number on my phone. It's Joe Jr.

"Hello?" I say.

"Dude," he says. "What's shaking?"

"Nothing much. Just leaving work now. What's up, man? You okay?"

"Uh—nah. You got room for a circus freak in your house?"

"Did you run away?" I ask. This makes Hannah's ears perk up. She's still very interested in running away. To anywhere. Apparently with any ASSHOLE, too.

"Not yet. But I'm thinking on it," he says.

"I wish I could, but I think my parents would freak," I say.

"I can do more than just clean fucking buses and run around being the talent's gofer," he says. "I'm just so ready to go find another show and get to use my own talent, you know?"

"You're not a dentist clown, are you?" I ask.

He laughs. "No."

"So what are you?"

He's quiet for a second and then he says, "What's your e-mail? I'll send you a link. You can check it out when you get home."

"Cool," I say. "I will." I give him my e-mail address.

"Sometimes I can't figure out what I'm doing here," he says.

"I feel the same way," I say. "Just without the clown dentistry part."

"Fuck this shit, man."

I answer, "Fuck this shit." And then we hang up.

I can't figure out if I helped him or not, but just talking to him made me want to run away tonight.

"So?" Hannah says.

"So... what?"

"Is he running away?"

I stop and look at her. Man, her freckles are gorgeous. "Why are you so interested in running away?" I ask.

She shrugs. "I just am."

"Isn't your dad coming to pick you up in a minute?" I ask. "I have to go to the parking garage," I say, pointing toward it. "You should be out front."

She looks down. "I told him I had a ride," she says. She looks at me and pushes her mouth over to the left, as if she's chewing on the inside of her cheek.

"With the asshole," I add.

"Yeah," she says. "I have a ride with the asshole."

I don't smile. I have all these thoughts. Crazy thoughts. Like, on the one hand, I want to kiss her passionately, like they do in movies, and just paralyze her with this feeling of how much I want to take care of her. On the other hand, she's like Tasha somehow. She's a girl, for one thing, and she wrote ASS-HOLE on my dashboard. And she hasn't apologized, so if I let her in my car and take her home, I will be like Mom and Dad, who never punished Tasha for writing ASSHOLE on my whole life.

"Look, I'm sorry," she says. "I'll clean it off tomorrow. I promise. I was just so mad at you!"

"Doesn't mean you had to do something crazy," I say.

She throws her hands up. "I'm not fucking crazy!"

"I didn't say you were. I said writing *asshole* on my car was crazy," I say. "But Saturday night, before I picked you up, you were walking right toward murder central to go to Ashley's house and you didn't care, so maybe you are crazy. I don't know."

We're standing still now—I think because I haven't indicated that I'm actually driving her home. I start walking down the block toward the parking garage and make a sign like she should follow me. The wind is harsh. I zip my coat to my neck and she wraps her scarf extra tight around her chin. Then she slips her arm into mine, and we walk, connected, with our hands in our pockets.

When we get into the car and I start it up and crank the heat, she says, "Dude, that's not hot yet. Now you're just blowing cold air."

I turn down the fan and rub my hands together to get warm. I stare at what she wrote on the dashboard. I look for something to say, but I can't find anything except the truth about how I'm feeling, which is: like an asshole. I sigh.

"That was dramatic," she says.

"What?"

"That big sigh you just did."

"You're sitting in front of the word *asshole,* which *you* wrote on my *car,* and you call me dramatic? Seriously. You—the girl who ran away to get murdered," I say. "That's some pot calling the kettle black."

"That's racist," she says.

"It is not," I say.

"It is. Totally."

"Fine. Then you're the snow calling the clouds white. Whatever," I say.

The heat kicks in and I turn the fan up and we both put our cold hands on the vents to get warm.

"You know," I say, "you're not the easiest person to talk to, either."

"Oh, really?"

"Yeah. Really. You could be nicer," I say.

"Well, at least I don't just disappear into another world like you do. Because that's just weird," she says. "And I want us to have a nice relationship."

I back out of the parking space and head down the exit ramp.

She asks, "Don't you want us to have a nice relationship, too?"

I point to the word ASSHOLE. But I smile, so she hits me lightly on the arm and says, "I promise I will clean that off tomorrow morning when you come get me for school. I have the perfect stuff to do it."

"Tomorrow morning? So part of this nice relationship is me being your chauffeur?" I say. Still smiling.

"Yes. And I promise to never break rule number three again," she says. "Unless you want to talk about it. Because I'm sure it will come up at some point, considering it must have messed you up really bad."

"Yes. Yes, it did," I say. "But I'm not as messed up as I was."

"Good," she says. "Because I'm getting more messed up every day living with my crazy parents and there's only so much room in this asshole's car for all our emotional baggage."

I laugh and she laughs and I don't feel like an asshole.

Until she's gone.

Driving home by myself, I feel like an asshole. In fact, the closer I get to the house, the more it comes on, as if my proximity to my mother and sister makes me into exactly what they need me to be.

Fuck that shit, Gerald.

When I get home, I get Joe Jr.'s e-mail and I follow the link to a YouTube video. It's titled *Great Trampoline Act*. Under it, the info says: *Two acrobats on a trampoline in Bonifay, FL.*

It's Joe on a trampoline doing flips and twists and other cool things with another guy who's dressed the same. I assume it's his brother, because they look alike. They have the act down and it goes for about two minutes. It was filmed in a big empty barn with no seats or people watching, but they're in costumes and they bow after each big trick as if there is an audience.

That's my whole life, right there—bowing as if there is an audience. I still can't pick my nose in my own bedroom, even though the guys from the TV channel came and patched up the little holes in our walls from the camera mounts ten years ago.

42

FRIDAY MORNING I am in Snow White's guidance-counseling office in Gersday.

"I want to get out of Mr. Fletcher's class."

Snow White the guidance counselor looks concerned.

"I mean, I love Mr. Fletcher," I say, and I look at him sitting to my right. "But I shouldn't be in the special ed room. It's a long story. It's just—all that stuff from my past and how my parents handled it and stuff. But I'm fine up here." I tap my head with my index finger. "And I want to go to college."

"Your grades aren't great. And you know your discipline record, so I don't have to tell you that." Snow White the guidance counselor tries to keep a straight face while pretending to be stern.

"But I can do it, right? I can go to college?"

"We'll try, Gerald," she says. "You just keep this positive attitude and stay out of trouble and it's totally possible."

I nod because my inner director told me to nod. This is the scene I want on TV. Boy makes good of himself. Boy takes a shit sandwich and turns it into a scrumptious meal. Boy calls himself on his walkie-talkie and says, *Dude—you're better than this. Why are you letting them do this to you?* Boy meets girl. Girl writes ASSHOLE on his dashboard and then erases it with magic junkyard solvent the next morning. Boy finds life worth living.

This should be a reality TV show. Except nobody would watch because it's no fun to watch normal people do normal things. Because happy stories aren't all that interesting. Because everyone wants to eat that shit sandwich, or watch other people eat it, along with exotic bugs and rotten eggs and diesel fuel and everything else producers can think of to keep viewers' thumbs away from the channel button on the remote control.

Not me.

I've eaten enough shit sandwiches, thank you.

▮▮▮▮▮

Hannah meets me at my locker at the end of the day. She has her phone in her hand and is reading text messages and says hi while I exchange some books for other books and stuff them into my backpack. I've spent the whole day in Gersday, pretending that I talked to the guidance counselor. I've spent the whole day looking for Lisi, but I can't find her anywhere.

"You ready for the big night?" Hannah asks.

I make a face like I don't follow.

"Rivals. Should be packed. Hockey—you know? Our job?" she says.

"Oh. Right," I say. "Shit. I forgot my pants."

She laughs.

"No. I mean I forgot my work pants. We're gonna be late," I say. "Shit."

"Can't we just go to your house and get them? It won't take that long, will it?"

We and *your house* just don't sound right in the same sentence. I can't take Hannah to my house.

"The mall. We can stop at the mall. I know where to go and I know my size. It'll be easier," I say.

"Easier than what? Going to your house to get a pair of pants? Seriously, Gerald. You've seen where I live. It can't be much worse than that."

"Uh. You—uh. Look. If we leave now, I can just stop at the mall. No big deal."

"I'll even hide in the car if you want," she says. "Is it *that* bad? You having a girlfriend?"

We walk down the hall toward the exit doors and Hannah seems sad now. I want to ask her what's wrong, but I don't want to fight again. I just want this day to keep going right. Straight to college. I want this day to just lead me to college.

"Does this have something to do with your chest?"

"My chest?"

"The bruises. I saw them. Last night."

"Oh," I say. "Shit. No. I box. That's from a fight I had on Monday at the gym. Guy was like a train."

"Mm," she says. Once we get into the car, she asks, "It's me, isn't it?"

"What? No. Shit. Of course not."

"I'm the junkman's daughter."

"You are not the junkman's daughter," I say.

"Then why can't we just go to your house and pick up a stupid pair of pants?" she says.

I look at my clean dashboard. I worry what she'll write on it if I say no.

"Fine. You're right. We'll go to my house. I can run in and get the pants and run out again."

"Exactly," she says. "You can thank the junkman's daughter for saving you fifty bucks, too."

I laugh. "Yes. Thank you."

As I drive, I finally find Lisi on the trapeze. I tell her about college and about how Snow White said I could go.

"Gerald?"

"Yeah?"

"Did you hear what I said?" Hannah asks.

"Shit. Sorry. I was spaced-out again. What did you say?"

"I said that I've never been in a gated community before," she says.

"Oh," I say. "It's really not as special as it seems. I mean, there's a gate. And a little booth with a security guard. That's about it."

"Sounds a lot like my house, eh?" She laughs.

"You know, it's not as bad as you think it is, your house. It's weird for you, but it's not like—a freak show or anything."

"If only they made a reality TV show out of us...then you'd see just how weird it is," she says.

I pull into the drive and stop at the gate. The security guard knows me, so he makes the gate go up without me having to enter my pass code into the box. He waves. Hannah waves at him and he smiles. I think maybe he's happy for me.

Hannah stays in the car and I run into the house and grab my pants. It takes me all of two minutes. Hannah says, "That was fast."

As I back down the drive, I catch Mom looking out the upstairs window like a woman from one of those old short stories they make us read in school. Like she wants to jump out.

43

EPISODE 2, SCENES 23-35

MIKE, THE KID from two doors over who Tasha was now "dating" even though it made Dad cringe every time Mom said it, was over at our house. His parents had signed a waiver so he could be part of the show.

He and Tasha were making homemade cookies together in the kitchen.

Dad was still at work. Mom was at the kitchen table yelling out the amounts and ingredients like the good, wholesome chaperone she was expected to be.

When I wandered into the kitchen, Tasha and Mike were having a great time, throwing teaspoons of flour at each other. And sugar. The director gave me the hand signal to stop and go away. I played dumb and kept walking in. I saw from the whiteboard next to him that they were on take three of the same scene, so I tiptoed in and played it very innocent and watched the scene unfold.

Only when Tasha took a wet-with-batter spatula and smacked Mike on the cheek with it did it begin to get ugly. He did the same then, with a spoon. She said, "Ow!" and gave him a warning glance. He said sorry, but didn't mean it. So then she said, "You better watch it, because I could pour this whole bowl of batter down your pants."

"Cut!" the director said. He looked to Tasha. "Pants? Come on. You're twelve!"

"Shoot," Tasha said. "I meant to say shirt, but pants seemed more real. Sorry."

"Mike lays in Tasha's bed all the time without his pants on," I said.

Everyone got quiet and looked at me. Then they looked at Tasha and Mike, who looked around the room. Mike looked as if he was figuring out which way to run. Tasha looked for the first person to hit. Mike was closest.

She slapped him across the face and then ran to Mom and buried her head in Mom's shoulder, leaving a glob of cookie batter on her sweatshirt.

Mom held Tasha at arm's length and said, "Is this true?"

"Of course not!" Tasha said. "You know Gerald is retarded. You said so yourself."

"I'm not retarded," I said.

"Are so," she said. "And you're gay."

Nanny transformed at that moment. She suddenly didn't

care what her hair looked like or whether her dress was the right color for the scene. She didn't care where her designer purse was or whether her bottled water was the right brand.

She told the cameras to stop rolling and took me and Mom into the living room, away from Mike and Tasha, who were still fighting in the kitchen.

"Calling a young child gay is *awful*," Nanny said. "It's an unacceptable word. Totally."

"The kid craps in my shoes and you say Tasha using the word *gay* is harmful?" Mom asked.

"Jill!"

"What?" Mom said.

"He's sitting right *he-ah*!" Nanny said.

"So?" Mom said. "You can see why I think there's something wrong with him, right?" Mom got up and went back into the kitchen just as Mike was running out the door.

Nanny turned to me and gave me a sympathetic look. "Was it true what you said about him being in Tasha's bed?"

"Yes," I said.

"And you were here, too? You and Lisi?"

I nodded.

"Right," she said. "I think I know what to do here, Gerald." She looked at me with a smile. Like a real nanny.

❚❙❚❚❙

The next day was the last day of filming. We had to do the usual end-of-episode family meeting. Dad was home from work for an hour, tops, still in his work suit, and doing that thing with his ankles that he does when he's stressed out. Like neck rolls, but with ankles. Around and around. Clockwise, then counterclockwise. His tarsal bones cracked each time, like popcorn. Lisi and I sat next to him.

Mom and Tasha were sitting together on the love seat. Ever since the day before, when Mike from two doors down broke up with her, Tasha had been stuck to Mom's side. The cameras were rolling and the director had already said we should just do the scene and he'd take care of it in the editing room.

"Let's *stah-t* with Gerald this time," Nanny said. "I think Gerald's come a long way, don't you?"

No one said anything.

"Well, come on, Faust family. Speak up!" Nanny said. "Gerald hasn't punched a wall in what? More than a year?"

"True," Dad said. "And he makes his bed every day and gets ready for school and does a lot around the house to clean up. That's true."

"That's right, Doug. He's come a long way if you think about where we were last year, am I right?"

The director nodded so they all nodded—except Tasha, who just looked like she was going to cry again.

I'd forgotten about punching walls. It was so episode one. I'd become the Crapper since then. Punching walls was for pussies.

"I think Gerald is awesome," Lisi said. "But I always thought Gerald was awesome."

Tasha said, "Well, he never crapped on your stuff, so you would."

We all looked at Tasha and at Mom, who was still stroking Tasha's hair like she was a prized dog or something. She didn't seem at all fazed, but then again, I'd crapped on her stuff, too.

The director walked over to us and said, "Look. We have to have this shot by four. It's three now. You had plenty of time to get all this family stuff out last night. You'll have forever to continue figuring it out. Can we just concentrate on the positive things that the show did for your family while we were here?"

He wasn't asking. He didn't wait for an answer. He just turned around and went back to his chair.

But the mere mention of last night made Tasha's lower lip curl out and quiver again. I don't know what they said or did to her, but Mom and Dad had her in Dad's man cave for over two hours, and then Mom and Dad fought all night long—or at least until I fell asleep.

It was about Mike from two doors down. I know that. I know it because Dad asked me and Lisi some questions before the meeting. *Did Tasha invite him in? Did he ever touch either of you? Are you sure he didn't have pants on? How long would they be in her room? Please describe the noises you heard, Gerald. Did Tasha have any clothes on? Describe those noises again?*

Nanny moved the scene forward. "You two did a *wondahful* job of keeping those house rules from my first visit in order. These kids know their chores and their responsibilities," Nanny said, looking at Lisi. "Which reminds me. I think I might have a late birthday gift in *he-ah* for you, Lisi," she said, reaching into a bag behind her and pulling out a wrapped gift.

Lisi sat forward. "Is it okay to open it now?"

"Of course," Nanny said.

When she opened it and found a set of walkie-talkies, Lisi screamed. We'd wanted them for years and Santa Claus had never brought them for us. She asked Dad to help her get the packaging open and put in the batteries, and then she handed one to me.

"Lisi to Gerald, can you hear me?" she said from the hall.

"I can't tell. You're too close," I said. "Go farther away so I can't hear you talking."

A few seconds later, she came through the walkie-talkie's speaker. "Lisi to Gerald. Come in, Gerald."

Nanny was smiling. Dad was smiling. I was smiling. I pressed the yellow button on the side of the walkie-talkie. "This is so awesome!"

"Now," Nanny said. "Gerald, you go off and play with Lisi. I want some time with the rest of the family."

I nodded and took off full speed toward the basement door, but then I stopped. I stood quietly where I could still hear the conversation and pressed the button on the walkie-talkie so Lisi would be able to hear, too.

"Tasha, I think we've talked enough about what happened here with the boy you invited over to the house," Nanny started. "But what we haven't talked about is your *behay-vyah* toward your *sis-tah* and *broth-ah*. I'd like to know what you think you can do to improve it."

222

I heard Dad sigh.

Tasha said, "I can't relate to them."

Mom said, "Lisi and Gerald are just so young compared to Tasha."

"I've met plenty of families who have far larger age gaps and the kids don't have as much trouble relating to their siblings," Nanny said. "At least they're not rude to one another. Tasha, you're quite rude to your *sis-tah* and *broth-ah*. I'd like to know why."

I could hear Lisi sniggering upstairs. If she didn't shut up, we'd be in big trouble.

"They don't love me," Tasha said. "Nobody loves me!" She started to sob again.

"That's silly talk," Nanny said. "We all love you. And I know being twelve isn't much fun, but it would be a lot *bett-ah* if you treated people more nicely and thought about them a bit. It's not that hard, is it?"

I didn't hear anything for a minute, and then Tasha said, "How can I relate to a retarded kid and a girl who doesn't do anything but read books? Seriously! I'm a woman now, you know? I have other stuff to think about."

"Like that—" Dad said. But then he stopped. But I think everyone knew he meant Mike.

"There are no learning-disabled children in this house," Nanny said. "Everyone here is fine! I could take you into some really difficult homes and then you'd realize how lucky you are. I get so cross when you say these things!"

"She's right," Dad said. "Every doctor we've taken him to says he's fine."

"And another thing," Nanny said. "You are *not* a woman, Tasha. Not for a while yet. You shouldn't be thinking you're a woman."

Tasha started to cry then. Mom said, "Stop making her feel bad! None of this is Tasha's fault. She didn't do anything wrong!"

"Yes, she did," Dad said. "She brought a boy into this house and—and—you know!"

Mom said, "Nothing bad came from it, Doug."

"He could have robbed us. Could have hurt Lisi. Could have done worse things than what he did," Dad said. "And what he did was bad enough. For Christ's sake, she's *twelve*!"

There was twenty seconds of silence. Tasha let out a few more sobs and Nanny told her to go to her room, so she did.

"Jill," said Nanny. "Look at me. You have to do something about your own *behay-vyah*. Everyone else here has changed, but you haven't changed. Gerald makes his bed every single morning. Lisi isn't any trouble. Even Doug does more around the house and has tried to help you through this. But it's really up to you now."

There was silence. Then Mom spoke. I think she was crying.

"When I was pregnant with Lisi—she was—you know. A surprise," she said. "I didn't think I could love another child as much as I loved Tasha. Tasha has her problems, I know, but I'm her mother. But—I mean, how can you have that much love for *two* of them? I just didn't think I had it. A lot of women feel this way. I've read articles about it," she said. "And

Doug was working all the time, so it was just the two of us. But then Lisi was born and I didn't feel anything for her at all."

This is when I switched the red button on the side of the walkie-talkie to OFF. If Lisi was still listening, then I didn't want her to hear that.

"I tried," Mom said. "I mean, I really tried. But I didn't have the patience for all that baby stuff anymore. The diapers. The spitting up. The night feeding. Doug? Do you remember? She never stopped crying."

He said, "Jill had a little breakdown. Or two." He sighed. "And Tasha didn't like being left out, either."

"And then, just as I'd potty trained Lisi, there was Gerald. God," Mom said. Then she started *really* crying. "It's normal for families to try again for a boy. Everyone said things to Doug about it. Like we had to keep going for our boy! And look at what we got. Look at *that boy.*"

I didn't need to hear any more. The way she talked about Lisi and me... was like we were pets, but without the whole reason you get pets.

I was stuck in the kitchen. If I made a move, they'd know I was there. So I stood still and tried not to listen as Dad explained Mom's trips to the shrink and how their marriage suffered.

I could hear Bony Nanny give Mom a hug. It was like a skeleton wind chime. "There's still time," Nanny said. "Just because they're six and eight doesn't mean it's too late. Tasha needs more discipline and those two just need love."

"They'll never love me," Mom said. "And I don't blame them."

When I heard this, I realized something. I was six, but I realized it and I shoved that realization deep down until I was old enough to handle it.

That realization: Her love was a lie, just like everything else.

The day I'd be old enough to handle it: my seventeenth birthday.

PART THREE

44

ON MY SEVENTEENTH birthday, I wake up thinking of Hannah. Not in that way. Okay, yeah, in that way, too. I almost told her I loved her last night on our way home from work. Our drives from the PEC Center the last few nights have been fun. We play loud music and Hannah sings. Over the weekend, we stopped at the baseball lot again and we lay on the field and looked at the stars. On Monday we stopped at the McDonald's and ate hot caramel sundaes. Last night, she was eating a long string of black licorice and she smiled at me in this way I can't explain. I had to remind myself not to go too fast. It's only been, like, two weeks. *She's not gonna love you back, Crapper. No one has yet.*

When I get downstairs, there's a card on the kitchen table for me in a blue envelope and it says *Gerald* on the front of it. Next to that is my lunch. Mom isn't around and I can't hear any rodent-reproduction noise from the basement, and I know Dad left at six today, because I heard him leave as I was getting up. So I grab my lunch and the card and stuff both into my backpack.

Happy birthday, Gerald.

Picking Hannah up for school this week has made my mornings earlier and berry-scented. We have to be in school by eight, but I pick her up at 7:15 so we have time together. She meets me at the end of her long driveway and we take off toward the back roads.

"Happy birthday!" she says.

"Thanks," I say. "What'd you get me?"

"I like that shirt," she says.

"Thanks. I got it at the mall this weekend."

"It's sexy."

"Don't start," I say.

"Right. Rule number five. I remember now." As she says this, she puts her hand on my leg. Near the knee. But still, it stirs me. She started doing this two nights after she cleaned the ASSHOLE off my dashboard.

"You know what I like about you?" she asks.

I don't say anything.

"You're a mystery, Gerald. I have no idea what you're thinking most of the time and I can't tell when you're here and when you're not here."

"I'm here," I say. "I'm driving the car."

"But the mystery part of it. I like that," she says. "Like—I'm the junkman's daughter and everybody knows that and it makes me easily recognizable. People see me and they think *junk*. They don't have to talk to me unless they crashed their car and they need a passenger's-side door for a 2001 Honda or something, you know?"

I laugh through my nose a little, because she's overlooking that I'm Gerald the Crapper. People see me and they think *crap*.

"See? Like just then. You thought something but you didn't say it. Mysterious."

"Just driving. To school, remember?"

"Let's skip!"

"School?"

"School *and* work. Why the hell not? Let's get out of here for the day and go somewhere exciting."

"Which would be?"

"I don't know. How about Philly? It's only two hours. We could walk arm in arm and catch an arty movie or something. Eat street-vendor hot dogs."

"That sounds nice," I say. I think of my Gersday Snow White guidance counselor. "But I should really go to school."

"Not so mysterious now."

"School's important at the moment."

"Unsexiest statement ever."

I sigh. "Can I ask you something?"

"Duh."

"Why do you want to run away so bad? I understand the junkman's daughter problem and all that, but is that it?"

"Is that it?" she says. "Dude. I am the original Cinderella. I cook. I clean. I wash. I scrub the fuckin' mildew out of the tiles in the shower. All the time, I'm cleaning shit. *Their shit*. I literally have cleaned up *their shit*. It's disgusting." She gestures wildly. "On top of that, I work and have to deal with all those hockey creeps at the PEC Center and go to school with a bunch of wankers. Seriously. Why would anyone want to stay?"

"Sorry."

"Eh. Life just sucks right now. Things will get better when Ronald gets home." Ronald's her brother. The one in Afghanistan.

"How so?" I ask.

"Well, as long as he doesn't come home in a bag, then my mother might get off her ass again. That would be a start."

We drive the rest of the way to school in silence. Content-birthday silence. Looking-out-the-window silence. Ignoring-the-lingering-pain-in-my-week-old-maybe-broken-ribs silence. When we pull into the parking lot and into my spot, she unzips her backpack and pulls out a small, wrapped CD-size box and a small card. "Don't open them until I'm gone," she says. Then she zips her backpack up and gets out of the car and walks into school.

I open the present first. It's a CD she made with a really classy-looking cover that says *Songs That Make Me Think of Gerald, by the Junkman's Daughter*. I know I don't have enough time to listen to it now, so I stick it in the glove compartment and open the card.

Her tiny writing—perfected from years of writing in her tiny book, I presume—lines the entire interior of the card and I realize I don't have time to read it now, either. But some words catch my eye as I close it. In the bottom right-hand corner, I see them. There's something about those words that forms a recognizable shape. Even in tight, tiny printing, which is how she writes. Then I close the card and stick it in the glove compartment along with the CD.

■ ▌ ▇ ▌ ▌

At lunch, she looks shy. "Hey."

"Hey," I say.

We spread out in the booth and she dumps out her bag. Two Kit Kat bars, a bunch of peanuts in the shell, a lollipop, and a stick of beef jerky. I dump out my bag. I'm completely embarrassed. Mom has wrapped all my lunch items in wrapping paper. She even put a ribbon and bow on the sandwich, which is on a roll, not on bread, so it's twice the size.

"Aw!" Hannah says.

We begin to unwrap my lunch. I shake my head because this is what my mother did this morning. She wrapped my lunch, when she could have been going to therapy or kicking Tasha out or reading a self-help article about how messed up she is. She could have been writing *I love you* on a birthday card, like Hannah did.

Instead, she wrote: *Who loves ya, kiddo?*

If it was a birthday e-mail, I'd have been able to hit REPLY and write *I don't know. Who?*

"Did you open my card?" Hannah asks as she chews on half my chicken salad sandwich.

"I didn't have time," I lie. "I figured I could do it later... before work."

"Cool," she says.

"Thanks, though. It was really nice of you."

She pulls out her little book and starts to write in it and her hair falls in front of her face so she can't see me smiling at her.

"I did open the CD, though. The cover is awesome. Did you make it?"

"I did."

"It's really great," I say, even though I'm thinking of her card the whole time. *She can't love you, Gerald. You are unlovable and you know it. She'll find out soon.*

"Thanks. Our Lady of the Junk appreciates compliments."

She's still hunched over, writing.

"So if I told Our Lady of the Junk that I think she's beautiful, that would be okay? She wouldn't come after me with a rusty old fender or a piece of farm machinery?"

She looks up between her strands of curl. "No. She wouldn't come after you with a rusty fender."

"Good. That's good," I say.

She looks at me for another second, then goes back to writing. She has on her glasses—they're fake with no prescription lenses. She wears them at the PEC Center now because she says people treat her better when she wears them. She told me this on Saturday. I didn't believe her at first, but now she shows me the chart she's been making.

"See?" she says, flipping open her little book. "On average, I get treated like shit thirty-one percent more often when I don't wear these."

"Is that what you do in your book?" I ask.

She puts it back in her pocket. "Yeah. And other stuff."

I leave lunch early because I want to see Fletcher on his own to ask him if he thinks I can get out of the SPED room and try to work on getting to college. I don't tell Hannah this. I tell Hannah I have to go to the bathroom.

"I'm going to hit the bathroom," I say.

"Don't hit it too hard," she says, still scribbling.

Deirdre is in Fletcher's room eating lunch by herself. She eats slowly and slurps soup through a straw from a thermos. We try some small talk, but she keeps talking about TV, and I keep telling her I don't watch TV.

"What's your fuckin' problem, anyway?" she asks after a minutes-long bout of silence.

"Meaning?"

"Why are you in here?" she asks. "You seem smart."

"It's a long story," I say.

"I've got all day," she says. "Nowhere to go." She flails her arms around her wheelchair as if to say: *See? Nowhere to go.*

"I don't know. I'm embarrassed. By—you know."

She looks at me, head cocked in that Deirdre way, a little

bit of her food stuck to her lips while she tries to chew faster so she can say something. She asks, "What do you have to be embarrassed about?"

"Dude," I say. But that's all I say. She gives me a look like she might cry . . . or kill me. I don't know which.

"I have to shit in my *pants*, Gerald. Do you know that? I have to *wear fuckin' diapers*. They call them *briefs* to make it sound better, but shitting in your pants is shitting in your pants."

"Sorry, Deirdre. I didn't mean to piss you off," I say.

"You didn't piss me off. You just made me aware of how embarrassed *I* should be if *you're* embarrassed."

It takes me a minute to figure out what this means. While I'm figuring it out, Deirdre says, "You know what you look like to me? You look like a kid who gets off on disappointment." She adds, "That's what you're embarrassed about."

I laugh through my nose. Not a ha-ha laugh. More like a wow-she-totally-called-that laugh. "Shit."

"You're all jacked up on being the world's biggest loser when really you could be kicking life's ass. What a fuckin' waste."

I think about kicking life's ass. I realize I have no idea where to start.

"Shit, you could be a TV star," she says.

I laugh again. A ha-ha laugh.

"Seriously. You've already got experience. You already have a name and people know you. You're fuckin' famous."

"I'm famous for shitting in my mom's shoes and for

punching someone on TV. That's not going to get me a job in TV," I say.

She rolls her eyes. "You obviously don't watch enough TV."

Fletcher arrives right when the bell rings, so I can't talk to him about anything, but talking to Deirdre helped me more than I thought it would. I can always talk to Fletcher tomorrow.

I ■ ■ I I

When we get in the car after school, Hannah asks, "Can we take the long way to work?"

The answer is yes. It always will be. Yes. Yes. Yes. I nod, and then I reach over to the glove compartment to get the card and CD and she stops me.

"Not yet," she says. "After work, okay?"

"But I want to hear the songs that remind the junkyard girl of Gerald."

"Dude, it's the junkman's *daughter*," she says. Then she opens the glove compartment and hands me the CD. "Just wait on the card. It's a lot of reading."

I can see, though, that she's noticed the open envelope.

45

WORK IS CRAZY busy.

Hannah moved to register #6 and Beth runs for us because she keeps telling us that we're "fun," which means that no matter how many hungry hockey fans are lined up in front of us, and no matter how many trays of fries she has to fetch from the hot table for us, we still make jokes and act goofy sometimes. Beth likes being goofy, too. I want to ask her what it's like to skinny-dip.

Close to closing time this guy comes to #6 with his girlfriend and asks Hannah for two beers. Hannah asks for his ID and he laughs as he gets it out of his wallet.

"I'd like to see *your* ID," he says to her. The hairs stand up on my neck when he says this. His tone is all wrong. I step away from my cash register and toward Hannah's. I become ready for confrontation. *I am Gerald and I was born ready to kick your ass.*

He gives the ID to Hannah. Beth moves over to tap the beers. "You need help doing the math, kiddo?" he says.

Hannah looks up over her glasses and says, "So you're twenty-two. Congratulations."

"They say men get better looking with age," the guy says.

Beth finishes tapping the beer and looks at the guy's girl-friend, who's staring into space like a bunny. "Really? I think women do, too."

"So what's *your* excuse?" he says.

As Beth hands him the beers I hope she spills one on him. Or drops them. Or throws them in his face. Hannah is just processing it. I can see her frown processing it.

"Time isn't going to do shit for you, asshole," I say. See? I'm good at this. *I have a switch and you can switch me on.*

He puffs up and says, "What'd you say to me, kid?"

"I said," I say. Then I raise my voice so the veins in my neck pop. "Time isn't going to do shit for your ugly asshole of a face, you big fucking tool." I smile. "Did you hear me that time?"

He stands there holding his two beers. His girlfriend says something I can't hear. *Let's go. Come on. We're missing the game.* He doesn't hear it, either. He's just staring at me.

He has no idea how fast I could put him in the hospital.

He puts the beers on the counter. "Where's your fucking boss?"

Beth raises her hand.

"I can make this a lot easier for you and just hit you first. You want that?" I ask. I really want to hit him, so I get right in his face.

He looks at Beth. "I want him fired."

Beth moves her ear closer and cups it. "I'm sorry. I'm far too ugly to hear you. Can you say that again?"

He stares at the three of us for a few seconds and then he picks up his beers and leaves.

Beth high-fives me. "You okay?"

I nod. "You're totally a babe," I say. "Don't listen to that asshole."

Hannah agrees. She's in some weird state of shock, though. I can tell by how she's still frowning. Like she's still living in a minute ago. I know time travel when I see it.

❚❚■❚❚

On our way to the parking garage, she says, "You scared me in there."

"What?"

"You scared me," she says. "You're—um—a lot more. I don't know. Nothing. Forget it."

"I'll forget it if you forget it," I say. I know neither of us will forget it.

We walk the block quietly.

She looks at me as we walk under a streetlight. "You're really handsome, you know that?"

I don't know what to say. I don't think anyone uses the word *handsome* anymore. I feel humbled by it. Because it's old and grandmothers say it, it seems classy and real and I feel... handsome. It makes me smile. And it makes me really want to kiss Hannah, but I don't.

In the car, I get to the glove compartment first and I pull out the card before Hannah can swipe it from me, which is what it looks like she wants to do.

I start to read the tiny writing.

Dear Gerald,

I know it's a little early for me to be saying this, but I think you're probably the best friend I ever had. This isn't saying much because I've never had a best friend. Once I thought I had a best friend, but then she started to get interested in clothes and we ended up not being friends anymore.

I like you a lot because you give a shit, Gerald. You really give a shit. I know we don't talk much about some stuff because of the rules, but I never felt like anyone could give a shit about Hannah McCarthy. Everyone knows I'm the junkman's daughter and I decided a while ago that I was okay with that because there's nothing I can do about it. And you are the boy from TV and there's nothing you can do about that. And today you turn 17 and I think it's about time that you know that you're the boy from TV and until you leave here, you will always be the boy from TV and I will always be the junkman's daughter. And I feel a bond with you because of this. Because neither of us is happy here and I want to find a way out. Of Blue Marsh. Of my life. Of my house, of my family. I want a way out. And it looks like you want that, too.

I know this girl from my old job and she wanted out of her family, too, and so she married a guy when she was 17. Don't worry. I'm not about to propose to you. But I also think that maybe we could find a way out early. I can't handle senior year. I can't handle another day as Cinderella. I can't handle one more day of living like the junkman's daughter. I want to be Hannah. And I want you to be Gerald and not some kid from TV.

Anyway, Happy Birthday, and know that I think you're my best friend and I hope that doesn't freak you out because I need you in my life right now more than I ever needed anyone. Because I'm pretty sure I love you.

Hannah

It's a small card and I hold it close to my face to read and I keep it there for a half minute after I'm done reading while I think of something to say.

"Ugh," she says. "I'm so embarrassed."

I put the card down between the bucket seats. "Don't be embarrassed. You're my best friend, too. I never had one, either. I'm just scared because if we go too fast, we could—you know—wreck it."

"Shit."

I look at her. "I think I love you, too, Hannah. Okay? I'm pretty sure, even. But let's just go slow."

We pause and look down for a few seconds. Hannah looks like she wants to say something.

"Is something wrong?"

"You scared me in there," she says. Again. I heard her the first time, on the way to the car.

"And?"

"And I can't love someone who would, like, you know. Hit people and shit."

"Jesus," I say. I say it because I instantly feel like the Crapper.

"I'm sorry."

"It's my birthday," I say.

"I know. I don't want to kill your buzz."

"Too late."

"But I'm serious. I'm not ready for visiting someone I love in jail, you know?"

"Jesus!" I say again. "What the hell are you trying to do?"

"I'm just telling you."

"Well, I heard you, okay?"

"Okay."

She looks scared now. Fuck. "And I'd never hit—like—you or anything."

"Shit," she says. "That's not what I meant, Gerald."

"I think it is."

"It isn't," she says, and I can see the tears welling up in her eyes, because the parking-garage lights are reflecting in them. "Look. Let's just try this again."

"Let's," I say.

"Come on. Don't be mad."

"Dude, you think I'm going to hit you one day. I think that sucks. It would suck for you if you were me, I guarantee it."

"I didn't say that."

"You didn't have to."

I pull out of the parking space and take off down the parking-garage ramp. Hannah starts to cry a little. *Happy birthday, Gerald.*

Once we get out of the garage and start driving toward the bridge, she starts to ramble. "Look, that was my fault and I'm sorry. But you scared me. I could see you nearly killing that guy. You had a vein popping out of your neck. And I know that your chest is still all messed up from boxing and it scared me and I didn't know you boxed and I don't like boxing because it's so violent and I don't understand why anyone would want to hit another person, so all of those things scared me, okay? And before you say it again, I don't think you're going to hit me," she says. "I think we're soul mates. Soul mates don't do shit like that."

"Now we're soul mates?" I don't know why I'm being so sarcastic. But I am. And I'm hurting her. And I can't stop. *Because you're an asshole.*

"Actually, I thought that as far back as three weeks ago."

"Three weeks ago we weren't even talking to each other," I say.

She pulls out her little notebook. "I can prove it. Want me to read you that part?"

"No," I say. "I believe you."

"So you're not mad?"

I sigh. I'm mad. *Zip code 00000.* But not at her. "I was just having a nice birthday and I didn't want to scare you. I was just playing around. I'd never have hit that guy." That is a complete lie.

"I'll read it to you," she says. "It's right here. Three weeks ago to the day."

I put my hand up. "Don't do it. That breaks rule number— what's the no-reading-the-book rule? Why didn't we number that rule?"

"Because it's a sacred rule."

"So then you can't read it to me. Put it back in your pocket."

Neither of us talks for a while, but she puts her hand on my leg again—near the knee—and it stirs me again, too.

I say, "Soul mates, huh?"

She says, "Yep."

I smile.

If she is my soul mate, then I have just saved myself years of searching. But I can't tell if she is or not, because I am wrapped in a lifetime of polyethylene lie-wrapping that denies me any possibility of knowing the truth.

We pull up to her driveway. She says, "You write your list of demands yet?"

"I tried to start," I say. "Big fail. Nothing I demanded made any sense."

"So? Do it anyway. If I was you, I'd have a long-ass list by now."

"I guess I'm not really good at demanding."

She gets out of the car.

"Thanks for the card," I say. "I thought it was funny that you said I give a shit. You know, because that's my life—giving people shits. Only those people never really appreciated it." I laugh. "But no. Seriously. Thanks for the card. It's sweet."

"You're welcome. And don't forget to listen to the CD."

"I won't. And that thing—the love shit," I say.

"The love shit? That's romantic."

"I mean, let's just keep going slow, okay? This shit scares me."

⚊ ⚊ ▆ ⚊ ⚊

When I get home, I go to the kitchen table and find my birthday present and a note. *Sorry we missed you!*

It's a gas card for three hundred dollars. I hear the loud TV downstairs in the basement and think about packing right now and going wherever three hundred dollars will take me.

Once I get to my room, I watch the amazing Monaco trapeze act twice before I go to bed. I count the spins and the somersaults. The performers are like birds. They have probably been forced to practice trapeze from the minute they were born, twenty-two hours a day, seven days a week, but they look free. At least, in the air they look free.

46

EPISODE 3, SCENE 2, TAKE 2

EPISODE THREE WASN'T a full episode. It was one of those let's-look-back-on-our-past-families-and-see-how-well-we-did episodes, and I couldn't have the world thinking that anyone in my house had done well.

No one had done well.

Mom still treated Tasha like a princess even though Tasha hit her all the time and had invented the pillow trick to scare Lisi and me worse. The pillow trick was when she'd take a couch pillow and put it over my face until I would start to kick and scream and nearly lose consciousness. Then she'd remove it and I'd be in Gersday, lying there with her invisible and Lisi by my side, looking concerned. Then Tasha would run to

Mom and tell her that I'd done something bad, and Mom would come in and scold me while I was mute, staring into space and eating ice cream with my favorite cartoon character or something.

Dad stayed away more. If that was even possible. The market was good then. Houses were flying. I overheard talk of storing money away like squirrels hiding nuts. He mentioned moving because so many people knew us now. *Reality TV stars.* Photographers would come to the end of the driveway and snap pictures. Articles would appear in the local paper. People would write letters to the editor. I was six, so I didn't know that then. I've since read some of those letters. Many were cruel. Some weren't. I'm pretty sure one was written by my hockey-lady/ketchup-coated dream mother.

Lisi was not okay. She feared for our lives. The pillow trick was avoidable, she reckoned, by staying in her room all the time, where Tasha couldn't get her. She read every book she owned a hundred times. She wrote things in a little locked diary and worked ahead in her textbooks.

Mom was not okay. Her eyes were empty. Translucent. She'd started walking for hours at a time. She even applied for jobs, but no one would hire her, since she didn't know how to do anything except fuck up her family. No one said that part. That part was mine.

When Nanny Lainie Church/Elizabeth Harriet Small-piece and the crew arrived on the first day, they walked in as if they owned us. Nanny didn't even bother wearing her Nanny costume. She was dressed in a dress that showed her every curve and her ample cleavage. The crew didn't mount any secret cameras on the walls. This was going to be a three-day-long visit, once and done, they said—just a way to reestablish the rules and make sure the family was doing okay.

The first scene with us kids in it was scene two. We were all washed and dressed and sitting at the kitchen table with Mom and Dad at the head seats and Nanny next to me, with Tasha and Lisi across from me and Nanny. All I could see was my invisible turds there in the middle of the table. It got me to thinking about the days when I put them there. Back when I was five, which seemed like a lifetime ago.

I felt older than seven.

What other seven-year-old could claim he'd escaped being murdered by his own sister at least a dozen times? What other seven-year-old could claim that when he went to school, he was seen as part movie star and part maniac? I couldn't understand if those kids in first grade had actually seen the show or if their parents had distilled it for them. I'm guessing both. Parents let their kids watch all sorts of shit they shouldn't watch.

"Nice to see you all again," Nanny started. "I'm very excited to hear of your *proh*-gress." Nanny said *progress* with the long *o* sound. I'd grown to love her accent even though I wanted to slap it right out of her mouth for her being so naïve as to think there had been any *proh*-gress.

"Tasha tried to kill me again last week," I'd said on take one. They didn't like that. Tasha protested. Things got loud.

So someone yelled "Cut!" and we started over and I was

given instructions not to speak until a question was posed directly to me.

Nanny looked worried, though. She eyed Tasha. She knew.

"Action."

"Nice to see you all again," Nanny said. "I'm very excited to hear of your *proh*-gress."

Mom smiled and said we'd been better behaved. She said she felt more able to handle the family now that house rules were in place and chores were still getting done.

Dad said he'd been busier at work than usual and felt that "the kids" were doing great. He said that he and Mom got to go more places together—once-a-month dates made possible by our newest babysitter.

"Gerald, how are you doing in school now that you're in first grade?" Nanny asked. This was my cue to say something that wouldn't ruin the scene and that would segue us smoothly into scene three, which would be an overview of our charts and chores and all the things Nanny had done for us. I was told to say *School is great. My teacher is really nice.*

But I thought about the question. *Gerald, how are you doing in school?* I thought about my answer. How do you *think* I'm doing? And why would I think you *really* care? What a load of bullshit.

"School would be better if Tasha wasn't trying to kill me all the time," I said.

"Cut!"

47

I DEMAND A *mother who isn't this person.*

When I tell her I'm sick today and not going to school, my mother responds with, "Well, I'm not letting this get in the way of my plans with your father." She bends her forehead into the shape of a *W.*

Dad sits there looking confused. I shrug and apologize.

"We RSVP'd to this wedding ages ago," Mom grumbles. "And we have to leave at ten."

"I'm sorry," I say again.

"You go pack, Jill," Dad says. "I want to talk to Ger on my own."

She leaves, still clearly disappointed in my behavior even though I haven't crapped in her shoes.

I demand to crap in her shoes. One. Last. Time.

"You okay?" Dad asks.

"Yeah. I just feel sick," I say. I point to my stomach.

"Hungover from birthday celebrations?"

"That was two days ago. And I worked, remember?"

He nods. "Anything you want to talk about?"

"Nah."

"You're not doing drugs, are you?"

"Jesus, no."

"Drinking?"

"Not unless you're there," I say.

"You got a girl?"

"Maybe," I say. "Nothing serious." My poker face is perfect.

"You're not going to bring her here while we're gone, right?"

"Never," I say, thinking of the screwing-rodent rodeo in our basement.

He looks at me, worried. "You sure nothing's wrong?"

I look at him, worried. "I'm sure everything is wrong," I say. "I just have to wait it out, like Lisi did."

"Huh," he says. As if I'm being unreasonable.

"Or we could buy that house with the pool," I say.

He sighs.

"Think about it," I say.

He looks at the clock and motions for me to follow him into his man cave, where he shuts the door behind us and opens the liquor cabinet. He pours himself a small glass of liquor and mutters about how Mom will drive anyway. It's nine o'clock in the morning.

"I hate going to weddings," he says. "Everyone is always so fuckin' happy. It's all about futures and celebrations and all these people acting like marriage is some dream-filled Twinkie."

"It isn't?"

He smirks at me. Before he can say another word, the racket starts. Quietly at first. *Ba-boom-ba-boom-ba-boom-ba-boom.* Slowly.

He swigs back the end of his drink and says, "Mom is leaving Tasha in charge. I know that sucks. If you want to sleep at a friend's house, that's fine with me."

He knows I don't have any friends.

"Call me if she does anything stupid," he says. *Ba-boom-ba-boom-ba-boom-ba-boom.*

"Do you have unlimited minutes?" I ask, and we both laugh.

▌▌▉▌▌

Once they finally leave, I pick Hannah up from school (she sneaked out the band room door and met me on the street) and we drive to Franklin Street. On the way there, I tell her about what I've figured out.

"I don't belong in Mr. Fletcher's class. I never did. I'm fine," I say.

She nods.

"But my mom wanted me to be retarded so Tasha would be happy. And she wanted Tasha to be happy because Tasha used to hit her all the time, and Lisi and me, and there's more stuff to the whole thing, but we can talk about that another day. I mean—what kind of mother wants her kid to be retarded?"

"Can we please start saying *learning disabled* or something?"

"But that's what she called me," I say. "It hurt and shit." *You know how your mother is.*

She squeezes my arm. "That totally sucks, you know?"

"But I'm fine, right? I'm not re—learning disabled, am I?" I look over at her as I drive. "Am I?"

"Gerald, did you ever think that her calling you that could have, you know, let her off the hook for all the shit she did to you? Like—the stuff from the show?"

"What do you mean?"

"This is totally going to break rule number three," she says.

"Go for it."

"Well, maybe she needed a reason for you to be, you know—doing what you did? So she decided that something was wrong with you, not her."

"You mean a reason for me to be crapping?"

"Yeah," she says.

"Huh," I say. Then my brain races. So, my mother needed me to be ~~retarded~~ learning disabled because it would explain why I crapped during *Network Nanny.*

Shit.

My mother wanted me to be retarded because it was easier than her turning into a good mother.

Shit.

▍▍▊▍▍

Nathan and Ashley are watching a National Geographic miniseries about the deepest parts of the sea. It's their day off.

Ashley isn't baking anything and Nathan says it's too early for beer. I find this ironic because I watched my dad drink straight Scotch at nine o'clock this morning.

I demand that Nathan and Ashley adopt me.

Hannah curls up in the chair that's surrounded by three fish tanks and says hello to Lola and Drake. She notes that there's a fish missing.

"Yeah. One of the Plecs died this week," Nathan says.

Hannah frowns. "Poor Luis. He was the best cleaner in the world."

I sit on the couch by myself and watch Hannah, mostly. She doesn't even know I'm watching her. She doesn't notice when Ashley offers her a soda before she goes to the kitchen. She doesn't see Ashley and Nathan look at her and laugh a little. She doesn't notice when her phone buzzes in her pocket. She's in those tanks, swimming around the algae-covered faux castle and the driftwood with her fish friends.

It's as if Hannah has a Gersday.

As I watch her, I realize that I'm tired and I close my eyes. Napping isn't something I do. Napping was dangerous in my house while I was growing up. Napping made me an easier target. No one here seems to mind, so I try it.

Next thing I know, Hannah is waking me up, asking what I want for lunch.

"It's on me," Nathan says. "I get a discount at the Chinese place."

"I'm not hungry," I say. Napping made me not hungry. I yawn.

"He can share mine," Hannah says.

A half hour later, we're all eating Chinese food around Ashley and Nathan's kitchen table. Nathan talks about his job as a driver for a local appliance company. Ashley asks Hannah if she likes working at the PEC Center.

"It's okay," Hannah says. "My boss is cool, which is a change."

"You work there, too, right?" Ashley says to me.

I'm still tired. My stomach is all twisted from my nap. "Yeah," I say.

"You want an egg roll?" Nathan asks.

When I say "No, thanks," he offers it to Hannah, who eats it in three bites.

I watch the three of them have a conversation about some news story they saw on TV about a high school junior who got expelled for a bomb threat. Nathan doesn't agree with Ashley about one part of it and Hannah does. They laugh while they disagree. There's calm—as if the ninety-nine fish in the house have taught these people how to live in the same tank without resorting to drama. They're just swimming, eating, living.

Maybe what we needed in the Faust household when I was little was an aquarium.

Maybe that would have made everything better.

And it's pretty hard to crap on an aquarium. I'm staring at the big one now and trying to figure out how little Gerald would have done that. Nearly impossible.

"Gerald?"

I look at them at the table and they are not Ashley, Nathan, and Hannah.

They are Snow White, Donald Duck, and Cinderella. I don't want this to happen, so I say, "Yeah?"

"What do you think about it? Do you think she should be allowed to go back to that school after what she did?"

I'm staring at Ashley, who is asking this question, but she is Snow White, with that fucking bluebird on her shoulder.

"Gerald doesn't watch TV," Cinderella says.

"Righteous," Donald Duck answers. He holds up his white wing for a high five. "That shit just makes you stupid anyway."

I high-five his wing and can feel the feathers.

I reach down and pinch my leg, but no matter how hard I do it, I can't snap myself out of Gersday.

Cinderella says, "Anyway, she only called in the bomb threat. It wasn't like she planted a real bomb. She had every reason to blow the whole school up, as far as I'm concerned. They all treated her like shit."

"That's no reason to freak people out," Donald Duck says.

"So freaking people out is now a crime?" Snow White says.

"Um, yeah," Donald answers. "Bomb threats are illegal."

I pinch my leg harder. I blink. I breathe in. Breathe out. I tap my foot. I dig my fingernails into my palm.

I am still sitting at the table with Snow White, Donald, and Cinderella. So I ask where the bathroom is and I lock the door behind me and stare at myself in the mirror. I am not a Walt Disney character. I am Gerald.

I am Gerald and I will never be anyone but Gerald.

I splash my face with water and flush the toilet and I look at myself one more time and I do not want to punch Gerald. Violence seems so out of place here.

When I return to the kitchen, I am relieved to see Hannah, Nathan, and Ashley cleaning up. No webbed yellow feet and no gaudy ball gowns.

"You want the rest of this?" Nathan asks as he offers me some lo mein.

I accept and sit down and eat it out of the white carton with a fork. They talk excitedly about watching *Jaws* next—a Friday tradition. Hannah makes her way to the chair in front of the big saltwater tank and touches the glass where a starfish has attached itself. I sit next to her, on the arm of the chair.

"Does he have a name?" I ask.

"He's an it. This species is hermaphroditic." When I look clueless, she adds, "It creates sperm *and* eggs."

"I know what hermaphroditic means. I just want to know its name," I say.

"Oh, sorry," she says. "I call it Sal. Could be short for Sally, you know?"

"Gotcha."

We stare at Sal for a while and she tells me the names of the other fish. Harry, Sadie, Kingsley, Bob, and the big clown triggerfish named Bozo.

"Don't they give you a feeling of hope?" she asks. "I mean, like one day we'll be free?"

I fail to see how fish trapped in a two-hundred-gallon glass tank should give me hope. I would think freedom for Harry and Sadie and Bob and Bozo would look more like the ocean where they belong. I don't say this. Instead, I say, "Free?"

"They have their own house. They have jobs. They have everything they want. They go on vacation in summer to Wildwood. It's just—it's just so much hope."

"I thought we were talking about the fish," I say.

"Oh."

"But yeah. They do give me hope, I guess. They're so nice," I say. "Are they always this nice?"

"Yeah."

"I'm not used to it," I say. "Like I said in the car, you know?"

She stares at the fish and thinks for a minute. "Shit," she says. "That thing I said about hermaphrodites. It was something like your mom would have said, wasn't it?"

I laugh. It's a real laugh. I check to make sure.

This makes her laugh, too.

"My mother probably doesn't know what a hermaphrodite is. Not unless it was in some article in a magazine," I say.

"You guys are missing the beginning," Ashley says. "You can't be here on a Friday and not watch *Jaws*. It's a house rule. Even you, fish girl. Come on."

Hannah and I sit in two different chairs. She sits where she can see her fish and the TV at the same time. I sit on the couch where I had my nap. Halfway through the movie—right when the shark starts chasing down Quint's boat—

Nathan goes to the kitchen and brings back beers for all of us and we sit there mesmerized until the very end.

As the credits roll, Hannah says, "I want to be a marine biologist."

"Hell yeah," Nathan says. "Do it. You'd be really good at it."

Ashley nods.

No one chuckles condescendingly and says *Marine biologist? Heh.*

What occurs to me at this second is this: There is a huge world out there. I only know my dumb family and my dumb house and my dumb school and my dumb job. But there is a huge world out there...and most of it is underwater.

48

WHEN I DROP Hannah off at her driveway, I tell her that I have an empty house for the night.

"Do you think it would be safe for me to come over?"

"I don't know," I say. "Probably not."

I demand to break rule #5.

I demand to kiss her today. Right now, even.

Then I lean in and kiss her on the mouth, and she parts my lips with her tongue and we break rule #5. For ten minutes.

I can't explain the thoughts I have about her on my drive home, but they are pretty hot thoughts. But then I'm soft inside. Like I'm filled with nougat or crème caramel. I want to tell someone. *I just broke rule #5. I am happy. I think I have a real girlfriend.*

I have no one to share that with. I have no friends. Joe Jr. would think I was a prude, only kissing a girl at seventeen years old. Beth is not my friend, she's my boss. No one in SPED class would care—or they'd just make dumb comments about it. Deirdre would make me feel bad because she's probably never going to break rule #5 in her life.

There is only one person I want to call right now, and she lives in Scotland and she left me here in this fucking mess and never calls me. My nougat hardens. My crème caramel turns crunchy. Why am I mad at Lisi? *Why?* All she did was follow through. All she did was exactly what she said she would do. She got out.

And it's not like I don't have a phone. It's not like I don't have fingers to dial her new number. I could have dialed her number a hundred times if I wanted to. Only I didn't because . . . what?

I thought I could do this alone.

I demand not to do this alone.

When I pass through the gate and wave to the security guard, he raises an eyebrow at me and I don't know why until I see our driveway, which is packed with cars. Maybe twenty of them, from the garage all the way down the drive. The extras are scattered around the cul-de-sac.

I stop and open my car window and I hear the music twanging away, rattling the neighbors' houses. I wonder how long this party's been going on. And how soon the cops will come.

I demand to not be here when the cops come.

I park and walk up the front yard to the door and when I open the door, the first thing I do is take a picture of the scene with my phone and send it to Dad's phone.

I make my way to the stairs, through the thick crowd of complete strangers in my house. Tasha is drunk. There are two kegs in the kitchen and a lot of bottles of liquor on the kitchen table. Some people are piled up on the couch making out. Others are dancing on the far side of the room where Danny has his stereo set up. I think one girl is dancing in her bra. I can't figure out what to do.

I get to my room and close and lock the door and stare at my phone. A minute ago, I didn't know who to call about how great everything is. Now I don't know who to call about how shitty everything is.

I dial Lisi's number.

As it rings, I do the math and realize it's, like, three in the morning where she is. But before I can hang up, she answers.

"Lisi," I say.

"Gerald? Is everything okay?"

I let the noise of the party downstairs filter through and hope she hears it.

"I need to get out of here," I say. "Like now."

"What's going on?"

"Tasha's throwing a party. There are rednecks all over our house. Mom and Dad are away. I think I saw two people doing it on the couch when I walked in."

"Shit."

"Can we talk about it now?" I ask.

"Sure. What do you want to talk about?" she asks. I hear a lighter flick.

"The time she nearly drowned me."

There's silence on the other end of the phone.

"Lisi?"

"I'm here," she says.

"Do you remember the time she tried to drown me?"

"Yeah."

"You said something that night. I remember it."

"You were, like, three, weren't you? How do you remember anything from when you were three?"

"I remember a lot," I say. "You said, *Now you can have baths alone, like I do.*"

"Did I?"

"Yeah."

There's silence. Well, not silence—the party is still thumping downstairs. "She did it to me, too," Lisi says. She takes a drag on whatever she's smoking. "Mom used to make us take baths together to save time. Tasha used to hold my head under the water. The last time, Mom caught her. Or—whatever. I was coughing and throwing up because she'd held me under so long. I think I breathed in water."

"Shit."

"Mom tried to get us to get in the bath together after that and I freaked out. I just lost it. I can barely remember it. You were, like, a baby. I wasn't even four, I don't think." She smokes and I try to block out the pounding of the country music that has just increased by at least ten decibels. "But I read about people like her in my psych class this semester, Gerald. She's a psychopath. Always was. Always will be."

I used to think this, but I never said it. Psychopaths are like the guys in *One Flew Over the Cuckoo's Nest*, right? Psychopaths are serial killers and mass murderers. I wonder if guys like that ever tried to drown their siblings in the family bathtub.

"A psychopath?" I say.

"Trust me. That's what she is," Lisi says.

"I can't figure out what that makes Mom," I say.

"I think it makes her the mother of a psychopath," she says. Then she laughs and I miss her laugh so much.

"I miss you," I say.

"Me, too," she says. "I don't miss being there, though. Obviously."

"Yeah."

"Do you have a plan?"

"You mean for tonight?"

"Tonight. Tomorrow. Life," she says.

"I don't know," I say. *I demand to run away with the circus.* "I have a girlfriend."

"That's great!" she says. "What's her name?"

My phone buzzes with a text. I tell Lisi to wait a second and I see it's from Dad. *Get out of there now. I'm calling the police.* That's what the text says.

"Shit," I say. "That's a text from Dad. He's calling the police. I have to get out of here."

"Do you have somewhere to go?"

"Sure. I have a mountain of friends who will open their door to me at ten o'clock at night." I grab my school backpack and shove in a few days' worth of clothing.

"No. Seriously."

"I'll be fine," I say. "Talk to you soon. I gotta go."

"Love you, Gerald," she says.

"Love you, too."

I say that as I'm walking out my bedroom door and Tasha hears it because she happens to be standing right outside my bedroom door like some kind of stalker.

"That your girlfriend?" she asks.

I pull my door closed so it locks and run past her toward the stairs. She grabs my arm. I wiggle free and get down the stairs. In seventeen years, I've learned the fine art of avoiding Tasha chasing me down the stairs.

"Dude!" she says. "Just stop. There's this girl. I want you to meet her."

On my way toward the door, I swing through the kitchen to get some food from the fridge. I know Mom made a big bowl of chicken salad and I swim through the drunk people to get to it.

As I grab the plastic bowl and a loaf of bread, someone is shoved into my back. I turn around to face a black-haired, henna-tattooed girl who can't be more than fifteen. Tasha's behind her and I can tell she's responsible.

The girl is wavering-drunk. She smiles. Tasha says, "She really likes you. She's just too shy to tell you at school."

I don't recognize her from school.

The girl lurches forward and kisses me, with Tasha so close her hand is nearly up the girl's ass like some sort of evil puppeteer, making her kiss me.

I keep my mouth shut and try to get out of her grip, but Tasha is egging her on. *Do it, Stacy! Kiss him!* It's a dare, I bet. *Kiss the Crapper.* I manage to twist myself away and head toward the doorway to the living room.

That's where I run into Jacko the fake Jamaican. He's smiling at me the way he used to at the gym before I kicked his ass. His face is still a mass of bruises, lumps, and cuts. I smile back because I'm still proud I did that to him.

"That's my little girlfriend you just kissed, asshole," he says.

It's the last thing I hear before he jumps on me.

Everything goes white. I don't feel anything. I am eating ice cream with Lisi on a trapeze. I am tap dancing with a blue-bird on my shoulder. The only sound from reality that seeps through to Gersday is Tasha's incessant laughter.

I demand to never hear that laughter again.

49

I'M NOT SURE what happened, but I find myself on top of Jacko the fake Jamaican, pounding my fist into his face. My fist is sticky. I can feel my skin stick to his skin for the split second when I pull away and make contact again.

Someone drags me off him.

He's conscious, but startled. His black-haired girlfriend is crying.

Tasha is still laughing.

I demand that Tasha stop laughing.

I lunge at her and grab her neck, which stops her laughing. She looks at me with crazy, fear-filled eyes. Part homicidal, part wounded forest animal. I think about what Lisi told me on the phone. I think about going to court for killing a psycho-path. I think about how the psychopath's mother has spent her whole life defending her little psychopath. Then I think about all that footage of my crapping, crapping, crapping. *No jury in their right minds would choose the Crapper over Tasha.*

I let her go and grab my backpack, my bowl of chicken salad, and the now-crushed loaf of bread and run out the door and down the packed driveway to my car. I drive away with the bowl of chicken salad between my legs so it doesn't tip over. I don't look back.

The road is bubble-gum ice cream. It's white with different-colored gum balls in it. It's bumpy. I put in Hannah's CD and crank the volume to louder-than-a-bomb. It makes my ear-drums vibrate so much, I get buzzing in my ears, so I turn it down. I feel something like sweat running down my cheek, and I wipe it with my hand and find it's stickier than sweat.

"It's blood, Gerald," Snow White says. "You should pull over and make sure you're not hurt."

"I don't know where I am," I say.

"You're near the shopping center. You can pull into the car park," she says. Snow White smiles a lot. She seems happy to live in a fairy tale. She seems happy to do all that housework for all those messy little dwarfs.

"How come you don't teach those little bastards how to do stuff for themselves?" I ask her. "They should know how to do shit for themselves."

Snow White looks confused. "Up here to the left, Gerald. Put on your indicator and get in the lane."

I put on my turn signal and get in the left-turn lane. The lane is made of butterscotch ripple. I want to put the hand brake on and get out and lick the road.

"Light's green. Turn now, Gerald."

I turn and find a huge, empty parking lot. The mall is beyond closed, and the only vehicles driving around here now are security trucks. I still see ice cream and Snow White.

She turns on the interior light and I open my sun visor's mirror. I see a small cut on my eyebrow. Snow White hands me the first-aid kit from the glove compartment and I open it.

"You're going to need a plaster for that," she says.

I look at her. "Say that again?"

"I said *you-ah* going to need a *plast-ah* for that, Gerald."

I pull out a Band-Aid and stick it on the cut. It's not bleeding that badly. I look myself over in the mirror and see that my nose has been bleeding, too, but as far as I can tell, no lumps or brokenness anywhere. I still feel kinda numb. I am so high on adrenaline, I have a spongy feeling all over my body.

"You're American," I say to Snow White. "Why'd you call it that?"

Snow White looks confused again.

"Americans don't say *plaster*. We say *Band-Aid*."

I look down at the road in front of my headlights. It is clearly tarmacadam. I look down at the bowl between my legs. It is clearly chicken salad. I am suddenly ravenous, so I reach back and pull out some bread from the bag and scoop up some chicken salad with one piece and plop the other piece of bread on top.

I demand to eat a chicken salad sandwich right now.

My phone buzzes with a text from Dad. *Did you get out?*

I decide not to answer him.

I decide the question is bigger than any question he's ever asked me.

Did I get out? Yes and no.

Get out of what? Do you really think I have a chance to get out of this shit?

50

"YOU WOKE ME UP," Hannah says.

"It's a long story," I say.

"What's a long story?"

"The story I'm going to tell you in a half hour when I pick you up."

"I'm sleeping."

"I'm leaving. Now," I say.

"To the circus?"

"To wherever. To whatever. I'm not going back."

I hear her sit up and switch a light on. "Seriously?"

"Yeah."

"You want me to come with you?"

"That's the plan," I say.

"I kidnap you. You kidnap me?"

"Yep."

"You got a list of demands yet?" she asks.

"A mile long," I lie.

"I don't have one yet," she says. There's shame in her voice.

"We have all the time in the world."

"Seriously, Gerald? We're going to do this?"

"Seriously, Hannah. We're going to do this."

She sighs. "Be here in half an hour?"

"More like twenty minutes," I say.

"How long should I pack for?"

This question stumps me. It reminds me that I haven't talked to Joe Jr. yet. It reminds me that this could be a complete failure. It reminds me that I'm seventeen and Hannah is sixteen. Underage runaways. *Incarcerated Ingrates. Locked-Up Lovers.*

"Gerald?"

"Yeah?"

"How long do I pack for?"

"I don't know," I say.

She says, "Okay." Then she hangs up.

▌ ▌ ▌ ▌

I am still pissed off at Snow White for being British. She shouldn't be anything but a wholesome, famous American cartoon character who washes seven dwarfs and all their clothing and their house and who mends their shoes. She should be happy being

American. She should be happy being famous, even though she's made herself a willing slave to seven little people.

Isn't that what fame is, anyway? Being slaves to little people? My slave name was the Crapper. My slave job was to crap and make millions of little people happy.

My other slave name was Gerald. My slave job was to make my crazy sister Tasha look smart by letting my mom call me retarded my whole life.

I pull over into a gas station parking lot to let time pass. I'm about ten minutes early. I pick up my phone and text Joe Jr. *Where are you in Florida? You never sent your address.* I send it even though it makes me feel like a moron. Would I give my address to him? Would Hannah give her address to anyone? Joe Jr. isn't going to send me his address. So, all I have is the tag on his YouTube video: *Bonifay, FL.*

I text Dad. *I got out.*

I make another chicken salad sandwich and eat it. Then I get back on the road to Hannah's house. She's waiting by the mailbox when I get there, her red backpack on her back, and wearing her leather jacket and a ripped-up pair of jeans.

When she flops into the passenger's seat, she says, "Shit. What happened to you?"

It reminds me that I have just been through what Roger would call "an incident," so I tell her everything. I even explain who Jacko the fake Jamaican is. About the boxing gym. About Roger. I stop short when my mouth tries to tell her about Tasha and how she tried to drown me and Lisi when we were little and how I escaped being murdered a lot. Something just chokes me when I try to say it.

"I can't tell if this is stupid or not," Hannah says as I drive toward the turnpike.

"What?"

"This," she says.

"If you're not okay with it, I can take you home," I say.

"I don't know."

I slow down and make a U-turn in a bank parking lot. I head back to her house. Can I tell you that my heart is breaking? My heart is totally breaking.

"I didn't tell you to turn around," she says.

"I don't want you to do anything you don't want to do," I answer.

"Can you pull over?"

I pull over.

"I don't want you to get mad, okay?" she says.

"Okay."

"But you were right. I lied about something. I don't think I can do this unless we talk about it first."

My heart continues to break and I'm so busy thinking about it that I don't stop to think what she might have lied about.

"When I said I wasn't scared that you could hit me. I lied. I was. You got so mad so quick and I have an aunt who had a husband who did that and I get scared of it. I'm sorry. I don't want to say anything else about it. I just had to say it."

Fuck. My FS levels go up and I do all the stuff Roger taught me to make them go down again, but this doesn't feel right. There is no way I can run away with Hannah now. She thinks I could hit her. As if I'm an animal or something. *You were a dumbass to think she could ever love a loser like you in the first place.*

Also, Gerald? She might be right. You never know.

"Gerald?"

I go to Gersday and I meet Lisi on the trapeze. Except she's not there. Tasha is there, in a blue sequined trapeze costume, so I leave Gersday in time to hear what Hannah says next.

"I do think I love you," she says. "I just can't figure out what will happen if we go, you know?"

My voice is a little louder than I want it to be. "What will happen if we go is: We will be gone. That's what you said you wanted, right? You wrote it in your birthday card. It's all you've bugged me about for two weeks, isn't it?"

"Shit. You don't have to be an asshole about it."

I reach into the tray between the seats and grab the Sharpie marker. "Go ahead. Write it again. At least you had balls when you did that."

"I have balls."

"But?"

"But I don't know," she says. I stop the car at the end of her driveway, where I just picked her up five minutes before.

"I have to get out of here now. That kid probably called the cops. That wasn't a boxing ring. Have a nice life, okay?"

She sighs. "Look. I don't want *another* person making decisions for me. I just want a minute to think about this."

"I don't have a minute."

She gets out of the car with her red backpack and stands there in my headlights, so I have to reverse into the road and do a U-turn in her neighbor's driveway. Then, when I drive back, she's standing there, in the road, and I can't go around her because she keeps moving the same way I steer the car.

I try not to be frustrated, but I'm frustrated.

"I don't have time for this!" I yell out my window.

"Let me in," she says.

"No."

"Let me in, Gerald!"

I stop the car. She gets in. Then she says, "You're totally in asshole mode right now."

"I just got my ass kicked."

"So?"

"So I'm tired. And I'm running away. I don't have time for your crazy shit right now."

"Stop calling me crazy!"

"I didn't call you crazy. I called your shit crazy."

We have a staring standoff.

We take off. Again.

▌▌▆▌▌

We're quiet for the first chunk of driving. I allow my adrenaline levels to drop. I try not to think about the police who might be on their way to find me. I try not to think about how Hannah thinks I could hit her.

I think Hannah has gone to sleep, but when I look over, she is wide awake, staring out the window into the darkness beyond the metal mile markers.

"Why do you love me, Gerald?" she asks.

"Wow. That's a question," I say. *Fuck*.

She doesn't say anything smart-ass or pleading and just keeps staring out the window.

"I loved you the minute I saw you at register number one. You were scribbling in your little notebook. You didn't notice me. I liked that."

"You love me because I didn't notice you?"

"Yeah. And because you're funny and sarcastic and you don't care what other people think," I say. "Do you know how long I've cared about what other people think?" I guffaw out my nose. "And the way you like the fish. I love that."

"The fish?"

"Nathan and Ashley's fish," I say.

"Oh."

I look over at her. "You okay?"

"Yeah."

"Really? I mean, we're about to run away together. You have to be okay or I'm taking the next exit and going back again."

"I'm fine. Really. I'm just trying to figure out what the fuck is going on," she says. "I can't tell if you love the real me or the fake me."

I see a sign that says EMERGENCY PULL OFF. I pull off.

I see Hannah's been crying and I hug her while she reminds me of rule #5, which in turn makes me hug her harder. I tilt her face up to mine. "I love the real you. I don't even know what you mean about the fake you."

"I have shocking news," she says. "I do care what people think."

I nod.

"And when I get out of high school, I want to do something fun—like they do in the movies or in punk rock songs. I don't want to do something just because some group of people decided that this is the process for baking kids. Preheat to three fifty and bake for sixteen years or until browned."

"We *are* running away with the circus, you know. That could be considered fun and not in the recipe for baking perfect kids."

"Except we have to go back to school, Gerald. We're juniors. It's only December. We have a while to go before either of us gets to run away with the circus."

I sigh. "You're a buzzkill."

"I probably just need sleep," she says. "Wake me up when you get tired and I can drive for a while."

"You drive?"

"Dude, I'm the junkman's daughter. Of course I drive. I even drove a bulldozer once."

She curls up and puts a sweatshirt between her head and the window and cranks her seat back a little so she can sleep. I pull back onto the turnpike and get going.

I realize I have no idea *where* I'm going, but I figure south is good enough. *South. I'm going south.*

Lisi's question rings in my ears. *Do you have a plan?*

51

EPISODE 3, SCENE 12, TAKE 17

BY THE END of the second day, Nanny started to storm around. None of her psychobabble bullshit worked on me. I tore down every new behavior chart she made to show off how great she was. I interrupted every time she tried to make us look like a fixed family. I made it a game.

"You're ruining the show!" Tasha screamed after take ten. "Just do what they tell you to do!"

Lisi pulled me aside after take twelve. "Do you want them to leave, Gerald? For good?"

"Yes."

"Then just do what they say and they'll get out of here. Forever."

I loved Lisi. But I couldn't do it. I couldn't do what they

said. They were wrong and I was right. They wanted a tame, loving child. I could give them one if only they stopped telling me what was wrong with me and let me tell them instead. *I'm living with a homicidal maniac.*

But they wouldn't shut up. So I had a crap fest. My final crap fest.

"Take seventeen!" the guy said, and he snapped down the wood.

"Gerald," Nanny said in her softest voice. "You know we all love you, right?"

I decided to make it fun. Make them think I was following their instructions. I nodded.

"And since we all love you, we want you to get *bett-ah*. And to get *bett-ah*, you have to listen to what Nanny tells you. Do you *undah-stand*?"

I nodded again while Nanny checked her hair in the on-set mirror she still carried around. "I understand," I said.

The director looked relieved. Mom looked at Lisi and gave her a thumbs-up.

"Right. Here's what's going to happen. You're going to apologize to Tasha for what you did to her doll, and then we'll go upstairs together and we'll start to figure out how to clean up her room."

I even followed her up the steps and stood at the door for the wide shot of Tasha's crap-covered walls. The smell was impressive. Repulsive. Just like Tasha.

"Where do you think we should start?" she asked me. "Maybe the walls?"

The director cued Mom, who said, "I still think I should

get professionals in to do it. I can call them. They can be here in a few hours."

Nanny put her hand up. "This is Gerald's mess. He needs to clean it up. It's part of his learning responsibility." She looked at me and knelt down to be right at my level. "Why do you torture Tasha so? She loves you. Don't you know that?"

I had so many things to say.

I had so many things to say.

Instead, I slammed my fist into Nanny's nose so hard it bled the minute I made contact.

"Cut!"

People gathered around her. Mom grabbed my arm and pulled me into my room. All I could hear was Nanny yelling, "Fuck it! Fuck it!" I heard her throwing things. I heard her slamming doors. Mom and I just stood there inside my bedroom door, listening.

Then Mom bent down and said, "Gerald, that's it. I think they're leaving. We're going to have to give all that money back."

I shrugged.

"We need that money, Gerald," she said, shaking me. "You have to go say you're sorry. We only have a few scenes left to tape. You have to do it."

"I don't have to do anything," I said.

She grabbed me by the arms and squeezed me so hard, I had bruises for a week. "You will apologize, and then you will go to your room for the rest of the day."

So we went out, her right hand still crushing my right

arm, and we looked for Nanny. The cameramen and crew were tossing all their equipment into the vans that were parked in our driveway.

Mom met the director on the way out. "Give us one more chance," she said.

"We have enough tape."

"But he's not fixed!" Mom said.

The director just laughed and laughed and looked right at me. "Good luck with that," he said.

I remember looking at the director and seeing his shiny shoes and knowing that my suffering had paid for them. My mother's words ran over my brain. *We need that money, Gerald.*

Nanny came out from the TV crew truck and Mom dragged me over to her and said, "What do you say?"

"Fuck you," I said. Mom squeezed so hard.

Nanny Elizabeth Harriet Smallpiece, still holding an ice pack to her nose, leaned down right then and said, "I look *forwah-d* to your *lett-ahs* from prison." Then she got in a waiting car and closed the door.

My mother was squeezing me so hard now I could feel pins and needles in my hand. She dragged me back inside and we watched, all five of us, as the entire show was emptied from our house and our lawn and our road. It took all of ten minutes. Mom squeezed my arm the whole time.

She sighed.

Dad said, "Rob said we get to keep the money, so that's something, anyway."

Tasha glared at me until I looked at her.

Mom said, "Apologize to your sister. Now."

I said, "Sorry, Tasha," because they were gone. Tasha's doll was disfigured. Her room was painted with shit. My job was done.

And so I went to my room and took a nap. A ten-year-long nap. The Gerald who didn't have to do anything he didn't want to do has taken a ten-year-long nap.

The Gerald who had control over his life is awake again.

Good morning.

How did you sleep?

52

HANNAH DRIVES LIKE a maniac. After Washington, D.C., when I got too tired to drive, I asked her if she had a valid license. She punched me in the arm so hard, it still hurts.

"I have my first demand," she says. "I demand people stop underestimating me."

"That's kinda abstract for a kidnapping note," I say.

She punches me again. It makes me uncomfortable, how easy it is to punch me like that.

"It is," I say.

"Just go to sleep. I'll get us around D.C. and we'll stop for some food, okay? Unless you plan on eating that chicken salad all day."

I curl up on her sweatshirt, which is like stuffing my face

into a berry patch, and I think of my demands. Her punches made me feel weird. My arm is still sore, and I realize I'll have to tell her she can't punch me anymore.

I demand to not be punched anymore. Even in jest.

|| ▌|||

I wake up to my phone ringing in my pocket. It's Dad. I ignore it. I check the time and realize that Hannah and I are late for work. I feel bad for Beth. We should have at least called her to let her know ... we were being kidnapped.

Which makes no sense.

"Welcome to North Carolina, circus boy," Hannah says. "You sleep like a dead guy. Who was that?"

"My dad."

"I turned mine off hours ago."

"Can we stop for coffee? Or something to eat?"

"You like crab?"

I nod. "Yeah."

"Then according to the billboards, we're about to find heaven."

I reach to her large cup of leftover coffee and swirl it around to see if there's anything left.

"It's cold," she says as I drink it back like a shot.

"And textured," I say. "Shit."

"Yeah."

"Woke me up, though," I say. I adjust the seat up and take a deep breath.

"Maybe they reported us missing and we're famous," she says.

"Been there. Sucks. Trust me."

The 2-4-1 Crab Shack is really a shack. We can get two-for-one crab legs all day long if we want. No limit. That's what the guy in the apron behind the counter says. No limit.

We get some. Hannah orders hush puppies, too, claiming that my life will change when I eat my first hush puppy. I pretend to like it more than I do, just to make her happy, because she's sitting here watching me eat it and yeah, it's okay. Really good. But it didn't change my life. *Welcome to the life of the Crapper.*

"Can I ask you a favor?" I ask. She nods while eating another hush puppy. "I know you think it's fine and cool or whatever, but could you stop hitting me?" I rub my arm to show her what I mean.

"Aw, come on. Have a sense of humor," she says.

I demand not to be told to have a sense of humor.

I look at her seriously. "Look," I say. "Tasha hit me all the time. Then I started hitting other shit, right? Does that make sense?"

"I guess."

"So hitting is out. I know you mean it to be funny and it is, but it reminds me of what I had to put up with and I just don't like it, okay?"

"Is that why that show came to your house?"

I shrug and feel awkward. "The show came to my house because my mom wrote them a letter. I was punching holes in the walls. That was because of Tasha hitting me," I say.

This makes Hannah stop gorging on crab legs. She looks at me. "You know, if the world knew what really went on there, people would understand why you were so messed up."

"I'm not planning on telling the world," I say. "Just you."

"Sorry for hitting you," she says. I tell her never to worry about it again and then go over to the counter and ask the guy in the apron for a pencil and a piece of paper.

I sit back at the table and look at her. "So what's your first demand?"

"More butter," she says, pointing at the plastic dish of melted butter in front of me. I slide it toward her. She's like a savage with crab legs. It's kinda sexy. "And I'm going to need a shower," she says. "Soon."

"I was thinking of stopping at a hotel for the night," I say.

"You thinking of breaking rule number five?"

"We already broke rule number five," I say.

"I'd like to break it more," she says, smiling even though her mouth is full of crabmeat. She goes back to chewing.

I clear my throat. "My first demand is a safe place to live. No more Tasha."

She nods and chews. "That's a good one," she says.

"I've only been demanding that since I was born, I think," I say. "Not like it ever worked."

"My first demand is that I only have to do my own laundry and I don't have to give my mom pedicures anymore. Her feet are disgusting and full of fungus."

I have no idea how she can mention this while eating, but I have to take a thirty-second break before I attempt my next mouthful of crab. I write down our first demands and think.

"And my second demand is that I don't have to go to college right after I graduate. I know they mean well, but I want a break. I don't even know what the hell I want to do, right? And they think being a marine biologist is *impractical*." I nod, and I write *I demand not to go to college right after I graduate.* "What's your second demand?" she asks.

"I don't know. It'd be nice if my mom stopped being sarcastic about my future. It's like she wants me to go to jail or something." *Oh God.* "Oh God," I say.

I feel like throwing up. How did I not see that before? *Fuck.*

"Gerald? You okay?"

I'm in Gersday. In Gersday, I am a family of three. Just me, Lisi, and Dad. I don't give a shit about ice cream or trapezes. I just want an escape from this thought. Then Snow White is there, and her bird says, "She wants you to go to jail because it will make her look like she was right all these years *lay-tah*."

Then the dwarfs show up.
GRUMPY: She.
SLEEPY: Wants.
HAPPY: You.
SNEEZY: To.
DOC: Go.
BASHFUL: To.
DOPEY: Jail.

"Gerald?"

I look at Hannah but I can't answer her. It's like I'm stuck in a time warp. I am stuck between Gersday, where I'm nineteen, and a 1937 Walt Disney movie, when my grandparents aren't even born yet.

She grabs my arm and squeezes until I can speak again.

"Shit. Yeah. I'm here. Wow."

"What the hell was that?"

"I just realized something really heavy," I say.

"And?"

"And I need a minute."

She pats me on the arm as if she can see something big is going on in my brain. I walk to the bathroom and have a pee. I look at myself in the small, dirty mirror while I wash my hands, and I smile. I don't know why I smile.

I feel like crying.

"I'm starting to think this list-of-demands shit is stupid," Hannah says when I get back to our table. She's doing it for me—I can see that. *She cares about the Crapper.*

"Yeah. What good is a list of demands if we're never going back?" I say.

Hannah makes a noise in the back of her throat. The noise says *Gerald, you know we have to go back.*

She takes out her notebook and starts to scribble something in it and I rest my head in my hands and close my eyes and think about what I demand.

I ask myself: *What do you demand, Gerald?*

None of my answers are possible.

I demand a different childhood.

I demand a mother who cares.

I demand a do-over.

When I look at Hannah, she is Snow White. She smiles and has a bluebird on her shoulder. The bluebird tweets.

I demand my own bluebird that tweets.

Snow White hands me the LEGO Star Wars set that Mom and Dad took away from me eleven years ago after I crapped on the kitchen table the last time. It's the *Millennium Falcon*. It's real. I wonder how I will explain this to Hannah—the *Millennium Falcon* appearing out of nowhere.

"Great," I say. "That's great."

"What's great?" Hannah asks.

I don't open my eyes. Or maybe my eyes are open and I can't see Hannah, because Snow White is clearly still sitting next to me on the bench.

"Gerald?"

I open my eyes and it's Hannah. No *Millennium Falcon* LEGO set. No Snow White.

"Shit. Sorry," I say.

"Where do you go?" she asks.

"I don't know," I say. "I go where I've always gone. This cool place." *Do not tell Hannah about Snow White and the bluebird.*

"What's so cool about it?"

"Tasha isn't there," I say. "And there's ice cream. And a trapeze."

This makes us both laugh and I feel like I got away with something.

I demand to stop getting away with things.

I grab another hush puppy and pop it into my mouth. I think about how messed up my mom must be. *My mom has a screw loose.* I take a second to pity her.

Holy shit.

My mom is pitiful.

Maybe hush puppies *can* change your life.

53

WE'RE DRIVING SOUTH. I check my phone again to see if Joe Jr. wrote back, but he didn't. All I know is to aim for Bonifay, Florida, and I hope, if he doesn't get back to me, that they're listed in the phone book. It can't be so hard to find a circus in its hometown, can it?

Mostly, we've been listening to music, but Hannah turns it down from time to time to badger me about letting her drive or to ask a question. She's tiptoeing around rule #3 since we talked about our dumb demands at the 2-4-1 Crab Shack.

"About my mom," I say, somewhere around the South Carolina border. "And Tasha." I don't know what to say afterward.

"Yeah?" Hannah says.

"Like—you could tell in the show that something was wrong? Like—when you watched it?"

"Oh yeah."

"Could you see that Tasha was nuts?"

"She was such a passive-aggressive. Totally. I could tell," she says. "It's complete Schadenfreude, dude, so most people are just watching for the thrill of being better off than the people in the show."

"Schaden-what?"

"Schadenfreude," she says. "It means when people take pleasure in others' pain or humiliation."

"Oh." Jesus. I had no idea there was a word for what I've suffered for my whole life. It's like being asthmatic but no one telling you until your seventeenth birthday the name for why you couldn't ever breathe. "I didn't know there was a word for that."

"It's German."

"I gathered that." I paused. "Did my mom look nuts, too?"

"I don't know. I never thought about it," she answers. "Is she nuts?"

I sigh. "Yeah. Pretty much."

"Isn't this breaking rule number three?" she asks.

I keep my eyes on the road and stay quiet for a second. "A lot gets cut out," I say. "From the show. Like—you only saw what they wanted you to see."

"A lot?"

"Like, almost all of it," I say. *Including all the shit that was important.*

We both stay quiet for a little while.

Then I ask, "Did Tasha really look crazy on the show? Because I couldn't understand why they didn't show that more."

"I'll be honest," she says. "They didn't make her look all that bad. It was really you they focused on. You know. You were kinda the star of that family."

"Great."

"Nothing you didn't already know, though, right?"

"Yeah. Still. It's such a bummer." *My life. My life is such a bummer.*

▮▮▮▮

After looking at the map while Hannah drove, I realized that Bonifay, Florida, is in the Panhandle, so we decided to get off I-95 and go west. We find a motel in western South Carolina.

Still no word from Joe Jr.

My dad has tried calling three times but didn't leave messages after the first time. The message he left is the one thing making me feel like this plan could work—kidnapping ourselves, demanding shit until something changes.

Isn't this what Nanny taught me? Isn't this the foundation of parenting responsible children? You demand proper behavior. And when they disobey, you punish them. I have done what any responsible parent should do...to my parents.

I demand their punishment.

Anyway, what Dad said in his message makes me feel like this might work.

We can work this out, Gerald. Any way you want.

I haven't even sent my list yet.

Dad doesn't know I'm in some motel in South Carolina about to have a shower for the first time since yesterday morning. He doesn't know I got my ass kicked in his living room last night. He doesn't know that my life has been a series of fails that could have been wins. *Nanny's coming! We're saved! Nope. Hannah likes me! I'm saved! Nope. Run away with the circus! I'm saved! Nope.*

"Gerald?"

I hear Hannah say that, but I keep staring out the motel room window, thinking about everything. *We can work this out. Any way you want.*

"Gerald?"

"Yeah?"

"You wanna take a shower together?"

I look at Hannah. She's naked.

I can't find anything to say, so I sit there and stare.

And as sick as it sounds, I can't get those thoughts of Tasha and my dad and my life out of my head. How can Hannah just stand there naked and not think about her junkman family? Is she a robot? Or am I just too emotional?

I demand to know if you are a robot, Hannah.

"Gerald?"

I stand up and strip off my clothes and we walk to the

bathroom, where the shower's been running. It's like walking into a foggy dream. A good, foggy dream.

I can't come up with words for what we do. *Kissing, touching, loving* all sound too intimate. We are not intimate people, but we fit, you know? We are breaking rule #5. Bouncing off each other. Like balloons.

And the best thing about being in a shower together is no one has to say anything.

54

"I SHOULD CALL my mom," Hannah says after we eat the Chinese food we ordered. "She's probably freaking out."

"Isn't that the point?" I ask. I'm sitting at the small, round table in our room with the paper from the 2-4-1 Crab Shack with our lame demands written on it. I'm trying to think of more.

"You don't understand. My mom can't live without me."

"Shit," I say. "You never put it that way before."

"It sounds so dramatic," she says.

"Do you have to give her special shots or something?"

"No."

"So she's not going to technically *die* without you?"

"No. But she's going to freak the fuck out," Hannah says. "And I don't want the police to come while we're sleeping."

"That would suck."

I break out in a cold sweat at the thought of what I just got us into. We are in a motel in South Carolina. We just took a shower together. The police could be looking for me because I beat Jacko's face into roadkill again, in my parents' living room. I dragged Hannah into this.

"That would suck?" she asks.

"Yeah."

I admit, I'm not all here. I'm picturing Hannah watching me get arrested outside this crappy motel in the middle of the night. It's playing like a movie in my head. A young Martin Sheen plays me.

Hannah goes out the door and stands at the railing that overlooks the kidney-shaped motel pool. It's closed for the season and they have a cover over it. I watch her through the front window of our room and I slip into Gersday, where nineteen-year-old Gerald knows what to do with a girl's body. Seventeen-year-old Gerald had some trouble with that back in the shower.

"We all learn as we go along," Snow White says. "I thought the whole thing was quite romantic."

I don't know where I want Snow White to take me. I don't want to go to the trapeze. I don't want to talk to Lisi about taking a shower with Hannah. That would be weird.

So I walk down the street by myself in Gersday. I am eating a strawberry soft-serve ice-cream cone. I don't have a family or any friends. At the end of the street is Hannah. She has a bluebird on her shoulder. She's wearing her leather jacket with the safety pin holding the sleeve together, and she hasn't brushed her hair.

Halfway down the street, Tasha walks out from an alleyway. She's pointing her finger at me and yelling horrible things in that insufferable Tasha voice. Then she pulls out a gun.

Shit.

Snow White, I demand you bring my ass back to reality.

When I look up from the table, I see the real Hannah talking to me. I realize she might be yelling. Her face is contorted with anger. I can't hear her.

She grabs her jacket and her phone and walks out the door, slamming it behind her. I tried to read her lips. I think they said *I'll be back in a minute.*

I sigh. I check my phone. I sigh again. I check my phone again.

I text Joe Jr. *Call me!* Then I erase the text before I send it.

I walk around the motel room. There is nothing to do except watch TV. And I don't watch TV, so I walk around more.

I go outside and look into the night. I make a mental note that if the pool was open for swimmers, I could jump from the balcony railing and land right in the middle. I wonder how many people have done that before.

Then I go back inside.

I am tackled by my own thoughts.

I try to find some pity for Tasha. I don't have any. I try to steal some from how I feel about my mom, but there isn't enough to share it.

I scream, "Fuck this shit!" and kick the chair over. Then I go looking for Hannah.

I check the motel property first. Vending-machines area, fitness center, lobby—not there.

I start to walk along the dark highway, and I realize about ten minutes into the walk that this is stupid and Hannah could have been kidnapped or something, so I jog back toward the motel. When I get there, I get my car keys and start driving.

I see a few people walking down the highway, and it makes me nervous. It's a Saturday night. I don't know what kind of a place this is. Is it the kind of place where girls who smell like berries could go missing?

I drive around for a half hour. I do not go to Gersday because in Gersday, Tasha has a gun and is trying to kill me. I do not go to Gersday because Gersday is the problem between me and Hannah. I can't go there anymore. I have to be here if I'm going to take showers with a beautiful girl, be in love with a beautiful girl, and run away with a beautiful girl.

Snow White can't be my guidance counselor. The roads will no longer contain pecans or chunks of bubble gum. I can't fly on the trapeze.

I finally find Hannah walking down a country road about a mile away. She has her earphones in and is rocking her head. I slow down and drive next to her and she gives me the finger without looking at me.

"Come on, Hannah," I say. I know she can't hear me.

"Hannah!" I say.

She keeps her finger raised, then she takes a left onto a smaller road and I miss the turn because she does it at the last minute.

I yell, "Damn it!" and turn the car around.

She's walking down the middle of the road when I get there. She won't get out of my way. I beep my horn. A lot. Little beeps, long beeps. She raises her finger again and keeps rocking out to whatever is playing in her ears. The road narrows. I stop and look around and realize that the road is about to become a path. I leave the car and follow her on foot.

She starts to jog. I start to jog. It's starting to feel creepy. I just want her to stop, but I know I can't physically reach out and stop her. We start to jog side by side. It's dark. We both trip a few times.

"Come on!" I yell.

She keeps jogging.

So I reach over and tug on the earphone wire and pull it out of her ear. The other earphone follows. She reaches down and unplugs them from her phone, so I'm left holding the earphones.

"Hannah, come on! I'm sorry! Okay?"

She stops.

"I'm really sorry," I say. "I get it. I totally get it, all right?"

"You don't get anything."

"Just come back to the room," I say.

She walks toward a streetlight that's beyond the path. I

can't figure out why a streetlight would be in the middle of what seems like wilderness.

"I trusted you," she says.

"I know."

"I don't have anyone but you."

"I know."

"Stop saying you know!" she yells. "You don't know!"

"Okay. I don't know," I say.

She throws her hands up. "Jesus!"

We walk—her two paces in front of me—through the last of the shrubbery and into the light. We have arrived at some South Carolinian version of paradise. There is a river with a series of perfect waterfalls. The streetlight illuminates a state park type of sign with a paragraph of information on it for tourists. She doesn't seem to notice paradise. She just sits down on the concrete, pulls out her book, and starts to write in it. I feel my face get hot.

"Hannah, I want to talk to you."

"Sorry, Gerald, I'm eating ice cream in my happy place right now." She keeps writing.

"Not fair."

"Nothing is fair," she says.

"I meant not fair that you used that against me."

"I know. And nothing is fair. So whatever," she answers, scribbling wildly.

My skin gets hotter. I sit down right across from her and stick my face in her face. "Hannah, let's talk. Stop writing. Come on. This is stupid."

She looks at me and even though she's glaring, I can imagine her in the shower, only two hours ago.

"You want to know what's stupid?" she asks. "What's stupid is me thinking a fucked-up kid like you could ever be my boyfriend. What's stupid is me thinking a fucked-up kid like me could ever be anyone's girlfriend."

I don't know what to say.

"So you want to talk?" she asks. "Talk." Then she goes back to writing in her book.

"I'm really sorry," I start. "I know I've been hard to talk to. I know I'm an asshole and stuff. I mean, I know I can't do that anymore. I have to stay here. I can do that. I don't want to be anywhere else." I want to tell her I love her, but I don't.

She keeps writing.

"And all that shit that happened to me, you don't know all of it, okay? There's more than you know and it's weird and fucked up and who doesn't come from a place that's fucked up, right? I just—" I stop, and watch her writing. She's not listening. My face gets hotter. "I just want you to listen to me," I say, and I snatch the book from her.

Her first reaction is to hit me—right in the chest where my ribs are still bruised.

I start to walk away with the book, and she screams.

"Give me the fucking book!"

"Not until you talk to me."

She walks over and tries to grab it from me, but I move it around my back.

"Give it here."

"Not until you talk to me. Look. I said I'm sorry," I say.

"You're not sorry enough," she says.

I stop and look at her. She's still beautiful, but this whole thing has taken the shine off her. She's human. Sometimes she can be a jerk. Sometimes there is no *why*.

I am also human. I toss the tiny book into the river like it's a Frisbee. Shocked, we both watch it fly in some sort of slow motion.

I can't believe I just did that. She can't believe I just did that.

When it hits the water's surface, neither of us says anything. We just stand there. The waterfalls are loud, but I can hear her breathing to stop herself from crying.

"Why did you do that?" she asks. Then she hits my arm really hard. I don't mind her doing that this time. I wish she had a silver Sharpie marker and could write ASSHOLE all over my face.

"I don't know," I answer.

She stares at me and I look past her toward the waterfalls. I wish I was the water. I wish I was the rocks. I wish I was the gravity that makes the combination of the two so beautiful.

Nature is so lucky.

People can look at it and think nothing. No one analyzes it. No one blames it. No one underestimates it. Most people respect it. When we look at an ocean after an oil spill, we don't smirk and say, "Well, look at the shithole you are now!" We pity it. We wish it hadn't happened. We hope it gets better and that the fish who live there don't die or grow babies who have two heads.

Maybe if we all saw ourselves as nature, we'd be kinder.

Hannah wipes her face with her sleeve. I sigh.

"I'm really sorry," I say. "Let's just go back now."

"I don't want to go back," she says. "I want my fucking book." She strips off her clothes and jumps into the river. Just like that. All I can do is stand there, my mouth open, but nothing coming out of it.

I have a bunch of completely unrelated thoughts. *I wonder if she'll drown. What does Beth look like naked when she skinny-dips? Are there rocks under the water? Should I jump in and save her? Is that why she did this? Why did I throw her book in the river? Why am I such an asshole? Should I stay up here and point to where it landed so she can find it? Can she find it? What if it's fifty feet deep already? What if she drowns?*

When she surfaces, she's laughing. Or crying. Or both. I point to where the book went in and she swims downstream toward something else. She swims out of the light. I get scared that she'll drown, so I start to take off my clothes, too.

I have no idea if I could save her, but at least if she drowns, I can, too.

And then we'll have solved pretty much all of our problems, right?

Or I can tell Beth I skinny-dipped and maybe she'll think I'm cool.

I jump in where Hannah did and there are no rocks. There is also no riverbed to get my footing, so I tread water for a minute and get my bearings. I can see her, about twenty feet away, heading for a series of rocks. The waterfall is about thirty feet behind us. It's so loud, it sounds like I'm next to a helicopter.

She sees me and her mouth moves like she's yelling something and then she swims away—toward the rocks. I think about eddies. I learned about eddies in eighth grade, sitting next to Tom What's-His-Name, before I ate his face. Eddies live near waterfalls and can pull you under in a second.

Hannah starts to scream and I can't see her that well. I swim to her to save her, but when I get there, all I find is her, clutching her tiny book above her head, crying and smiling— the same way she was when she first jumped in.

This is the first time I realize how cold I am.

I mean cold like the temperature, but I mean cold inside my heart, too. I can feel it beating in there for the first time in years. My whole life, it wanted to beat for real. It wanted to experience *what happens after*. Even if it was jail. Even if it was Nanny punching me back. Even if it was Tasha finally drowning me. Even if it's me drowning in this river, right here, right now.

It's like my life has been a chain of dull disappointments. One after the other. And I grew so cold I could eat What's-His-Name's cheek right off his face. I grew so cold because the climate in FS is downright arctic. They say angry people are hotheaded, but we're not. We're cold. All over.

I I ▆ I I

I look around at my surroundings. *How the hell do we get out of here?*

Hannah floats on her back downstream a little. She finds a clearing on the shore. There is a pair of shoes there. This indicates to me that we are not in some way-out place where no one will find us if we drown. We are in a well-lit, popular bathing spot. I guarantee you a few people have broken rule #5 on this very shore.

Hannah sits there naked. Soaked. But still smiling. Even at me, which is weird considering I'm the asshole who threw her book in the water. As I approach, I see her staring under the surface and I see a familiar look. She's talking to the fish— even the ones she can't see and the ones she hasn't named.

"I'm sorry," I yell as I pull myself onto the rock where her feet are.

She stares past me into the water.

We sit there, naked and cold, for a few minutes before I figure out how to pull us back to the edge we jumped off. I stand up and work my way around to a place that seems like a rock ladder. It's slippery, but it works. Hannah keeps staring into the water, so I don't even care that my dick is the size of a peanut. I start to climb and in five steps, I am able to pull myself up. I walk over and pick up our clothes and I meet her back where I climbed out. I call her name a few times, but she can't hear me over the waterfall.

I dry myself with my T-shirt and put on my pants. Then I sit there until she's ready to go. It seems like a half hour, but it isn't. She just holds the wet book and stares into the water. And then she gets up, climbs most of the way herself, and then she takes my hand and I pull her the rest of the way.

She gets dressed while she's wet. Her mood is unclear. When she starts to walk, I follow her.

"Come on," she says.

"But—" I say. *But what? What are you going to say?*

"Come on," she says again, and she takes my hand and walks me quickly back toward the path we traveled to get here. I don't understand why she isn't yelling at me. I don't understand anything. We get in my car and I drive us back to the motel. She doesn't say anything and just combs through her wet hair with her fingers and looks at the road ahead while quietly allowing tears to drip down her cheeks. I don't say anything but I don't go to Gersday, either. I am 100 percent *here*.

When we can see the motel up the road a ways, I clear my throat. "You're sure you don't just want to drive home?" I ask. "We could pick up our stuff and be back by tomorrow."

She lets a minute pass. "I thought this was, like, the perfect idea, you know?" she says. She sniffles.

"Okay," I answer.

"I was serious when I said I thought I loved you. I meant it." I notice the past tense in this sentence. I dread what she'll say next. "I don't know if running away was the answer, but I'm not going back. Not today, not tomorrow. I have needs, you know?" she says.

"Yeah. I know. That's why we did this."

She starts to cry again and I start to cry, too. I think she's surprised. I'm not sure she knows what to do with a crying boy.

In nature, crying is okay. Waterfalls cry all the time.

We hug each other when we pull into the motel parking

lot. We cry until nature makes us stop crying. A pressure has released from my chest. I feel lighter. Hannah doesn't look like she feels lighter, though. She still looks worried.

We get back to the room and change into drier clothing. Hannah turns the heating unit on and places her wet book on top, standing it up so the pages will dry. She doesn't say a word to me about it. I turn off all the lights except for the bathroom light, and I leave the bathroom door open. Hannah sits at the table in front of our stupid, pointless list of half-witted demands.

"My mom's probably tracking me with my phone," she says. I walk over and squat next to her chair and put my arm around her back.

"Let's turn it on and see if she's texted today," I say.

"I already did."

"So?"

She hands me the phone, text messages from her mother lined up like battlefield soldiers. Hundreds of them.

Where are you?

Come home now!

I need you!

Where's the milk?

Where's the cereal?

Where are my pink-and-blue-striped socks?

Your father has a headache and I can't find the aspirin.

I'm calling the police.

I think you were kidnapped.

Were you kidnapped?

Is it your brother?

Did he come to get you?

Both of you get back here now.

Your father needs his asthma medicine, where did you put it?

The police say I can't report you missing until I know for sure you're really not at work. I called that place, but your boss won't tell me if you're there.

Your boss is a bitch.

They don't believe me that you were kidnapped.

KIDNAPPER! Give me my girl back!

I need her!

Don't do anything bad to her! And if that's you, Ronald, get your ass home and bring Hannah with you.

Where are you?

The police say they can trace you with your phone.

They told me to tell you that.

Don't tell the kidnapper.

Where's my white bra?

And Dad's striped sweat socks?

I forget how to turn on the stove.

Can you call and tell me how to turn on the stove?

Hannah eats cold chicken fried rice while I sit on the edge of the bed and scan through the texts from her mother. I stop a few times and look at her, realizing that this goes far beyond Cinderella jokes and junkman's-daughter CDs. I don't think I ever realized that Roger was right when he said that I can't see anyone but myself. I thought it was something *we could work on.* But it's not.

I never thought anyone could have a worse life than the

Crapper. I never thought anyone would have as good a reason to run away as the Crapper. I never thought anyone would have as much reason to cry as the Crapper. I know about the starving kids in Africa and war-weary refugees and women getting stoned to death for stepping out their front doors. But they have always been at arm's length. As I stare at Hannah's phone and the texts from her mother, I realize I am a selfish asshole. *But so is everyone else.*

"What's she saying here about your brother?" I ask.

Hannah just nods as if there's music playing inside her head.

"No pressure. You can tell me whatever you want when you want. Plenty of shit I haven't told you yet."

She keeps nodding to the imaginary music and wiping silent tears between bites of Chinese food.

"Want me to tell you something first?" I offer. She keeps nodding to the music. "Tasha tried to drown me in the bathtub when I was three. Maybe more than once. I don't know. She did it to Lisi, too. She used to try and suffocate us all the time."

"Shit," Hannah says.

"Yeah. Lisi says she's a psychopath."

"Shit," she says again.

She keeps nodding, so I start nodding, too, as if the same song is playing inside both of our heads. She stops eating chicken fried rice.

"My brother went AWOL before he got shipped to Afghanistan. He's down here somewhere. In the South. We haven't heard from him in over a year."

"Oh," I say.

"He's mentally—uh—slow—just a little," she adds. "So we weren't sure if, you know, he just got lost or really ran away. Or if something . . . else happened. No one can tell us."

I demand that Hannah and I get do-overs.

"It's why I hate the word *retard*."

I demand that no one uses the word retard *again.*

"It's why I do all that stuff for my parents," she says. "The whole thing kinda drove them crazy."

I keep nodding until she comes and sits on the bed next to me. There are two beds with rust-colored bedspreads that are stiff from being new or from being unwashed; you choose. We break rule #5 again. And again. And again.

55

HANNAH FINDS A radio station that plays 100 percent 1960s Motown music on our way through Georgia. Hannah seems to know a lot of the words to Motown songs. I find this surprising for the punk rock junkman's daughter, but maybe nothing is quite as it seems.

Just like me.

Hannah puts her hand on my thigh as I drive. It makes me think of what happened in our motel room. It makes me want to get another motel room. It makes me want to get married. *Slow down. Slow down. Slow down.*

Once every hour, she pokes me in the leg and says, "I can't believe I saved my book" or "I can't believe we jumped into that river" or "I can't believe you threw my book into a fucking waterfall, you asshole." I tell her I'm sorry every time, but she doesn't care because she has it in her pocket, dry and safe, although some pages are illegible. She's not mad, and I find that impossible. *How can she not be mad?*

I want to talk to her about my plastic-wrapped heart and how I think she's unwrapping it, but I think it's stupid. Anyway, it's more than my heart that's wrapped. My mouth is wrapped. My brain is wrapped. That's how it works when you grow up in the land of make-believe. To survive, you wrap and wrap and wrap until you're safe. *Gersday is full of shit. Nothing is real.*

The sky is bright and blue and the clouds are huge. The sun is warm. I was cold at the 2-4-1 Crab Shack yesterday, whereas now I'm hot. I roll my window down a bit more. Hannah keeps singing what I think is Little Stevie Wonder. Something about everything being all right.

I demand that everything be all right.

My phone rings and Hannah says, "It's your dad."

"Shit," I say. "Just let it ring."

She turns down the music. "I'm starting to feel bad."

I find a place to pull over on some empty back-country Georgia road. I kiss her—nothing slobbery like last night. Just a love-kiss on the lips to make her feel better.

"Are we really going to ever finish that list?" I ask. "I don't want to go back. Nothing is ever going to change."

She looks at me and smiles. "I left it at the motel. In the trash can."

"Good," I say.

"None of our real demands are sane enough to write down, right? I mean, how can I write *please stop going crazy and using me as your house slave for everything?*" she asks. "How can you make your sister not a psychopath?"

"I really only have one demand after last night."

Hannah looks intrigued.

"I want you to be my real girlfriend."

"Oh, that." She seems blasé.

"I want to trust somebody. You know? I want to be trusted *by* somebody," I say.

She nods.

"I want a normal life," I say. "Does that make sense?"

She looks at the road and answers. "I want to be Nathan and Ashley. I want to have a job and a house and cookies and aquariums," she says. "Remember, like playing house when you were little?"

I never played house when I was little. Unless you count playing *people in your house want to drown you.*

"I never liked aquariums until we went there," I say. "We never had pets."

"Fish aren't fucking pets," she says. "They're, like, birds, but in water or something. Manifestations of freedom."

"In a tank."

"But they don't know they're in a tank," she says.

"Right. But we do."

I feel her staring at me when I say this and I smile a little. *It would be nice to be a fish and not know I'm in a tank. It would be nice to share my tank with Hannah. It would be nice to grow gills so I can breathe underwater.*

"Can I drive now?" she asks.

The back roads of Georgia are bumpy and sometimes they twist. Hannah handles them all at higher speeds than I would and she puts in the Gerald/Junkyard Daughter CD and cranks it and tries to give me a punk rock education, but I can't hear her over the loud music and the bluebirds on my shoulders.

I haven't been to Gersday all day and I don't want to go. The bluebirds have come to fly me back, but I ignore them.

I find I like punk rock music. It's a sort of sound track for my life. I think the screaming guitars and the yelling, incoherent singers would fit perfectly over those YouTube videos of the *Network Nanny* me—acting out, punching shit, crapping, and crying.

I text Joe Jr. and I lie. *Dude, I'll be in FL in a few hours. Near you. Can we visit?*

I see my dad has texted me again.

Some woman called saying that you kidnapped her daughter. Just come home. We can work it out, I promise.

I read that one to Hannah. She expresses surprise that her mother had the capacity to even find Mom and Dad's number.

"It's unlisted," I say. "So she must know someone." Then I think. "Or my dad is lying. That wouldn't be a first."

She turns up the music again. I position myself so she's the only thing in my view. She's shed her leather jacket and has on a men's white T-shirt and those same ripped-up jeans and a pair of round-toed boots. She has her sleeves rolled up because it's hot. With the windows open, her hair is flying around and it's wild. Her face is perfect. Cheekbones high. Eyes big. Lips full. Looking at her knocks the air out of me sometimes.

I watch her like she's a TV. No. That's insulting. I watch her like she's a great work of art in a big museum. I stare and try to figure out the mystery.

The mystery: There are other beautiful girls with perfect skin and big eyes and all that shit. Why Hannah?

Why do I feel like I can't breathe without her?

Some kid did a speech on pheromones in tenth grade. I think maybe this is why I love Hannah. She smells right or something. Not the berries, but the Hannah. The Hannah smell.

I turn down the music. "Do you believe in pheromones?"

"Isn't that a little like believing in oxygen?"

"But do you believe that they bring people together?"

"I guess. That's what they say, right?"

"Yeah." I turn the music back up, but I know it's more than that. More than science. I love Hannah. I need her the way she needs me. She's here to save me and I'm here to save her. And somehow, the Creator of the Universe put her at register #1 and me at register #7.

56

WE STOP AT a diner right outside Marianna, Florida. I have this dumb idea in my head. I want to talk to Dad. I want to see what he's really so willing to do. Or maybe, more accurately, I want to tell him what I'm not willing to do. I want Hannah to call her mom and make sure the police aren't after us. I admit I got a horrible feeling in southern Georgia when I saw a police car and reminded myself of the Gerald mantra for the last three years: *No jail no jail no jail.*

I demand a better mantra.

Hannah is eating grits with her all-day-breakfast eggs and bacon. I am eating a BLT and potato chips.

"I want to call my dad," I say.

"So call your dad."

"I was waiting until I had the list," I say. "But then we ditched the list."

"The list was stupid. We can't demand anything. We're the fish in the tank, Gerald."

"We are?"

"Yeah."

"But we know we're in the tank," I argue.

"Exactly."

"So what the hell do we do? Just keep running?"

"We have to go back," she says.

"Shit."

I demand to grow gills.

"Yeah," she says. "So, will we call them at the same time?" She checks her phone. "There's decent reception here."

"I don't know," I say. "I wanted something symbolic to send to him. Something that means I'm serious."

"Like leaving didn't make him think you were serious?"

"I don't know. I just thought we'd have a list, I guess."

Hannah grabs a napkin from the shiny stainless-steel napkin dispenser and pulls out her pen. She writes:

We've kidnapped ourselves.
We're safe.
We're sick of how you treat us.

She takes a picture of the napkin with her phone. We make it lighter and more contrast-y through some app she has, and we crop it, but we leave in the random pepper shaker because it seems to add to the whole thing.

She sends it to me.

Once I get it, I attach it to a text for my dad: *I'll call you later*. We count to three and hit SEND.

⁣ ▌▌■▐▌

We stay at another motel because I don't feel comfortable barging in on Joe Jr. late at night. Plus it gives me time to send him two more texts. I even call him twice, but he lets it ring out. While Hannah is in the bathroom, I try to look the circus website up on her phone, but the reception is terrible.

Breaking rule #5 again puts me in a new state. Magic. Postal abbreviation MG. It doesn't need a zip code because it's too big.

But just like FS, it follows you around.

⁣ ▌▌■▐▌

As we drive into Joe's circus town, using the address I scribbled on a napkin from the lobby where I looked up the website on the computer this morning, we are both still in MG. I aim to keep it that way no matter what awaits us.

I called my dad last night.

He said he didn't think the kidnapping note was funny.

"I won't come back until Tasha is gone or I can live somewhere else," I said. "I'm willing to move into my own place. I think I can find a roommate."

"I've been fighting with your mother since Friday night," he said.

"Good for you. A little late, though, don't you think?" I asked.

"Will you tell me where you are?"

"Nope."

"You know that's my car, officially."

"So?"

"So I can have you arrested for stealing it."

"Geez, Dad."

He was silent.

"Did you really take a girl with you? Is that who this *we* is on your little note?" he asked. I could hear him squinting.

"I didn't take her. She ran away with me. Big difference."

"You know that won't look good on your record."

"Since when does having a girlfriend go on a kid's record?" I said. "I'm sick of having such a messed-up life."

"Me, too," he said. I wasn't sure what he meant.

"Look. I'm going to go now. But I'll call you tomorrow night," I said. "Think about what our life is like at that house. It's not safe there, Dad."

"That's going a bit far, isn't it?"

"Call Lisi. She'll explain. I'm not coming back until I don't have to live with Tasha anymore. Sorry to be dramatic or a douche or whatever you want to call me, but it's just time I stand up for shit, you know? Just talk to Lisi. She'll tell you the truth."

I hung up then, thinking it was good to end on something

edgy. Maybe then he wouldn't drink himself into a coma and forget the whole conversation happened. Maybe if he heard it from Lisi, he'd know it was true.

Hannah's mother panicked at the note, but she also wrote some sane things sandwiched between her insane things.

I still can't find my white bra.

I'll find other help.

This isn't fair to you.

We're eating cereal because I can't use the stove.

I'm afraid of the stove.

We should have asked other people to help, too.

We're sorry.

Hannah just stared at the texts as if she couldn't see the sanity there. I said, "Now *that's* progress."

"You think?"

"Beats what my dad said."

"Which was what?"

"He isn't taking it seriously at all."

She ran her fingers through my hair and curled it behind my ears, which put me back in MG. MG is a hundred times better than Gersday. For one thing, it's real. We broke rule #5 a few more times before we took off this morning for Joe's house.

As we're driving up the road to our destination, I realize that Joe Jr. either doesn't know I'm coming or doesn't want me to come. Hannah doesn't know this, or else she does, and doesn't care. I am either about to fuck everything up or make it better. That should be my motto for this whole trip.

An hour later, Joe has us cornered in some sort of barn, where the trapeze rigging lives among trampolines and nets and straps, and the decorations on the walls show decades of circus history. I can't help but stare at them while he yells.

Hannah and I hold hands.

I don't think she likes him yelling like this, but I don't mind, because I like how honest he's being.

"What the $%#* did you think you'd $%#*ing find here? A $%#*ing job? A new family? Did you see those assholes out there? You really want a bunch of circus freaks to be your new family? And what the hell can either of you do, anyway? Nothing. You can't do shit. You work at a food stand. You can make change and fry shit. How's that any good to us? And how's working with us any good to you?

"And next time you drop in on people, why don't you call first? $%#*. I could have at least warned them that you were coming so they'd be more sane."

"I called like twelve times. You need to turn on your $%#*ing phone," I say. "Anyway, I like your dad."

"Then you're an idiot," Joe Jr. says.

"Which one was your dad?" Hannah asks.

"The biggest prick you saw today."

"Stop, Joe. He's not that bad. He has redeeming qualities."

"Like what? Being able to $%#* over his own family for money? Working us like $%#*ing animals?" Joe looks toward the door as if he's afraid someone might hear him. "Look. If I was you guys, I'd get the $%#* out of here now. Before he puts you to work and you can't get out."

"Come on, Joe. It's not that bad," I say.

"Dude, get out while you can. You have everything to live for up there in New York."

"Pennsylvania."

"Right," Joe says.

I look at Hannah. She doesn't seem concerned that my friend doesn't know where I live. "Can I try that?" she asks, pointing to the trampoline.

"No $%#*ing way," Joe Jr. answers.

"You don't have to be a douche about it," Hannah says. "Shit. Gerald here thought you were his friend."

I look at him and shrug.

Joe sighs and crosses his arms. "Yeah. Well, friends tell each other how it is. And this is how it is."

I stare at Joe. I try to figure out what I'm doing here. Why I came. Why I dragged Hannah along. What we're going to do now. I stare at the trapeze. I try to picture Lisi and me. I try to picture ice cream, but it's all gone now. All that Gersday. MG has completely landed me in the present. No more future Gerald at nineteen. No more bluebirds.

Joe looks like he feels bad now. "Look. You can stay in our chalet. Just for the night, though, okay? Big Joe will kill me if he thinks I invited you."

Only circus people can get away with calling something a *chalet*.

57

JOE'S FAMILY EATS together at a huge table in the main house. There are four chalets that surround it at a distance, and an uncountable number of sheds and barns. Joe introduces us as his "friends from New York" and we are introduced to two other sets of visitors—a couple from Colorado and a couple from England.

Joe's mother says, "All the way from England!"

They have accents like Nanny's. I instantly want to coat their plates with toilet water.

Then Hannah puts her hand on my leg under the table as if she sees that their accents grate on me. Her hand reminds me that I am in Florida in 2013, not on TV in 2002. It's hard to remember sometimes that a normal life is possible for the Crapper. Joe's family doesn't recognize me. Yet.

"I think the $%#*ing French act sucks," Big Joe says. "It's all $%#*ing fire and flashy but there's no talent in it. So what if some guy jumps through a $%#*ing ring of fire? Jesus! It's been done to $%#*ing death."

"True," Joe Sr.'s wife says. "It's been done a lot."

"I don't know," the Englishwoman says. "I think it's sweet the way they're imitating the old animal tricks. The ball balancing and all that. It's cute. Arty."

Joe Sr. looks at her as if she's an idiot and goes back to eating his roast beef.

At last count, Joe Jr. has five siblings. It seems all of them are married. The only people who seem to notice Hannah and me are the kids, who are eating in the adjacent room, having a loud conversation of their own. Twice now, a little guy—maybe four or five years old—has come up to me and given me some of his clay.

There's something about the tension around the adult table. It's like they're all about to kill one another, but something is stopping them. Maybe it's the fact that they have company *all the way from England!* Maybe it's the fact that they have a TV on—a flat screen mounted to the wall behind Mrs. Joe's head—that's airing the day's local news. Something about an alligator. Something about a shooting. Something about an accident. Something about a bald kid with cancer.

Then a story comes on about tonight's finale in *Dance On, America!*, a reality TV show, and Mrs. Joe says, "Oh my god, if Helen doesn't win this show, I'll be so angry."

"She deserves it," someone says.

"I like Jennifer. I think she'll take first place," a sister says.

"Yeah. Jennifer."

"Jennifer can barely stand up straight," someone else says. "Helen totally deserves this win."

Mrs. Joe nods at this and can't keep her eyes off the newsshow footage from last week. Two women in dancewear evening gowns, grinding and doing the latest pop-dance moves.

"Helen is too old," a brother says.

His wife smacks his arm. "Age shouldn't matter. You're such an idiot."

"She's not that old," a sister-in-law offers. "She's only twenty-nine, I think."

"Like you're twenty-nine."

"$%#* off," the sister-in-law says.

"Jennifer is better at the sexy stuff. Helen is better at the older-woman stuff."

"Christ," someone says. "The older-woman stuff? What the $%#* does that mean?"

"It means more men will vote for Jennifer," a brother-in-law teases.

"No doubt."

"Do you guys ever think about anything other than sex?"

Most of the men in the room shake their heads.

"Helen is more talented. If she loses, then I'll lose faith in the whole world. She deserves it," Mrs. Joe says.

I think: *Wow. And I thought I was the only one who was allowed to base my faith in the whole world on reality TV.*

"Sex sells," a sister says.

"It's why you married me, right?" her husband says.

She hides her head in her hand and says, "Not in front of my parents, Don."

Joe Sr. says, "How'd you think we brought you all into the $%#*ing world?"

The sister's face gets redder with embarrassment. "Oh god."

"I'm just saying Helen is a better dancer. It's *Dance On, America!* It's supposed to be about who the best dancer is."

"I think Jennifer is the better dancer," a brother says.

"That's because you're a man."

"You're a $%#*ing idiot," he replies.

"And you're a lazy asshole," someone says.

A sister—the youngest-looking one, maybe in her early twenties—stands up and throws her empty plate at the floor to shut everyone up. It works. We all stare at her. "Who gives a $%#* about *Dance On, America!?*" she says. Everyone looks at her, ready to pounce on whatever she says. Then she smiles and looks at her boyfriend/husband, who's sitting next to her. "We're $%#*ing pregnant!"

After the loud response and the many claps on the back and hugs, the women start clearing the table. I excuse myself and go back to the chalet. Hannah stays. Joe Jr. eventually shows up at the chalet and knocks on the door before he lets himself in.

"Sorry," he says. "My family is a freak show."

"Not really," I say.

"Totally. We'd be candidates for some reality TV show. People would love to watch us fight over who's going to win $%#*ing *Dance On, America!*"

I chuckle. He senses my mood.

"You okay?" he asks.

"Yeah. Just taking a break. It's been a weird week," I say.

As Joe Jr. takes out a cigarette and lights it and then digs around in the kitchen of the chalet for an ashtray, I try to figure out what day it is. I think it's Monday. I ask, "Is it Monday?"

"Yep."

"Shit," I say.

"You supposed to be somewhere else?" he asks.

"Kinda."

"I was serious when I said all that shit today, Gerald."

"I know."

"You have choices. You have so many things you can do," he says, spreading his arms wide. "So many things."

"So do you," I say. "Are you chained here? I think not."

He takes a drag on his cigarette.

"The reason I stayed friends with you is because you were like an escape," I say. "When the shit hit the fan at home, I could dream of coming down here with you. We could clean the buses together. We could bitch about your dad together. You could teach me how to smoke."

"That's exactly why you shouldn't be here. You don't want to learn to smoke. You shouldn't want to live like this," he says. "You're either born into it, or you're not."

I think about what I was born into.

He drags on the cigarette again. "And being born into it isn't as great as it seems. But it means I have something. Like roots, but not roots."

"Do you know who I am?" I ask. I feel like I don't have control over my mouth.

"What do you mean? Like—should I?"

"Maybe. Depends."

He looks at me more closely. "I don't recognize you from *America's Most Wanted* or anything. You're not in trouble, are you?"

"Do you remember a little kid named Gerald? From *Network Nanny*?"

He cocks his head to the side to think better. "Nope. I don't remember that," he says. "When was it on?"

"When we were little. Probably six or seven," I say. "The kid crapped on stuff all the time."

Joe Jr. cracks a smile. "Oh! The Crapper! I've heard of him but never saw him. Dad makes jokes about how bad the talent is sometimes and says he might as well have got the Crapper for the second act and stuff like that." He nods as if this is all great until he realizes that I might be the Crapper. "Hold on," he says. "Is that you?"

I raise my eyebrows and smirk.

I demand to be the Crapper and be proud of being the Crapper.

"Shit," he says. "Sorry."

"You're not the only person who grew up in a circus," I say.

"And maybe my staying here wouldn't be as bad as you think, you know?"

"Except that you can't. I mean—it's the off-season. We don't go anywhere for another month and a half. We sent the crew home. There're no paychecks until we start again."

"Oh," I say, and I feel a distant relief because I didn't really want to clean buses for minimum wage anyway.

"Yeah," he says, then stubs his cigarette out in the ashtray.

Once we get out into the darkness, he says, "No shit—you're the Crapper?"

"Yep."

"I never saw you in action. I've heard stories, though."

"I bet."

"You're not going to crap in my chalet, are you?"

I hit him on the arm. "Dude. I'm seventeen."

"So?"

"So, no, I will not crap in your chalet," I say.

"Why'd you really come down here?" he asks.

"We wanted to run away, so this was as good a place as any. Plus, I've been watching this video." I stop here. I don't want him to know about my obsession with the video.

"Porn?" he asks.

"No!" I say. "Shit."

"What's wrong with porn?" he asks.

"It's a trapeze video. From Monaco," I say.

"It's $%#*ing incredible, isn't it? The one with the Chinese girls?"

"Yeah." I nod. "$%#*ing amazing."

We walk to the main house and don't say much more. There's something about Joe Jr. that makes me know that we'll be friends for life. I can see me taking my kids to his circus. I can see us drinking beers on a summer night in my backyard or something. We stand outside the back door of his house and listen to the family arguing. It's loud. Someone bangs a table. There is cackling laughter. There is outrage and more laughter.

"Welcome to my hell."

"You can always come to New York with us," I say.

"I thought you were from Pennsylvania."

"I thought you thought I was from New York."

We look at each other. I think: *Why did I just make it easier for him by saying I was from New York?*

I demand to demand that I am from Pennsylvania.

I demand to stop being such a $%#*ing pushover.

"Forget it," I say. "I mean you can always untie your roots and come visit us, wherever we end up."

We walk into the loud celebration. Someone has found a bottle of champagne to celebrate the new baby-on-the-way. Someone else is still talking about how Jennifer shouldn't win and that the world is an oversexed mess because of people like Jennifer.

Hannah is sitting in the middle of all of it on her own, smiling. When she sees us walk in, she smiles even wider. I take my place next to her at the table and we hold hands.

She says, "I always wanted a big family."

I don't know if this is some weird hint about babies and

our future, but I don't care. I can't think of one seventeen-year-old guy who wouldn't be freaked out by this. But I'm not. I can totally see us having a big family. I can totally think of our future—how we'll do what we want and be what we want. Surrounded by aquariums, eating cookies, not being pushovers.

58

DEAR NANNY,

I KNOW THIS WILL DISAPPOINT YOU, BUT I AM NOT
WRITING YOU THIS LETTER FROM PRISON. I AM
WRITING TO YOU FROM A CHALET WHERE I AM
VACATIONING WITH MY GIRLFRIEND, HANNAH, AND MY
ONLY FRIEND, JOE. THE REASON HE IS MY ONLY
FRIEND IS BECAUSE AFTER WHAT YOUR TELEVISION
PROGRAM DID TO ME, IT WAS PRETTY IMPOSSIBLE TO
MAKE FRIENDS.

I WENT TO AN ANGER MANAGEMENT COACH FOR A
WHILE AND WE USED TO WRITE YOU LETTERS, BUT

NONE OF THEM WERE REALLY ABOUT WHAT I WANTED
TO SAY TO YOU. THEY WERE ABOUT WHAT HE THOUGHT
I SHOULD WRITE. MOSTLY ABOUT MY ANGER. I HAD A
LOT OF ANGER. I KNOW YOU KNOW THAT BECAUSE I
HAD IT LONG BEFORE YOU EVER GOT TO MY HOUSE
WITH ALL YOUR CREW AND CAMERAS AND CHORE
CHARTS, BUT I WAS ANGRIER AFTER YOU CAME.

MY SISTER TASHA DID HORRIBLE THINGS TO MY
SISTER AND ME. SHE TRIED TO KILL US A LOT. I
THINK YOU KNEW. I'M NOT SURE WHY YOU DIDN'T
REPORT IT OR DO MORE ABOUT IT, BUT I KNOW IT'S
ON YOUR CONSCIENCE, NOT MINE. LISI IS OKAY. SHE
LIVES IN SCOTLAND NOW. I AM ALSO OKAY.

I HOPE YOU REMEMBER HOW FUN I COULD BE. I
WAS PLAYING WITH A FIVE-YEAR-OLD LAST NIGHT
AND I REMEMBERED BEING FIVE AND HOW MUCH FUN
IT IS BECAUSE WHEN NO ONE IS CHASING YOU TRYING
TO HURT YOU, THE WORLD IS PRETTY MUCH A LAND
OF FUN. I WAS FUN, ONLY THEY EDITED THAT PART
OF ME OUT OF THE SHOW.

I MET A WOMAN LAST MONTH WHO RECOGNIZED
ME AND SHE HUGGED ME AND SAID SHE WISHED SHE
COULD HAVE TAKEN ME FROM MY HOUSE AND TAKEN
CARE OF ME BACK WHEN YOUR SHOW AIRED. I TOLD
HER THAT I WISHED SHE WOULD HAVE, BUT THAT I'M
OKAY NOW.

THAT'S WHY I'M WRITING TO YOU. I'M OLD
ENOUGH TO GET AWAY FROM ALL THOSE PEOPLE IN

MY TOWN WHO BELIEVED WHAT YOU SHOWED THEM AND WERE TOO SHALLOW TO SEE ANY DEEPER. WHY DO YOU THINK THEY DO THAT, NANNY? DO YOU THINK THEY LIKED WATCHING ME SUFFER BECAUSE IT MADE THEM HAPPY TO SEE A LITTLE BOY SUFFERING? DO YOU THINK IT'S BECAUSE IT TOOK ATTENTION AWAY FROM THEIR OWN SUFFERING? DO YOU THINK THAT THEY WERE JUST DUMB AND LOVED SCHADENFREUDE?

BECAUSE WE WERE SUFFERING.

LISI AND I TOLD YOU.

YOU ASKED AND WE TOLD YOU.

AND EVEN THOUGH YOU KNEW AND DIDN'T DO ANYTHING TO HELP ME, I'M OKAY. AND I WANT YOU TO KNOW THAT I HOPE YOU'RE OKAY, TOO.

SINCERELY,
GERALD FAUST

Hannah called her mother while I was writing. She went outside and paced while she talked. Her mom asked her aunt to find them some help, including help for Hannah's mother's increasing mental issues. The aunt went to a few places and thinks she'll be able to find some solutions. Anyway, Hannah's mom isn't sending her a hundred crazy texts a day anymore.

I call my dad in front of Hannah. This is what she hears.

ME: Yeah.

ME: Okay.

ME: Huh. Okay.

ME: I guess.

ME: Yeah, I'd do that.

ME: Are you? Does it make you happy?

ME: She probably just didn't want to get involved in the drama. She'll talk to you again. Don't worry.

ME: What day is it again?

ME: I guess by Thursday if we leave today.

ME: Thanks.

When I hang up, she stands there waiting for the story, but instead of telling her, I hug her and say, "I told Joe I'd meet him in the barn. I'll be back in an hour."

"But are we leaving? Today? Didn't you just say that?"

"If you want to, then yes. If you don't, then no. We can do what we want."

59

"YOU JUST JUMP," Joe Jr. says. "And hold on to the bar."

He's sitting in a chair on the edge of the makeshift ring. Thirty feet below me.

I'm standing on the tiny platform with the bar in my hands. My sweaty hands. I hook the bar to the hook at the side and I cover my hands in chalk for the fifth time.

"Come on," he says. "There's a net. Nothing to be worried about."

I close my eyes and see Lisi on the other side. I promise myself ice cream if I do this. Any flavor I want. All I have to do is jump. My hands get too sweaty again, so I hook the bar up and rechalk. This happens at least four more times.

Joe Jr. starts to play on his phone and has stopped encouraging me. He looks so small down there, in his tiny chair. His phone is the size of an ant. He is the size of a large spider. The net is so far away.

I look at my hands. Very chalky, but not shaking.

I look at the other platform—across the rigging. Snow White is sitting there with her bluebird. She also looks small, but not as small as Joe Jr. or his phone. She is superimposed— unreal. Not really there. She's just a projection.

I sit down on the platform and think.

I have a conversation in my head. It's about never having to see Tasha again because I demand that.

I demand to never see Tasha again.

Tasha has a screw loose and no one knew what to do about it, so they hid it, fed it, and then ended up a slave to it.

I feel bad. For me and Lisi. For Dad. For Mom, even. Maybe even a little bit for Tasha, who has the loose screw. I feel bad for everyone involved.

And now the conversation in my head is about Hannah. About how having her in my life changes everything. Before Hannah, no one would ever love me. I was too angry. Too violent. My past was too fucked up. My future held no hope.

No one ever said it. But they meant to. *I look forward to your letters from prison.*

But Hannah changes everything.

I stare down at the net and then at Joe Jr., who looks up periodically to see if I'm standing again. Then he goes back to his phone. I look back at the projection of Snow White, and all that's left is her bluebird. If the bluebird could talk, it would tell me what it sees. *Chickenshit.*

I stand up, chalk my hands one last time, and grab the bar—and then I jump. All in one motion. One split second. Just like how I ran away. Rash decision. Hasty action. Off the top of my head. Not Prescribed by a Medical Professional. I just get up, hang on, and jump.

My first swing is when I realize those girls in the Monaco video must be stronger than Clydesdales. I can barely make the rig swing. In fact, I have no momentum at all. I try, but I look like I'm having some sort of fit. In mere seconds, I am a straight, rigid seventeen-year-old hanging still from the end of a trapeze bar in the middle of a circus barn in Florida.

It's kind of fun, except my shoulders are about to separate.

Joe Jr. laughs. "You did it! You $%#*ing pussy! You did it!"

This makes me laugh a little, but laughing makes me weak, so I stop. Then I realize I'm hanging twenty-five feet above the ground.

I demand to trust the net.

But I don't trust the net.

My chalky hands have a firm grip on the bar. In fact, they feel like they *are* the bar. My hands have *become the bar.* And that's fine because I'm not letting go.

"You ever coming down?" Joe Jr. asks. I bet he's done this a hundred times before. No big deal to Joe—just dropping into a net that barely seems there.

"No," I say. "I think I'll stay here forever."

"Your shoulders are going to $%#*ing burn soon. And your wrists."

"How do you know?"

"I just do," he says.

"And your fingers are going to peel off one by one and you'll drop. No stopping gravity, man. It's $%#*ing science."

"Shut up," I say.

"I'm going to go and make out with your girlfriend," he says, then gets up and walks toward the door. "When you finally decide to let go, drop ass-first. Then roll to the edge," he says.

I laugh because Joe Jr. is funny. I'm also terrified that the net is broken and I'm about to willingly fall to my death. For the first time in my life I don't think this is funny. I don't shrug off dying as if it's some dare. I don't want to die. I have a plan.

I let go.

Falling feels like Gersday. I think I scream, but I'm not sure. As I fall, I unravel from my plastic wrap. It floats through the air above me because it's lighter, and I see it twisting there like smoke hangs in the air above Joe Jr.'s cigarettes. I land in the net with a small bounce. I lie there for a few minutes, staring up at the bar, now suspended in the middle of the rig. It looks so small. After a while, I hear things happening outside. A truck or a tractor or something. I hear yelling. Big Joe screaming "$%#*, $%#*, $%#*!"

I roll to the edge of the net and flip myself over it and onto the floor. I think about climbing to the platform again, but I know I have to drive home today.

"About time," Joe Jr. says when I walk into the chalet. Hannah is there, packed and ready to go. "She wouldn't kiss me, dude. You've got yourself a $%#*ing gem there."

*I deserve a $%#*ing gem.*

60

IT'S A SURPRISINGLY easy transition. Dad sends Mom and Tasha on a four-day all-inclusive vacation, and we move out over the weekend while they're off getting suntans or pedicures or whatever loose-screw people get in all-inclusive Mexico.

"I think it's the only way," he'd said. "Your mother hasn't really heard anything I've said in years."

Dad and I talked about everything last night. Then we called Lisi and told her what was going on. She told me she might come home for Christmas if she could stay with Dad and me in the new house. When I hung up, Dad and I talked about Tasha. How she used to hurt me and Lisi. How she probably still hits Mom. He looked numb and didn't say much, and just listened. He had a tear in his eye when he hugged me at the end. He told me he was sorry.

"Your mother always said it was just you two exaggerating," he said.

"I don't really want to talk to them again," I said. "Is that okay?"

He said it was okay, but I guess we both know there will be times I have to talk to them again. I can almost picture the day my mother is on her deathbed and I say something kind and poignant like "I know you never meant to hurt me. I know you were doing the best you could with what you had." *What woman looks down at her pregnant belly and expects a psychopath?*

We're moved in by Sunday night. Dad wasn't a pussy about it, either. He took what was his. The car. The gym equipment. The stereo system. We emptied his man cave into the truck, and we emptied the entire contents of my bedroom and the guest room, which will be Dad's new bedroom suite. He took all of his clothing and the Ping-Pong table. He even went into the attic and took everything that came to him from his parents. He got his mother's engagement ring out of Mom's jewelry box. And her two quilts from their closet.

My new room is closest to the pool. This morning I swam some laps and sat in the hot tub for fifteen minutes before I took a shower. I was at the breakfast bar before six thirty. Dad bought frozen waffles and real bacon. He stuffed the fridge full of shit Mom would never buy. I eat four waffles and three strips of bacon. He eats the same thing. I will be fat in three months. I pretty much don't care.

We leave at the same time for work and school. It's a shorter drive to Hannah's from here. It's a shorter drive to everywhere. There's no security guard to give me judgmental looks on my way out. At night, from the third-floor deck, you can see endless stars because the sky isn't polluted with gated-community security lighting. And no one knows us here. No one cares. I have no idea why we ever stayed in that other house for so long after *Network Nanny*. It's like no one ever thought about how freeing it would be to get the hell out and start over. Or maybe some of us didn't want to.

■ ■ ■ ■ ■

When Hannah gets in the car, we kiss good morning. She smells like berries. This makes me smile like crazy.

She writes in a new little book—one that isn't water-logged. When I bought it for her in Virginia, on our way home, she told me she was sorry that she had kept her family a secret from me. I didn't know what to say, so I just hugged her.

We all have secrets, Hannah.

I missed six days of school, but I don't have that much to make up. Dad will come in later today for a final meeting with the guidance counselor, Fletcher, and me. I'm going to college. I'm taking the first step by getting back into regular classes. Best Monday ever.

But in SPED, I feel like I'm leaving behind a whole family. Fletcher tells them I have something to say and I get up and sit on my desk and say, "I'm leaving today."

"I thought you left last week," Kelly boy says.

"Yeah," Jenny says.

Taylor is rocking.

"I don't mean leaving Blue Marsh. I mean this room. I'm going into other classes," I say.

"About fuckin' time," Deirdre says.

Jenny looks like she's going to have a fit.

"I'm still going to come by and say hi, you know?"

"Bring cupcakes," Karen says. "It's the least you could do."

"Yeah," someone agrees.

"Just go, Gerald," Jenny says.

I see Deirdre's foot has come off her footrest, so I kneel down and put it back where it belongs. When I stand up, there's nothing left to say. I pick up my backpack and head for the door.

Fletcher says, "I like chocolate cupcakes, Gerald."

I nod and close the door behind me. When I get outside, I'm scared to death. My first class is Language Arts and I have to talk about *Romeo and Juliet* and I'm not sure I can be what they want me to be. But I'll try.

❚❚■❚❚

"You okay?" Hannah asks me at lunch.

"Fine," I say, but I'm smirking like crazy and she smirks back and it's really hard not to ask her to marry me on the spot. *Slow down. Slow down. Slow down.*

"Craptastic got a girlfriend! You know what to do with

her?" It's Nichols. We ignore him and keep smiling at each other.

"I want a rematch in Ping-Pong soon," she says.

"Why bother? You're playing two guys whose entire third floor is home to a Ping-Pong table."

"Because it's fun," she says. "It's not about winning all the time, you know." She's eating a sandwich that we bought at Quik Mart on the way to school. "I was distracted last night. I think I was worried about impressing your dad."

On our way home, I drive her to the new house and we play two games of Ping-Pong. Then we break rule #5. Then I take her to the deck.

I think, *I demand that we get married*. I plan on thinking this for a long time before I ask it. But it feels nice having a goal and working toward it. If I think about it, Nanny taught me that with all her stupid charts. And Hannah taught me that with her little book.

It's never a bad thing to have a list of demands.

61

THE PEC CENTER is crowded on Wednesday for Dollar Night. Hannah and I come straight from school so we'll be early to pay back Beth for being so cool with us leaving her short for over a week. We tell her what we did after she gives us a warning about how she'll have to fire us if we ever do that again. Lucky for us, there's a pool of cashiers to choose from at the PEC Center. It's not like we're highly trained brain surgeons.

"Sounds like an adventure," Beth says while she hands me the large ketchup containers over the counter. Hannah organizes the other condiments and then sets to work wrapping the first batch of hot dogs.

She's at register #6. I'm still at register #7. I told Dad I was going to be coming home late. He's all over the place since Mom came back from Mexico and found us gone. She goes between threatening to take him for all he's worth to sobbing into his voice mail for ten minutes at a time and I know he sees it now—that up and down. The instability she worked so long to pretend wasn't there.

"Gerald swung on the trapeze," Hannah tells Beth. "We stayed in a chalet."

"A chalet?" Beth says. "Sounds fancy."

We don't tell her that it is just circus jargon for a prefab house.

"We went skinny-dipping," I say.

"Not quite," Hannah says. "It was more of a rescue mission."

Beth shrugs, and shakes her head as if she's thinking, *Those madcap teens.*

The night is a blur of Dollar items, complaints about Dollar items, and running out of liquid cheese, like, three times. Beers. A lot of beers. Beth has me tapping my own now and I tap Hannah's, too, because she doesn't look eighteen, even with the extra black eyeliner she's been wearing.

Beth lets us go out during second period. Hannah gets her new little book and starts to write in it in the smokers' alley. I stand there with my hands in my pockets, feeling the cold. Christmas is coming. Dad and I decided on no tree in our new pad. Hannah says she's going to bring us a small one anyway because everyone should have a Christmas tree.

"What are you writing about?"

"Just stuff," she says.

"Good," I say. I say that because I like when she writes in her book.

I lean against the freezing brick wall and take a deep breath and exhale the fog into the alley. Gersday is warmer. Lisi is in her leotard and about to swing high on the trapeze and I'm in the ring watching. Hannah is next to me. Holding my hand. Breaking rule #5. I can see it from here, so I don't have to go in. Gersday is like a show now.

"How much longer do we have?" Hannah asks.

I shrug. "As long as we want, I guess. Break should be soon, though. So—"

She grabs me around my neck and kisses me and I grab her around the waist and kiss her. We become one person when this happens. One warm person.

Then the door opens and it's a smoker. Only it's not just any smoker—it's Hockey Lady.

"Gerald!" Hannah hasn't let me go yet, and I don't let her go, either. "Look at you," Hockey Lady says.

"Is it the end of second period yet?" I ask.

"Nah. We're just losing so bad I came out before the rush." She lights up a cigarette.

"I'm Hannah," Hannah says.

I nod and say, "My girlfriend," as if this isn't obvious.

"That's great," Hockey Lady says.

There's an awkward moment between the three of us. Hannah giggles.

"I wanted to thank you for talking to me that first night," I say.

"You're welcome," Hockey Lady says.

"It really helped me," I say, remembering all the sobbing I did on her shoulder.

"Glad I could help."

Then Hannah says, "We'd better get back in."

"The rush is coming," I explain.

Hockey Lady nods and then winks at me on my way through the door.

"Who's that?" Hannah asks as we walk back to stand five.

"Just some viewer I met once."

"Oh," she says.

I hear myself say this and I like it. *Just some viewer I met once.*

Just some viewer.

As I sell sixty more chicken-fingers-and-fries orders and tap ten more beers and sell two little kids some hot chocolate, I see them all that way.

Viewers who will never know the truth. Viewers who don't really matter. Viewers who just didn't have anything better to do on Friday nights a decade ago.

I look at Hannah over on register #6. She is more beautiful than anything I've ever seen. When she looks at me she is the opposite of a viewer. She can see *inside me*. She makes me see *into the future*. I can see myself graduating next year—war paint and all, pushing Deirdre up that ramp they'll have to build. I can see myself in ten years, married to Hannah, maybe a baby or two if she wants some. I'll have a job that isn't counting hot dogs. I won't have to see Tasha or my mother again if I don't want to.

It's like Gersday, but better.

It's real.

I'll eat real strawberry ice cream.

I'll be somewhere else. My own Morocco or India. My own Scotland.

I'll be just another human on a planet full of humans, but better equipped because I have demands.

For my family.

For my life.

For the world.

For myself.

What acceptable behay-vyah.

What acceptable behay-vyah.

ACKNOWLEDGMENTS

Huge thanks to the usual suspects: my supportive family and friends, the fantastic Michael Bourret, the genius Andrea Spooner, Deirdre Jones, Megan Tingley, Victoria Stapleton, and the entire team at Little, Brown for making me feel like a superhero.

Special thanks to Heather Brewer, Andrew Smith, Sara J. Henry, Beth Kephart, and Ellen Hopkins, who write beautiful books and who are beautiful friends.

To every fan, librarian, teacher, bookseller, and blogger who has supported my work: Your support means the world to me and my gratitude is galaxy-sized.

AN INTERVIEW WITH A.S. KING

How did you come up with the idea for Gerald Faust?

The character of Gerald Faust came to me in the shower one morning. My characters are often brought to life by a question. In this case, the question that came to me in the shower was: *If one in four children is suffering abuse of some sort in this country, then is it fair to assume that kids on reality TV reflect this same ratio?* The question that followed was: *Does that mean that we adults are being entertained by children who are in danger behind the scenes? What does this say about us?* I think about deep stuff in the shower, apparently. In this case I saw Gerald completely, in a flash. I saw how angry he was—how they used him on the show, how everyone believed what they saw, and how his home life was slowly killing him and yet no one knew about it.

I was rushing, trying to make it to Princeton, New Jersey, to be interviewed on TV. I had thirty minutes to get dressed and ready, and I used twenty-five of those minutes to write the prologue of *Reality Boy*. It's safe to say I drove to Princeton with wet hair and a voice recorder on the passenger seat.

⸭

Like Gerald, the main characters in your previous books Everybody Sees the Ants *and* Ask the Passengers *live in dysfunctional families. Do you feel like all families deal with some kind of dysfunction, or are you drawn to writing about these kinds of families in particular?*

In twenty years of writing novels, I've never thought, "Hey! I should write about dysfunctional families!" I am drawn to writing about real life, and I reckon families are not just a few people who live in a house. One can't overlook the landscape of where the family lives, the history of that landscape and that family, as well as what might be going on in the present-day story that triggers those histories. I don't think Astrid's family in *Ask the Passengers* was all that dysfunctional. I don't really think Lucky Linderman's family was dysfunctional, either. Not in the same way that Gerald's family is. The Fausts (for the record, I got the name from a street sign I passed on the morning I got the idea for the book, and I liked that it's German for *fist*) are truly dysfunctional. There is abuse here. There is mental illness here. The Fausts are a bit different from other families I've written about.

▌▌▆▌▌

Do you have a kind of "Gersday" that you go to when life becomes too much to handle? Did you ever consider running away to the circus?

I do not have a Gersday. I'm one of those workaholic types who can't stop for ten minutes without doing something. Anything. Today, I took a break for fifteen minutes, and rather than a power nap, I chose to pay the family bills. So, no Gersday here, though paying the bills does make me feel a lot better. Maybe my lack of Gersday is my Gersday.

As for the circus, I've done that. I know my way around the territory pretty well, thanks to a family friend who runs Ireland's oldest circus. It's the hardest life ever, as adorable and fun as it may sound.

▌▌▆▌▌

Your books seem to appeal to a wide audience of teen and adult readers. What do you hope they will take away from Gerald's story?

I think all readers, regardless of age, will take what they need from any story they read. I know that's a wide look at a specific question, but that's how I see it. I do not write my books for a specific age group. I just write books that might make readers see things in a way they hadn't before.

Readers who are not dealing with anger issues or dysfunctional family situations can still find important ideas in Reality Boy, *such as the significance of making demands. What are some demands you make of your own life?*

Demands, I got 'em. Here's my list.

1. Respect
2. Kindness

Not the longest list in history, but I believe most other demands I have can be sorted out with respect and kindness. Do no harm. Take no shit.

Gerald begins to imagine what his life will be like in the future at the very end of the story when he thinks about someday proposing to Hannah. Do you know what his life is like ten years after Reality Boy *closes? Or do you not think about your characters beyond the final page?*

I think about Gerald a lot. I think he has a long way to go. For example, at the moment when the book ends, Gerald has latched onto Hannah as someone he will be with forever—as someone he wants to *marry*. This is an intense thought brought on by having a person he can trust, and who trusts him, for the very first time. I don't think this intensity is necessarily healthy for Gerald, but I think it's realistic for him to want to marry Hannah and be with her forever because of what he's been through and how much he loves her.

Anyone who has been in a long-term relationship knows that things will get harder in spots, and I'm not so sure Gerald is ready for that yet. He needs to stay in school, stay in anger management or counseling, and he needs to continue to look for a way out of the area where everyone knows him, or a way to deal with this infamy. I think Gerald and his father moving was a good first step. But beyond that step, Gerald needs to find a place where he isn't the Crapper anymore—whether he moves far away physically, or he becomes more accepting of the fact that his youth, as much as it sucked, was his reality.

We have this judgmental way of looking at the idea of leaving a home or a family, and our society has reinforced this idea that if we "run away," we are "running away from our problems." In some cases, though, to face certain problems (in this case, two family members who are not mentally stable and who are not going to face up to their issues) the family members who are capable of facing reality must realize that leaving *is* a viable option. Some environments *are* harmful. As fellow humans it is our job to judge less and encourage more when others choose to remove themselves from harmful environments.

So, yes. I think a lot about Gerald. I hope he finds peace. I do know he graduates, because he and Glory O'Brien (from my next book) go to the same high school.

⬛

There is a teaser for your next story, Glory O'Brien's History of the Future, *in the back of this book. What can you tell readers about it?*

Glory O'Brien's History of the Future is about two friends who are vastly different but who are brought together through extraordinary circumstances. On the night when they drink a strange concoction, they begin to see visions of the past and the future when they look at people. Ancestors and descendants. Glory O'Brien, our narrator, wishes she could see a future for herself past high school graduation, but she can't. Though what she *does* see is the next American civil war, and it's terrifying.

DISCUSSION GUIDE

1. Which character in *Reality Boy* do you best relate to and why? Which one is the hardest for you to understand or sympathize with and why?

2. When Gerald needs to escape from the world, he goes to "Gersday." Do you have a place like that where you can retreat to in your head? Do you think it can be a healthy thing to do when you get overwhelmed, or is it more of an unhealthy coping mechanism?

3. Gerald's mother bears a huge part of the blame for what happens to her family, but what about Gerald's father? How does he let his family down? Do you think he redeems himself at the end of the story?

4. The adults who are supposed to look out for Gerald and understand him (his parents and his anger management counselor) are the ones who exacerbate his problems. But there are several adults (the hockey lady, Gerald's boss, his special education teacher, and Hannah's friends) who seem to know exactly what Gerald needs. Can it be good to reach out to a wider circle when you don't get the support you need from the people you are close to? Or should you try to make your closest relationships work?

5. Hannah believes that Schadenfreude—a German word that means "taking pleasure in another's misfortune"—drew viewers to *Network Nanny* to watch Gerald's dysfunctional family. Do you agree? If so, do you think this term applies to reality television shows in general? Why or why not?

6. Gerald realizes in the middle of the novel that he doesn't know how to demand things. What do you think he means by this? Do you know how to make demands? Do you think your demands will

change over time, or will there be certain demands that you always have?

7. Lisi leaves home to study overseas as a way to escape her home life. Do you think this was fair to Gerald? Should she have stayed to help him, or does she need to protect herself first? How do you think Gerald feels about Lisi leaving home and rarely making contact with the family?

8. Do you think Gerald and Hannah are a good match? What works well in their relationship, and what do they have the most trouble with? Are there people in your life whom you sometimes don't get along with but can't imagine living without?

WOULD YOU TRY TO CHANGE THE WORLD IF YOU THOUGHT YOU HAD NO FUTURE?

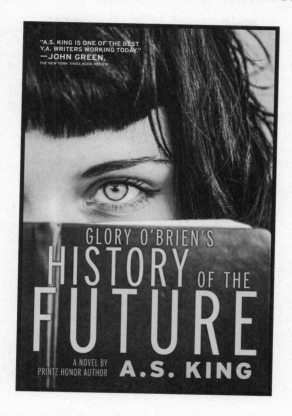

A.S. King's latest masterpiece is an epic story about freedom, feminism, destiny, and a girl coping with devastating loss at long last.

COMING OCTOBER 2014

Turn the page for a preview!

PROLOGUE

The clan of the petrified bat

So we drank it—the two of us. Ellie drank it first and acted like it tasted good. I followed. And it wasn't half bad.

When we woke up the next morning, everything was different. We could see the future. We could see the past. We could see *everything*.

You might say, "Why did you drink a bat?" Or, "How did you drink a bat?" Or, "Who would do something like that?"

But we weren't thinking about it at the time. It's like being on a fast train that crashes and someone asking you why you didn't jump before it crashed.

You wouldn't jump because you *couldn't* jump. It was going too fast.

And you didn't know the crash was coming, so why would you?

Hippie weirdo freaks

Ellie Heffner told me that the day she graduated would be the day she left her family and ran away forever. She'd been telling me that since we were fifteen years old.

"They're freaks," she said. "Hippie weirdo freaks."

I couldn't argue with her. She did live with hippie weirdo freaks.

"Will you come back and visit me, at least?" I asked.

She looked at me, disappointed. "You won't still be here then, will you?"

I had one week to go. Three more school days: Monday, Tuesday, Wednesday, and optional Baccalaureate on Friday and then a weekend wait to graduate on Monday. I still got postcards and letters from colleges and universities in the mail every week. I still threw each of them away without opening them.

It was Sunday night and Ellie and I were sitting on the steps on my front porch facing her house, which was across the road.

"I don't know," I answered. "I have no idea where I'll be."

I couldn't tell her the truth about where I thought I'd be. I almost did a few times, weak times when I was gripped by fear. I'd almost told her everything. But Ellie was . . . Ellie. Ever since we were little, she'd change the rules of a game halfway through.

You don't tell your biggest secrets to someone like that, right?

Anyway. I had a week until I graduated. I had zero plans, zero options, zero friends.

But I didn't tell Ellie that either because she thought she was my best friend.

It was complicated.

It had always been complicated.

It would always be complicated.

The origin of the bat

The bat lived at Ellie's house. We saw it first on a weekend that February. She pointed at the tiny lump of fur lodged in the corner of the back porch and said, "Look. A hibernating bat."

We saw it again in March and it hadn't moved. We talked about the bat's upcoming awakening and how it would soon swoop to the surface of Ellie's pond and eat newly hatched insects and touch its tiny wingtips off the water.

But spring came and the bat didn't move. Didn't swoop. Didn't seem to be dining on any of the tasty neighborhood pond bugs. One of its elbows—if that's what bats have—stuck out a little, like it was broken or something. We talked about how it might have an injury or a birth defect.

"Like the way I can't bend this finger down all the way since I broke it," Ellie said, showing me her right-hand index finger.

Life on Ellie's commune was different. They used hammers before they could walk. They didn't have any plastic. They swung on a homemade swing with a wooden plank as a seat. They played on the frozen pond without adult supervision and had chores that involved livestock. Ellie was in charge of chickens. One time when she was seven, she broke her finger while hammering a door hinge on a chicken house back into place.

I was convinced that the bat was out of hibernation and was simply nesting there at night in the exact same place under the eaves of her back porch. If we were in any way smart, we'd have stayed until dusk that night to watch the bat leave in order to answer our curiosities about it, but we didn't. Ellie had commune chores and a secret boyfriend. I had reluctant homework and senioritis. We were happy believing the bat was fine.

When we met on Easter Monday in late April, the bat was still there, elbow pointed to the eastern horizon like it had been since winter. Ellie found a stick and poked it and then sniffed the stick.

"Doesn't stink," she said. "And there are no flies or anything."

"Don't bats have fleas?" I asked. "I heard they carry fleas and ticks and stuff."

"I think it's dead," Ellie said.

"Doesn't look dead," I said.

"Doesn't look alive, either," Ellie said.

She poked it again and it didn't move. Then she nudged

the stick up into the siding where she could force the whole bat out with one slice and it fell into her mother's sprouting summer lilies. Ellie reached into the lime-green and came out with this oddity—perfectly intact, still furry, still with eyeballs, still with paper-thin wings folded like it was resting.

We leaned down and looked at it.

"It's petrified?" Ellie said.

"Probably more like mummified," I said.

She ignored my correction and placed the bat on the picnic table and went into the house and got a jar. I took a picture of the jar. I named the picture in my head. *Empty Jar.*

"It's so light," Ellie said, weighing the bat in her palm. "Do you want to hold it before I put it in?"

I put my hands out and she placed it in my palm and we looked at it. Even though it was dead, Ellie seemed to see it as a new stray pet that needed a mother or something. When I put it in the jar, she sealed the lid and held it up and said, "I christen thee the petrified bat! Hear ye, hear ye, the petrified bat is king!"

"Might be a queen," I said.

"Whatever," Ellie said. She inspected it through the glass. "It's alive and dead at the same time or something."

"Yeah."

"It's the closest I've ever come to God," Ellie said.

"Amen." I was being sarcastic. Because Ellie said stuff like that sometimes and it was annoying. Because we were seventeen and this was silly, us finding a bat and acting like it was something special. This was what nine-year-olds did.

But then something serious came over me. I said, "Hold on. Let me see it." Ellie handed the jar to me and as I looked at it—a tiny lump of mummified fur—I said, "Maybe it *is* God."

The bat was dead but somehow it represented life because it looked alive. It was mysterious and obvious in one hollow, featherweight package.

"We'll put it in the shed," Ellie said. "My mom will never find it there because that's where we keep the cleaning supplies."

Ellie's mother didn't believe in cleaning.

My mother was dead, and I had no idea if she was ever a clean freak or what.

The ballad of Darla O'Brien

My mother wasn't conveniently dead, like in so many stories about children, whether they jarred dead bats or were attracted to beasts in woodland castles. She didn't die to help me overcome some obstacle by myself or to make me a more sympathetic character.

She haunted me—and not in some run-of-the-mill Hollywood way. There were no floating bedsheets or chains clanking in the night as I tiptoed to the bathroom to pee.

My mother, Darla O'Brien, was a photographer. She haunted the walls of our house with pictures. She was always there and never there. We could never see her, but every day, I saw her pictures. She was a great photographer, but she never became famous because we didn't live in New York City. Or that's what I've heard she said.

Getting dead didn't make her famous either.

Regardless, having a dead mother isn't convenient, especially when she died because she stuck her head in an oven and turned on the gas.

That is not convenient.

Although, I'd argue that there is some convenience in having a death machine right there in your kitchen waiting for the moment you finally get the nerve to do it. I'd argue that's more convenient than a fast-food drive-thru. You don't even have to leave your house to stick your head in the oven.

You don't even have to change out of your bathrobe.

You don't even have to take your kid to preschool where it was Letter *N* Day and she was ready to show off her acorn collection. You don't have to remember to do anything but breathe in and breathe out.

That's about as convenient as it gets.

What's inconvenient is: Living in a world where no one wants to talk to you about your dead mother because it makes them uncomfortable.

What's inconvenient is: Not having a mother at middle school graduation. Not having a mother when I tried to figure out how to shave under my arms. Not having a mother when I got my period. My dad was helpful; but he's a feminist, not an actual woman.

I always knew that one day, it would be inconvenient as hell not having a mother at high school graduation. The last few weeks of senior year were filled with all the girls in my homeroom talking about buying dresses and shoes and all I could think about was how small those things seemed.

I sat in homeroom thinking *Shoes. Dresses. Disposable bullshit.*

I sat in homeroom thinking *Where am I really going, anyway?*

Though my yearbook photographer duties were over because the year's book was done, I still carried my camera with me everywhere. I took candid shots of those girls talking about their dresses and shoes. I took pictures of my teachers trying to teach near-empty classrooms. I took pictures of the people who thought they were my friends, but who I'd never let all the way in.

I didn't let anyone sign my yearbook. I decided: Why fake it?

Everything tasted like radiation

Ellie hadn't been to public school with me since we finished the eighth grade, and in the four years since, she'd said, "Homeschooling is faster because there's no repeating everything all the time," about eleven trillion times to me. Maybe it was true. Maybe not. Seemed to me homeschooling was just another way to keep all those kids in the commune from seeing the real world.

I didn't like the real world, but I was glad I knew about it.

Darla O'Brien didn't like the real world either, so she stuck her head in an oven.

My dad loved the real world. He ate it up. Literally. He weighed two hundred and forty pounds now. Not a bad weight unless you were five foot four and 120 pounds when you started out.

Dad had never replaced the oven. Not even with an electric one. Our kitchen had never had an oven since Letter *N* Day. Just a freezer full of food that could be cooked by the microwave.

Everything tasted like radiation.

Ellie wouldn't come to my house if we were cooking because she believed microwaves gave you cancer. She never could understand why we didn't have a huge stove like they had on the commune—a stove that could pickle and blanch and reduce fruit into jam for the winter.

"It's not like that could happen twice, right?" she'd said once. By *that*, she meant Darla sticking her head in the oven.

I'd answered, "No. No, I guess that couldn't happen twice."

But it could. Right? There were still two people left in my house. I was one of them. Whenever I thought about what Ellie had said, my guts churned. Sometimes I got diarrhea from it. Sometimes I threw up. It wasn't as easy as *it can't happen twice*. Anyone who knew anything about what Darla did knew it sometimes *did* happen twice because it's often hereditary. But Ellie just said things without thinking. That was hereditary too.

Ellie's mother, Jasmine Blue Heffner, believed that the microwave oven was no different from an atomic bomb because it was invented by defense contractors during World War II.

I figured by the time Ellie applied to colleges, she'd either be smarter than me from learning *so much faster* in homeschool, or she'd be so brainwashed by Jasmine Blue that she would score badly on her SAT because she believed a microwave oven was the same as an atomic bomb.

Ellie might have defended homeschooling to me, but deep down she knew what she was missing. From the day she stopped getting on the yellow school bus with me she started complaining about the commune. It was as if school was her one real-world connection, and cutting it off made her feel like a bird in a cage.

She asked about what other girls were wearing to school. She asked about makeup. She asked about boys, TV shows, social media sites, dances, sports games.

Mostly, she asked about sex, even though we'd just turned fourteen.

"Did you have health class today?" she'd asked.

"Yeah."

"Did you get the rubber demonstration yet?"

"Today we learned about meth," I'd said.

I told her that real sex ed wasn't until eleventh grade and she looked disappointed. "I think that's too late to learn about sex."

"Yeah. By then, we know everything already," I'd said.

We knew enough. I had the Internet at home. (Ellie did not have the Internet. Jasmine Blue believed the Internet was an atomic bomb full of porn and lies. In that order.) By fifth grade, we'd Googled it. First we Googled *penis*. We looked for images. That was the day we found the butter penis. A penis carved from butter—anatomically correct. We made jokes about it. *What good is that if it melts? Bet it tastes better than the real thing.* We wondered why anyone would sculpt a penis out of butter. But then we found penis cakes, penis candy molds and penis lollipops, and we figured adults were gross.

That's as far as it went in fifth grade. Adults are gross. Nothing more to it.

We made a promise that day. We promised to tell each other the minute we had sex. Both of us doubted in fifth grade that it would ever happen, but if it did, we swore we would tell each other and talk about it.

In middle school, before homeschooling, Ellie became an expert, as if she was preparing for the most important event of her life. She got her friends to buy her the latest women's magazines and she'd talk about orgasms and balls and *how to please your man*. She would sometimes give the magazines to me to keep for her. I had a box of her contraband under my bed. Mostly magazines and eye shadow. A condom that a random boy gave to her. A weekend section of the newspaper with a page of exotic dancers, with names like *Leather Love*, *Lacey Snow*, *Shy-Anne*, who would perform at the local lap dancing bars. I looked through the magazines sometimes, too. In front of Ellie I pretended I wasn't interested. But I was.

In front of everyone else, I pretended I didn't care about all the stuff girls start to care about in middle school—the right clothes, shoes, mascara, hair products, sex—but I did. I was interested in the *why. Why? Why do we care so much about this?*

I wasn't sure why I cared about not caring. Or why I didn't care about not caring.

I figured it had something to do with what everyone else was avoiding talking about, which was Darla. Maybe had Darla still been around, she'd have given me a direction. Or something.

Jasmine Blue's homeschool sex education was contained in a simple mantra. *If you do it too early, you'll regret it.* I watched as each mention made Ellie more curious and more rebellious and more determined to have sex just because she wanted to test Jasmine's theory.

"What do you think it's like?" she would ask me, even though she knew it made me uncomfortable to talk about it. I think she figured since she was fourteen and curious, so was I.

"I don't know," I'd say. "I don't really care."

"You don't *care*? Really? Come on. You care."

I didn't care.

"What about that kid on the bus you used to crush on? Didn't you ever think about doing it with him?" she asked.

"Markus Glenn?"

"Yeah."

"Don't you remember? He was such a perv."

She picked at a fingernail that was bothering her. "What'd he do again?"

"The porn guy."

"Ohhh. Yeah. Him," she said. "So, who do you like now?"

"Nobody."

I never told her that after Markus Glenn showed me those pictures on his computer in seventh grade, he asked me to touch him there where his shorts were sticking up like a tipi. When I wouldn't touch it and I told him I was going home, he said, "You're never going to be a real woman acting like that, you know! Anyway, you're flat as a board!"

I didn't tell her that from that moment forward, I never even wanted breasts because then kids like Markus Glenn would look at them. I didn't tell her that from that moment on, I sometimes didn't know what a woman was really supposed to look like.

"You liked one kid in your whole life? I don't buy it."

"I told you. I don't care," I'd said.

I picked up my camera and held it at arm's length and took a picture of myself not caring. I called it: *Glory Doesn't Care*.

HE'S NOT THE BOY YOU SAW ON TV.

REALITY BOY

A NOVEL BY PRINTZ HONOR AUTHOR
A.S. KING

"A.S. King gets better with each book."

—stackedbooks.org

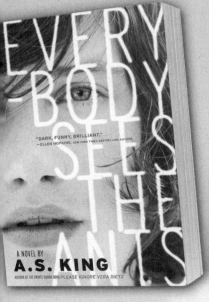

"DARK, FUNNY, BRILLIANT."
—ELLEN HOPKINS, New York Times bestselling author

A NOVEL BY
A.S. KING
AUTHOR OF THE PRINTZ HONOR BOOK *PLEASE IGNORE VERA DIETZ*

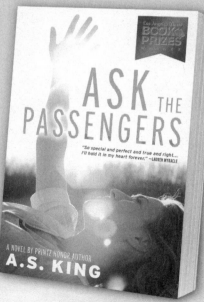

ASK THE PASSENGERS

"So special and perfect and true and right...
I'll hold it in my heart forever." —LAUREN MYRACLE

A NOVEL BY PRINTZ HONOR AUTHOR
A.S. KING

three powerful stories that will keep you thinking long after the last page,
from Michael L. Printz Honor author A.S. King

ABOUT THE AUTHOR

A.S. King is the author of the highly acclaimed *Reality Boy*, which was a *New York Times* Editors' Choice book, appeared on five end-of-year "best" lists, received five starred reviews, and was a YALSA Quick Picks for Reluctant Young Readers book; *Ask the Passengers*, which was a Los Angeles Times Book Prize winner, received six starred reviews, appeared on ten end-of-year "best" lists, and was a Lambda Literary Award finalist; and *Everybody Sees the Ants*, which also received six starred reviews, was an Andre Norton Award finalist, and was a 2012 YALSA Top Ten Best Fiction for Young Adults book. She is also the author of the Edgar Award–nominated, Michael L. Printz Honor Book *Please Ignore Vera Dietz* and *The Dust of 100 Dogs*, an ALA Best Book for Young Adults. When asked about her writing, King says, "Some people don't know if my characters are crazy or if they are experiencing something magical. I think that's an accurate description of how I feel every day." She lives in rural Pennsylvania with her husband and children. Her website is as-king.com.